CHRISTINE HART

The Compendium

The Variant Conspiracy, Book 2

Prologue

Late afternoon sunlight brightened the red brick ruins of a chapel next to a large Gothic church. The road signs and surrounding architecture were British. Past the ruined and new churches, the road led to an archaeological site ringed with remains much older than the battered chapel. A couple walking up from inside the excavated pit spied the chapel ruins and the woman gestured with delight. Her words inaudible, she pointed from a brochure in her hand, up to the ruins and back to the paper.

The man nodded and they made their way towards the churches. As they grew closer, I recognized them. Ivan and my mother walked arm in arm, young and happy. Ivan had a kind of warmth and energy to him. His face was tanned and speckled with ginger beard stubble. He wore a plain grey T-shirt and faded blue jeans. I almost didn't recognize him. My mother looked equally different in a sundress dotted with small flowers. Her cheeks were pink. Wavy brown hair cascaded down her back, shimmering in the sunlight as she moved. As my view of them zoomed in, their voices grew louder.

"Let's take some pictures here too. The light is still good enough." My mom reached into her shoulder bag and pulled out her camera.

"Sure, whatever you like," said Ivan in a thick Russian accent.

My mother walked ahead, twirling through the building's fragmented structure. She paused to snap a picture, dialed the film ahead, turned, and snapped another picture. The open walls and setting sun cast hard shadows against the glowing brick.

"I know this one isn't as old as the Roman ruins, but isn't it soooooo lovely to have something to walk through? It's so much easier to *feel* this place. I hope the pictures turn out. Photos never do a vacation justice."

"Your pictures will be perfect," said Ivan.

Mom looked through her brochure again, examining the text. "It says here that both the current church and the adjacent ruins are heritage sites. The 'new' church is an excellent example of eleventh-century architecture. The ruins of the original building date back to the year 689."

Mom's voice held a sense of wonder uncharacteristic of the woman I knew. She kept walking, looking up and around with her hands clasped against her chest, leaving Ivan to play with the settings on his manual camera. My view expanded again, drifting upwards to an aerial vantage. A dark spot inside the excavated Roman remains flickered to life and traced my parents' path, pursuing them like a fluid shadow.

"This one is interesting," said Ivan as he came to a plaque on a pedestal under a window of a partial wall. He read something I couldn't make out from my viewpoint. He scratched his chin and then rested his hand on the plaque.

Ivan's body straightened with a jolt as he stood with his hand planted firmly on the weathered stone. The shadow caught up to him, flowing along the ground and up through the pedestal. Ivan shuddered as he absorbed the dark blur. He stood like a statue with his hand on the plaque until my mother came back to him.

My viewpoint shifted and I saw a cold smirk on Ivan's face. His suddenly pale skin matched the familiar man I had worked for in Victoria.

"Hon, what are you doing over here? We're missing the best light on the other side of the building. The sun will set in a few minutes!"

Ivan looked at my mother's face and then dropped his gaze to her belly. He reached out a hand to touch her. As soon as he made contact, he broke into a grin.

"What's gotten into you?" Concern filtered into my mother's face.

Ivan said nothing and the image switched off.

Chapter 1

"Where's my crystal, you fuckin' moron!" A woman screamed outside my window.

I rolled over in bed and grabbed my new phone. The time read 7:53 AM against a serene night sky. I sat up, rubbed my eyes, and looked at the chipped old mirror on the opposite wall.

My decision to dye my hair back to my natural color hadn't worked out perfectly. The box I'd chosen - Darkest Chestnut Brown – was supposed to convert my easily recognizable faded blue streaks into something mundane. Now, my whole head looked several shades darker than its original cinnamon. My face seemed paler than usual against the flat dark brown frame. I looked like a goth girl without her make-up. My amber eyes appeared a bit warmer than normal, making me smile.

The lump of covers remained motionless on the other bed. Faith's purple dreadlocks poked out of the blankets like a hairy anemone. My twin brother Ilya had suggested we divide our accommodations along gender lines, for comfort and privacy. Nobody contradicted him. I knew he was worried about romance drama, and by extension, the angst he had to overhear in our heads.

Faith rolled around and threw off her blanket, as though she sensed me watching her.

"Even four stories off the ground, we just can't escape the neighborhood charm," I said. "At least we got to sleep in a bit today. The curtains are thick enough to keep out most of the early morning sun."

"Too bad they can't block out junkie drama. Ilya better be right about Ivan having tested on these assholes," said Faith.

Everyday life in Vancouver's downtown east side had been notorious since my childhood. Discussions about Vancouver in my northern hometown of Prince George frequently referenced East Hastings Street as nothing short of the gateway to Hell. I felt uneasy with every step I took on the crowded sidewalks.

"How long did Ilya say we could stay here? Wasn't it about a month, factoring in the cost of food for everyone?" I asked. "I think our room is four hundred dollars and the guys' room is six hundred."

"Sounds about right," Faith said. "His estimate accounted for staying at other hotels in other cities, didn't it? I hope so, because the longer we stay here, the less money we have for the next place. And considering the fact that we've got one window with a view of a boarded-up sushi joint and a weed dispensary covered in iron bars, I think we're getting ripped off big time."

I changed from my nightshirt and pajama sweats into jeans and a fresh shirt. I brushed my freshly dyed hair up into a dark ponytail. Faith had slept in the clothes she wore the previous day. I felt relieved as she finally dug some fresh clothes out of her bag and changed into a new pair of cargo pants and her other black T-shirt.

We stood next to each other in front of the mirror as we flicked through cosmetic bags applying eyeliner and eye shadow. I added lip gloss while Faith added copious swoops of mascara, narrowly missing her eyebrow ring with each blink.

"So … I had a dream about Ivan last night. And my mother. I think Ivan was possessed or something."

"Awesome. I guess it doesn't matter now that he's dead." Faith adjusted her nose stud while examining her reflection. "Still, hold that thought for breakfast. The guys will want to hear if you've got new info."

I had to give my reluctant roommate credit for her capacity to absorb weird and unpleasant news in stride. I wondered if I would become numb to bizarre things once I had been in the variant world as long as Faith had.

We met Ilya, with my almost-boyfriend Jonah, and my estranged crush Cole in the hotel lobby. My heart sank as I took in Jonah's form. His skin had a gray undertone and his once stunning arctic eyes had faded to the color of pre-dawn sky. He'd been healed after his bone-breaking fight with Innoviro's most dangerous thug, but he clearly wasn't his old self. As an aquakinetic, I knew Jonah needed a steady supply of fresh water, but even that was no longer enough to keep him healthy. Our would-be relationship had ebbed when we discovered that his touch drained me of life and energy - and that he was slowly dying of an unstable genetic mutation.

Cole radiated strength, his biceps bulging through a fitted army-green T-shirt. His fresh crew cut had transformed him from skater to would-be soldier. Ilya was the shortest and slimmest. His shaggy cinnamon hair and lean build mirrored my own–exactly as my twin should look.

Ilya had already picked out our breakfast spot, a greasy spoon in the heart of Chinatown. As we exited the Bella Maria, I could barely suppress the urgency I felt to flee from the pedestrians on the street. I had always known Vancouver's downtown east side was one of the worst neighborhoods in Western Canada. Yet how could I properly prepare myself to function in ground zero of Vancouver's addiction and mental health problems?

We followed Ilya silently past too thin people scratching their arms, some smoking cigarettes or pipes, a few sitting on the sidewalk with empty stares, or rifling through shopping carts. The chatter of arguing and mumbling blended with the engine sounds of traffic. Cars, SUVs, and buses all rumbled past without stopping. We walked until abandoned buildings and barred storefronts gave way to overstated Chinese architecture advertising curios, fast food, travel agencies, and wire transfers.

Ilya turned into a small diner under a simple yellow sign with red letters, the English words "Hung Fat" printed below larger Chinese characters. Air thick with grease pervaded the room and several strips of overhead lighting were burnt out. Cole gestured to a vacant window table and we all took seats.

"So what made you pick this paragon of nutritional bounty?" Jonah picked up the typed menu.

"I read some reviews online that the food tasted great but the service was terrible. Meaning we'll get a decent meal with practically no attention from the servers," Ilya said, "and if the workers here don't speak English, we can probably talk freely."

"Couldn't we take some food back to our rooms again?" said Cole.

"I figured we'd have a little field trip after breakfast today. We should leave your car behind in case we encounter any Innoviro staff on site that might recognize it. There's a bus stop just down the street."

"So you're in charge now, Ilya?" Faith demanded.

"Does it matter?" I asked.

"Where do you want us to go?" Jonah looked at Ilya, ignoring the sniping and the glares Faith and I shot at each other.

"We're going to find Irina's warehouse, the one she saw in Brad's head," said Ilya.

"I still don't have anything to go on, apart from a few vague landmarks," I pointed out.

"Exactly. We have landmarks," Ilya said. "You were on the North Shore, between the bridge and a pile of sulfur. So let's go find the sulfur. It should be in a light industrial area. Or we'll get as close to the bridge as we can."

"Sounds like a great way to get mugged." Faith tossed her head, purple hair flying.

"It's a decent idea." Jonah smiled at me over his menu. "Irina might see something new if we hit the right spot."

"We've got nothing better to do," said Cole.

"Good. The bus that picks us up outside will turn towards West Van after the Lion's Gate. We'll get off at the first stop on the other side of the–," Ilya's forehead crumpled and his face screwed in a confused frown.

"What do you hear?" said Cole.

"Let him listen, genius," said Faith.

"Variants?" said Jonah.

"Only one, I think. A boy. The one that just went by on a bike a moment ago," said Ilya.

"How can you tell?" I said.

"He's worried about his skin changing color in the sun. I could be wrong. Maybe he gets bad sunburns," said Ilya.

"Should I run him down?" said Cole.

"I think that would draw attention even in this part of town," said Jonah.

"Let's worry about tracking variants later," I said. "I'm keen to try the 'new vision' tactic on the North Shore. Oh, and speaking of new visions, remind me to tell you about my dream where Ivan and Mom hang out around some ruins."

"Good. And I will," said Ilya.

The bus that picked us up near Hung Fat an hour later was almost full. We crammed in like sardines, nudging between passengers and grappling for bare handrail space. The bus driver's frustrated voice came over the PA system asking passengers at the back to keep moving backwards, but it had almost no effect.

I clung to a rubber hand loop attached to a railing above my head. My face was angled away from my friends, but I could see out the window between a schoolgirl's shoulder and the cap of an elderly man on the seat facing me.

We rolled out of Chinatown and into the heart of downtown. Vancouver's glass towers loomed overhead bigger than ever. The bus crept along the urban street until residential condos and a marina replaced the financial district. I saw a sign for the Lion's Gate Bridge in time to stave off a claustrophobic panic attack.

Driving slower than a tractor, our bus edged onto the bridge while the green pole and cable structure reached up into the sky overhead. I felt like a small-town girl more intensely than I ever had in my whole life.

The sea came into view below the bridge and across the water, I saw my bright sulfur pile glaring out of the landscape ahead. I felt relief when the ding of the stop cable pierced the din of voices and the bus engine. We stopped at the first bus stop after the bridge shrank away behind us. We stepped off the road and into a ditch to get our bearings.

"So, who knows this area best?" I asked the group.

"Aren't *you* supposed to know where we're going?"

"Cut her some slack, Faith. This angry rebel thing is getting old." Frustration filled Cole's voice too. I hoped our lack of direction was the problem rather than my choosing Jonah over him, futile as the choice had become.

"I don't know how close we can get to this giant yellow pile. It's probably part of an industrial site," I said. I looked around for signs of machinery in the landscape.

"She's right. We won't be able to walk right up to the sulfur," Ilya said, "But we can walk around under the bridge on this side. We might be near enough."

"We don't even know if getting close to these landmarks is going to work." Jonah rubbed his tired eyes.

"You've still got the letter, right?" said Cole.

"Yeah, it's here in my bag." I patted my backpack.

"Then, let's go for a walk," said Ilya, clapping his hands.

We followed Ilya in a line. Nobody spoke. The tension eased as the blaring sun took center stage in my mind. I hadn't expected heat and high UV in Vancouver. Without the cover of downtown towers, we baked slowly under the early summer sky.

In a few minutes, Ilya led us off the road onto a grass-lined dirt path with a view of the open space under the north end of the Lion's Gate Bridge. "Well, I think this is as good as it gets."

The dirt path opened up to a concrete landing. We stopped at the bridge's shadow, facing the ocean inlet. Under the near midday sun, we stood almost underneath the grid of green steel. Trees flanked us on the right, rising high enough to block out the ocean-side, industrial, and real estate to the west.

"Should we go right?" Jonah gestured in the direction where the giant sulfur pile should be located.

"Yeah, we've already got a ballpark idea here. Let's start walking," said Cole.

"Feel free to do your vision-quest thing." Faith lifted her purple dreads in a medusa-like pose, mocking my authenticity.

I frowned back at her. Then, I fished the letter out of my backpack and looked around as the others walked ahead. Apart from recognizing the bridge, probably because of its iconic status, the area was totally unfamiliar. I took the letter from its envelope and ran my hands across the typed surface. Nothing happened. Voices carried from the group ahead, but I had fallen behind them. I wanted to take in everything around me; I drank in the scents of lilac, brackish water, and motor oil; I felt the cool air above the pavement at my feet. And I picked up a black piece of rubber that looked exactly like a bottle stopper.

The road dissolved around me, but my vision didn't take me far. I found myself back in front of the rundown warehouse building. The bay door was closed this time, but daylight added detail to the neighborhood. The cream-colored stucco building had no signage to suggest ownership or occupancy. The sulfur pile seemed farther away. I scanned the face of the building for a street number but saw nothing. I turned around and around until I caught sight of a street sign. Aspen Lane! I opened both palms to force my physical hands to drop the rubber stopper and end the vision.

"Stop!" I shouted. "We're looking for Aspen Lane!"

Everyone came to a halt and turned. I looked down at the stopper on the ground, and then at my sweaty hands covered in dirt left by the rubber nugget. I grabbed the stopper and shoved it in my pocket.

"I see it! It's the next road up here," Ilya called out.

Anticipation flooded my body and I started running. I prayed to the universe that this warehouse would be the last stop in our weird quest.

Chapter 2

At the intersection of Bridge Road and Aspen Lane, I saw my precious cream building half a block away. The yellow sulfur pile peeked out behind the structures in the distance, barely visible as the coastline curved into the inlet.

I suppressed the urge to run. In broad daylight – and real life now – discretion was essential. "It's the plain cream building ahead, the one with the brown trim."

"You're sure?" said Ilya.

"I am. I had another vision." I presented the grubby piece of rubber on my palm. Ilya walked over to the building while the rest of us hung back.

"Where did you get that?" Cole frowned in disgust.

Faith's nose wrinkled and light glinted off the metal stud she always wore. "It looks like garbage."

"No, it looks like the kind of stopper we used in the lab." Jonah leaned in for a closer look and I caught a whiff of the musky aftershave I'd come to crave.

"I found it on the road back there." I handed it to Jonah and pointed at the spot.

Ilya returned from evaluating the entrance. "The lot is fenced around the sides and the back. If we want in, we'll have to either hop the fence or pick the lock on the front door. There's nobody in there. Nobody I can hear, anyway."

"What about those loading bays? I could try lifting the door if they're not alarmed," Cole said. "Anyone watching will think we've got business there."

"Good idea." Jonah rubbed his whole face.

"But there's no way to know if there *is* an alarm." Faith crossed her arms. "I can check to see if electric current is near the frame, but doors like this are probably rigged with motorized openers."

"If an alarm starts, can you cut it off?" I asked Faith.

"I'd have to find the right circuit and melt it."

"We're expecting this place to be abandoned, right? I say we go for it," said Jonah.

Cole nodded and walked to the nearest bay door. He gripped the large metal handle at the bottom and pulled it up as though it were made of paper. Cole stopped the door about three feet off the ground. We all froze, waiting for a wail or a siren. Nothing came.

"Good to go!" Ilya smiled.

"I'll go in first. We still don't know if this place is empty," said Cole.

He ducked under the door into the dark open space. We waited in silence. Faith and Jonah peeked in after Cole. I looked up and down the street to see if anyone was watching. I scanned the windows of the few parked cars around us. I squinted at building windows in the distance in both directions.

"Nobody noticed us. There are a few bookkeepers in that building." Ilya gestured to the nearest structure. "And that one," he said pointing at the warehouse across the intersection, "has one forklift driver and a handful of packers, all of them concentrating on what they're doing."

"You can tell all of that from listening briefly?" I said.

"It's easier to block out thoughts from people standing next to you if you cast a broader mental net, so to speak." Ilya grinned at me. "But you were practically yelling your panic about someone watching us."

I looked away, blushing as I remembered what else I'd been thinking about. Even after practicing with Rubin, I'd never get the hang of someone listening to my private thoughts.

Cole emerged from the open bay door, brushing his hands on his thighs. "The place has been stripped. Looks like it might have been a grow-op of some kind, but it's hard to be sure. There isn't much here, but we can poke around."

"Irina got a vision from a piece of rubber trash. Anything is a potential lead now." I heard a hint of desperation in Jonah's voice.

"Let's get on with it then. Out here we're waiting for an audience," said Faith.

I slipped under the door easily, being the shortest of our group. The others followed and Cole slid the door shut behind them.

Row upon row of long rectangular basins stretched from one end of the warehouse to the other. Only a few desks in the corner nearest the entrance suggested any kind of office presence.

I reached into one of the basins and dusted dry dirt off the side. Cole was probably right. This looked like a growing facility, but what could Innoviro want with plants? Had Ivan planned to change our world so much he'd need new plant life? Or would his group of variants need new food sources?

The terrifying part of Innoviro's transformative projects was the veritable sea of inadvertent problems they could create. Ivan wanted a legacy of chaos and he seemed accustomed to achieving his goals. Could plant extracts spark or enhance variations? I never did learn the ingredients of the lavender liquid Tatiana and then Brad both shot into my arm.

I turned from the dirty basins to the three desks in the corner. The laminate-coated fiberboard frames of each workstation had only cables protruding from holes in the surface. Phones and computers had been here but yanked out unceremoniously along with the plants when the previous tenants left.

One desk held a few papers. A brochure for pizza and a real estate notepad. Another had a pen. A personal possession! I picked it up.

The room around me flickered and the basins were full of plants again, under hanging fluorescent lights. Slender aluminum tubes reached up over the basin edges like large insect arms. A bell jingled off to my left and a fine mist burst out of the arms in unison.

I walked up to one of the basins full of tiny lush bluish ferns. A small plastic label in the dirt declared RESISTANT STRAND 122B. Farther down the line, I could see a kind of evergreen seedling.

As I got closer to the evergreens, I saw glints of red in the spiky leaves and tiny spindly pods on the branches. Flies buzzed around the plants and I saw one of the pods open like a glistening green mouth. A fly landed inside and the mouth snapped shut. I shuddered as I contemplated the size those little mouths could become if they grew proportionate to the rest of the tree.

I turned around to the desks in the corner. No longer bare, one was occupied. A balding man sat at a computer with his back to me. I walked as quickly as my vision self could manage.

The man typed furiously as I came around the desk to face him. He was older and slightly overweight with a ring of straw blond hair. He looked up at the door behind me and frowned. I turned around to see Tatiana and two men enter. I recognized one of the men from Innoviro, but the other was a stranger. Both wore plain slacks and golf shirts. Tatiana wore her typical pencil skirt, buttoned blouse, and stilettos.

The bald man stood to greet Tatiana and his height struck me. The man was tall, even while slouching. He looked defeated, dominated by the displeased look on Tatiana's face. She opened her mouth and the scene evaporated. I was back in the dim empty version of the warehouse. Everyone was staring at me. I lifted my pen for their perusal.

"They were cultivating weird plants. And Tatiana showed up. She looked grouchier than usual." I closed my eyes and rubbed my temples. "The guy sitting at this desk was responsible for the place. Tatiana was about to give him hell when my vision ended."

"Did you learn anything else? See anything else?" asked Ilya, leaning towards me.

"So all we know now is that this was some kind of variant grow show." Faith swooped her arm at the empty basins.

"Did you see any printed material? Anything with a name

or an address?" asked Jonah.

"The guy at the desk had an ID badge clipped to his breast pocket, but I couldn't make out anything on it," I said.

"So, where are we going next?" said Cole. He rested his hands firmly on his hips.

As my friends started to argue about the chances of successfully tracking down any Innoviro activity, I opened and closed drawers in the bald man's desk. I reached the top center drawer and a plastic-sheathed card slid forward. The bald man's face looked up at me next to bold print, **Dr. Kingston, George T.**

I picked up the card and the angry voices beside me were silenced. I stood in a lush meadow watching Dr. Kingston survey a small field of bizarre plants. The carnivorous evergreens and their giant mouths loomed over teal-blue ferns with pearl flowers. A glass and screen enclosure held large colorful bees that shimmered as though bathed in a slick sheen of gasoline. It looked like an alien planet, surrounded by BC's steep coastal mountains.

A portable plastic table behind Kingston held specimen jars with plant fragments and a stack of pizza boxes with RIVERSIDE PIZZA HOUSE printed in bright red letters. I moved to step closer to Kingston and a hand grabbed my arm, pulling me back to the North Vancouver warehouse.

"What happened? Why did you–," I stopped.

Jonah lay unconscious on the ground.

Chapter 3

Ilya released my arm and I dove to the ground next to Jonah. Faith and Cole were already kneeling beside him.

"What happened?" I asked again.

"I don't know. He collapsed," said Cole, checking Jonah's pulse.

"It's not that hot out. We weren't running," I said to Jonah's unconscious body, as though my rationalization would wake him.

"We're even near the ocean for fuck's sake!" Faith yelled as she pushed her hair back from her forehead.

"We can't take him to the hospital," said Ilya.

"Let's get him back to the hotel," I said.

"How are we supposed to get him there? Carry him on the bus?" Faith shrieked.

"Faith, put a lid on it unless you want cops over here!" hissed Cole.

"Cole will carry him over his shoulder and Ilya will make Jonah look like a duffle bag," I said.

"We'll get him in a cab. Cole and I will keep the 'bag' on our laps," Ilya said as he tapped on his phone.

Our hotel room was an inadequate clinic and we were feeble medical aids, but we all agreed not to resort to a hospital unless Jonah took a turn for the worse. Faith took the first shift with him, holding his hand firmly and stroking his hair gently. I bit my lip and said nothing. I balled my fists, digging into my palms hard to keep me from slapping her. I reminded myself that I needed to debrief Ilya and Cole about the garden in the field, so I turned my back on Jonah's sick bed.

"I was about to tell you before Jonah passed out. They've transplanted the seedlings from that warehouse into an outdoor field. Kingston supervised the whole thing. I still don't know what they're doing with the plants, but they had a mutated strain of honeybee there as well—shimmering like a metallic rainbow. They were beautiful." The image of the bees drifted back into focus. How could something so magical be malicious?

Cole flicked the thought away with his hand. "Those plants could be some benign little side project."

"I don't think so. In the warehouse vision, Tatiana looked pretty intense. I don't think she bothers with silly-little-nothing projects."

Ilya gently removed the ID badge from my backpack. "Is this the same guy?"

"Yeah, and he wasn't working alone, although he seemed to be in charge."

"Irina, did you see or hear anything to help us find the place?" said Ilya, staring intently at the badge.

"The mountains were pretty steep, and close to the site, compared to the mountains north of the city. But we might be able to find the Riverside Pizza House. Kingston had a stack of pizza boxes like he'd been living off them."

Ilya handed the badge to Cole, who examined it while Ilya turned on my laptop.

"I've never seen this guy. I don't think he ever came to the Victoria office. Not while I worked there. I'd remember a dude like this," said Cole as he peered into Kingston's face.

Ilya found a website for Riverside Pizza in Hope, a mountain town that could easily hide a meadow. Google Maps told us we could get there in an hour and a half with no traffic.

"We should take my car this time. The Greyhound might take us to this pizza place, but if we're lucky and Irina has another vision, we'll need wheels to get out to a secluded grow site," said Cole.

"*We* should take the car." Ilya gestured with his thumb between me and him. "*You* should stay here with Jonah and Faith. She'll need your help if Jonah takes a turn for the worse."

My stomach sank as I looked over at Jonah's sleeping form. Faith heard us, but she didn't look up.

"Are you comfortable loaning us your car to leave the city?" I asked.

"After everything that's happened in the last couple of weeks, sharing my car seems like the smallest risk," Cole answered.

I felt like I dragged all my friends into a zero-sum game. Stopping the work Ivan had started would force us to sacrifice far more than we could afford. I massaged my face and sighed.

"We're all in this because we want to be. We know there will be sacrifices–we've made quite a few already. And remember, I can speak for everyone," said Ilya, tapping his temple with one hand, and placing the other on my shoulder.

"Will you get the hell out of my head already?" Heat filled

my face.

Cole tossed his car keys to Ilya and I stole one more glance at Jonah. Faith's focus on him didn't waver, while I felt Cole's dark brown eyes on me. And Ilya could hear every angst-ridden thought. We had to focus on Ivan's legacy and Innoviro. Our lives were going to get worse before they got better.

Vancouver's mid-day traffic slowed our progress to a crawl. I knew Ilya could hear my thoughts, but I couldn't stop them from racing around in my head. I wanted to know where I stood with my friends, and with the man I'd started to love, however foolish the feeling might be.

I stared out the window and Ilya stayed silent until the roller coasters of the Pacific National Exhibition appeared on our left.

"Would it make you feel better if I told you something embarrassing and personal about myself?" Ilya kept his eyes on the road ahead.

My head snapped in his direction.

"When you're this intensely upset, I can't block you. Probably doesn't help that we share near-replica DNA either," said Ilya.

"Is that why you ran away from Ivan? Because you couldn't block him? I thought you said you had a hard time hearing his thoughts," I said. "Wait, I think I know why!" I clapped my hand over my mouth.

"Seriously?" said Ilya.

"I wanted to tell everyone at breakfast, but we were all focused on the North Van outing. I had a dream about Ivan getting possessed. Or infected maybe. My visions are usually pretty literal. I've seen him with demon eyes too, in other dreams."

"Where did it happen? What was he doing?"

"He was visiting ruins with Mom." I stopped as I said the word, remembering that she was dead. And that Ilya would never know her. I forced my grief away and shoved my mind's eye back to the dream. "I think they were in England. He touched a stone and a dark shadow shot up from the ground and into his body. It changed him. The expression on his face changed, hell, even his skin color faded," I said.

"That might explain why his mind always felt so different, so … brutally wild. After the other night … I guess we'll never know. Then again, we should operate on the assumption he's still alive. We both know how strong he was. Or still is, regardless of how he looked when we left him," said Ilya quietly. "But, back to my offer to bare my heart and soul, do you want to hear my embarrassing confession?"

"Sure, why not? You'll still have the advantage, but I've got to get used to it at some point."

Ilya continued staring at the highway ahead, looking as though he was reconsidering. I gave him credit for bravery in my mind, hoping to give him courage.

"Yeah, this is pretty good. At least you'll probably think so." He paused again before saying, "I'm still in love with Faith."

My first thought was, *Oh, good luck with that one.* I regretted the thought immediately.

"Don't you think I know she's got a thing for Jonah? If *you* can tell, and everyone else can tell, what do you think *I* have to listen to?" Ilya looked over at me briefly with raised eyebrows.

"I thought you broke up with her," I said gently.

"I did. I couldn't handle her temper. I didn't think I'd have trouble getting over her." Ilya's voice revealed his frustration.

"Well, she is a touchy gal," I said cautiously. "You deserve someone who loves you back." I wanted to say more, that if he won Faith back, it would help us both. But Jonah's unconscious face popped into my head and I cringed at my selfishness. I sat on my hands as though it might help me bottle up my thoughts.

"You think she's a bitch. But you'd rather her with me than pining for Jonah. Don't hold back. I know what you think anyway." Ilya gripped the steering wheel harder.

"Are you going to do anything? Do you want to tell her?"

"I'd been planning to let you and Jonah get more established before I said anything. I'm not interested in competing with Jonah. Of course, now that you're pushing him away– ."

"Was he ever in love with her?"

I was instantly sorry I'd asked. I didn't want the answer to be yes.

"Honestly, I don't know. He and I aren't that close. He felt an intense attraction to her for a brief time. Remember though, the fleeting things people think and how they feel deep down can get muddled together. If interpreting thoughts came easily, if emotions and intentions were straightforward, my mind-reading would have kept me and Faith together. If you think it's hard to be friends with someone who knows your every thought, think how hard it would be to date that person. She always waffled between embarrassment and anger around me."

"I guess if psychic powers aren't much of a relationship enhancer, mind-reading might not be either."

Ilya didn't reply, but increased speed as the urban traffic broke up and the street turned into a highway.

The road to Hope led through Vancouver's suburbs, through outlying cities, into farmland, and up against rugged mountains. The lush foothills and sharp peaks loomed higher and higher as the valley narrowed.

Ilya pulled off the highway at a sign for Hope's city center. "According to the map, this pizza place should be across from a park. Can you check your phone?" I tapped on my map app and searched again.

"Turn right past the gas station at the next intersection." We rounded the corner and saw a large chalkboard tent sign for Riverside Pizza House on the sidewalk.

I noticed the emptiness in my stomach. "Are you hungry?"

"Sounds like we could both eat. Let's go see if we can get a lead with our lunch." Ilya handed me the ID badge I'd found at the warehouse. "Here. For inspiration."

The interior of the pizza place greeted us with sparse retro diner décor. The building smelled of fresh bread, herbs, and roasted green peppers mingled with hot oil. A carved wood sign instructed us to seat ourselves.

A young family had the best table next to the storefront window. Ilya and I grabbed a table for two nearest to the register. I put my hand in my pocket to feel Dr. Kingston's ID badge. With my free hand, I plucked a menu out of the spice rack in front of me and the diner disappeared.

I sat on the passenger side of a pickup truck. Dr. Kingston drove. Two Riverside boxes rested between us on the bench seat. Soft classical music drifted out of the speakers on the dashboard. We were on a gravel road in the woods.

We reached a fork in the road. And a sign! We could turn right to access Jewel Lake. Or we could turn left onto a Forest Service Road. Kingston turned left. The road grew rougher until the rattling frame and struggling engine drowned out the trumpets and violins. The drive continued until the forest had practically swallowed the road. And then we burst out of the trees into the alien meadow.

I let go of the menu and ID badge and snapped back into the Riverside Pizza House. "I know how to get there!"

"Lower your voice." Ilya pushed air down with his hands. "I know you're excited, but we're surrounded by civilians."

An annoyed teenage girl appeared next to our table. "Can I get you anything?"

"We'll take a pepperoni and a vegetarian. To go, please." Smiling, Ilya appeared polite, but I knew he was listening to the server. She finished writing, looked at Ilya, and then at me with a lackluster expression. I decided that she must dislike tourists.

"I hope she does think we're tourists. We wouldn't want our faces to stand out in her memory," said Ilya after she had gone.

"I guess if Innoviro has other mind-readers working for them, and if Innoviro is looking for us, all those people would need to do is ask about us. Even if a civilian wanted to lie to someone posing as a private investigator or bounty hunter, they'd think the truth anyway."

"Exactly," said Ilya.

We took our pizza boxes back to Cole's car. I found Jewel Lake on my phone while I related the details from my vision and savored a slice of pepperoni pizza.

Minutes later we were back on the Trans-Canada Highway looking for a turn-off to Jewel Lake.

"Watch the route closely as we go. I want the exact fork in the trail from your vision." Ilya drove slowly through the lake's parking lot.

A gravel road at the end of the lot was blocked off by a thick chain that read NO ADMITTANCE STAFF ONLY hanging between two yellow concrete posts. We both scanned the lot for signs of travelers or park staff. The few cars in the lot were all unoccupied. There were no pedestrians, so I slipped out of the car and lifted one end of the chain off its post. Ilya drove through and I hooked the chain back in place.

I hopped back in the car and snapped the door closed. "The vision starts on a gravel road. So far, so good. But go slowly. We're going to make a lot of noise."

"This is me you're with, remember? To everyone outside, there is no car, no noise."

"I keep forgetting about your illusionist side." I looked out the windows all around, unable to shake my concern.

We reached the fork in the road and the signpost from my vision in a few minutes. The Forest Service Road got rougher than expected, as though the forest had grown since my vision of Kingston driving.

The path narrowed and the trees closed in. We bounced and rattled through claustrophobic foliage. But like my vision, we burst out of the dense forest into an alpine meadow full of exotic trees and ferns. Kingston was nowhere in sight.

We got out of the car and walked towards the open-air workstation. A portable canvas canopy had been erected to shield occupants from the sun for the few hours it loomed overhead daily. We reached the workstation and found the stack of pizza boxes intact. No notes, files, vials, or specimens were visible. Kingston's truck was gone.

"Should we collect some samples for ourselves?" I said, feeling helpless.

"What would be the point? We're not looking to do any testing. We don't have access to a lab anyway." Ilya paced around the meadow, eyeing the mountains.

"It seems like a waste. To come here and have nothing to show for it," I said bitterly.

"Hang on!" Ilya walked to the rows of teal ferns. "That's not nothing!"

He pointed at a pair of shoes attached to horizontal ankles jutting out from the edge of the ferns.

Chapter 4

"He's alive!" Ilya said as we closed the gap between us and the body.

"Doctor Kingston?" I cried out. "George Kingston?"

We brushed the ferns back to see his whole body. Kingston looked up at us with a pained expression. He tried to speak, but blood dribbled from the corners of his mouth.

"What happened? Who did this to you?" I said.

"You don't have to talk. I'm a telepath. Think what you want to tell us," said Ilya.

I waited through the excruciating silence, wringing my hands, hoping Kingston communicated something. "I'm so sorry … for everything. We will stop Tatiana, I promise. And Casey and whoever else they're working with, it's why we're here."

I knelt down and took Kingston's hand, hoping for a vision of his attack. My focus paid off and the field around me shifted. I saw Kingston look up from pruning a plant. Casey walked forward with a menacing glare. He flexed his arms snapping them open into four new limbs without breaking stride. Terror seized my heart as Casey closed in, arms ready. I dropped Kingston's hand to slip back to the present. I took a calming breath as I looked from Kingston's face to Ilya.

"Do you have a copy of *The Compendium Transmuto*? Or do you know who does?" I said.

Kingston gingerly reached into his pocket and pulled out a thumb drive.

"He says it's not *The Compendium*, but it's a snapshot. And he says they took the bees. We have to find the bees." Ilya still held Kingston's hand.

"Is there anything we can do for you?" I met Ilya's gaze and he shook his head. "We could take him to a hospital in Hope."

We sat in silence again for a painfully long moment.

"He's gone," said Ilya.

I looked down at Kingston's large limp body before I glanced over at the workstation and the bee habitat I'd seen in my vision. The image of a chameleon beetle from the Capitol City Motel flashed through my mind. I'd seen two engineered species of insects. Who knew how many more were created? There could be more plant species too. We needed *The Compendium* to be sure.

I walked over to the workstation table and punched the stack of pizza boxes. I shouted as the cardboard went flying. I kicked one of the table legs again and again until it snapped up and the table collapsed.

Ilya touched my shoulder. "We should get out of here."

"Let's go check on Jonah," I said.

At the Bella Maria we found Jonah awake, but weak. Ilya

insisted on resuming his patrol of the Downtown Eastside and took Cole for protection. To my surprise, Faith volunteered to join them. Jonah and I were alone at last.

"So you found another research site." Jonah sat up in bed.

"And we found Doctor Kingston," I said.

"Did he help you?" asked Jonah.

"He did. He gave us a thumb drive with Compendium documents on it before he died of what looked like internal bleeding." I showed Jonah the small plastic rectangle on my palm.

"I'm so sorry."

I shook my head. "I've seen two people die in the last week. Technically, I also witnessed my parents' death last month. I don't think I'm handling it very well."

"Nobody expects you to watch people die and just bounce back. If you did, there'd be something wrong with you." Jonah reached a hand to me, but I shook my head.

"I'll tell you what I'm never going to see. You are not going to die on my watch."

"I'm not dying. I overdid it a bit. And then I went for a walk in the sun. I wasn't being smart." Jonah smoothed the blanket down on either side of his hips.

"Please, please take it easy. We don't know when or *if* we will find a treatment to help you. I know you don't want to lie in bed while the rest of us investigate, but there's no choice."

"I'll stay in bed if you'll join me." Jonah tried to smirk at me, but it wasn't convincing.

"It's not a good idea." I looked at the wall to avoid Jonah's eyes.

"You never know, I might drain you again and we'd be trading places. Kiss me, Irina and it could be you in this bed."

Jonah cocked his head with another weak smile.

"That's not funny. We both know that won't happen. The last time we were together, you did start to drain me, but I think I hurt you too. The injections Tatiana and Brad gave me made me stronger in general." I looked down at the ground.

"You didn't hurt me."

"You're still too weak for us to get close again, Jonah. I won't risk it."

"How about we lie together for a while? Nothing heated. We can watch TV. I'll pull the sheet up between us and if I start to feel weaker, I'll let you know." I let my gaze connect with his. Jonah looked at me intently with those glacial eyes. "I promise."

I stared back helplessly, grateful Jonah didn't have a mind-reading gift. We had established that he was attracted to me too, but I couldn't imagine he felt as strongly about me as I did about him.

I got into bed with him, on top of the bed sheet. I let him wrap his arms around my sweater. I clicked through television channels until I found an episode of *Doctor Who*. "Here. Let's have something stranger than us for once."

Ilya, Cole, and Faith walked in moments after *Doctor Who* ended. Cole carried grocery bags full of food. Ilya had a whiteboard and Faith had a full cardboard tray of to-go coffee cups.

"Okay." Ilya propped the empty whiteboard up on top of the dresser. "We need to get organized and develop a plan of attack."

Cole began shelving groceries. "We're fumbling around playing catch-up, but you can be damn sure Ivan knew exactly what his next steps were."

"We'll never catch up to him, let alone get ahead if we're roaming and groping in the dark," said Ilya.

"The first thing I'm going to do is copy everything on this thumb drive to Irina's laptop." Faith distributed coffee cups. "From there, I'll run a script cross-referencing what I pulled off the Innoviro server and plant doctor's thumb drive. Any common terms might be important."

I had to remind myself again of Faith's high intelligence and why she had been a part of the Innoviro team.

"For now, we'll have three columns." Ilya drew lines on the whiteboard with a black dry-erase marker. "Facts we know, questions we have, and actions we need to take."

"This feels like corporate life all over again," I said, half-joking.

"Until recently that life was all we knew. We have skills and education we should put to use here. Ivan hired us for the same reason," said Cole.

"My father – our father, sorry, Irina – used variants to further horrific goals. If he's capable of achieving what he wants, the destruction will be catastrophic. Nothing short of an apocalypse." Ilya wrote on the whiteboard.

Faith clicked on my laptop. Cole started making a meal.

I suddenly felt proud of my friends. I was a mess, but here they were, fresh from losing their jobs and homes, plunging into a dangerous mission with only their wits and morals to guide them. "I wish I had more skills and knowledge to contribute."

"Speak for yourself," said Jonah. "You can still have visions. I'm useless as long as I'm bedridden."

"You guys aren't useless. We're all here for a reason," said Cole.

Did he mean we all had motivation? Or did he think a higher power had brought us together? I didn't have the energy to probe for an explanation. Ilya and Faith hadn't looked up, still concentrating on their work.

"I need some air." I got up out of bed. Being cuddled up to Jonah with Cole and Faith in the room had gotten uncomfortable. "I won't be gone long."

I ducked into mine and Faith's room. I put my phone in the front pocket of my backpack and slung one of the straps over my shoulder. I heard the jingle of my 8-ball keychain.

The keychain had been a gift from Gemma. How ironic it seemed now. My little sister, who no longer knew who I was, had given me a trinket to play a predict-the-future game. I decided to ask it a question for fun.

I set the backpack down on the end of my bed and picked up the ball between my thumb and forefinger. I closed my eyes to concentrate on a question, but I was instantly transported to a lawn in front of a stairway leading to a long rectangular building made of a castle-like grey stone center and elegant modern glass wings on either side.

Clock hands moved rapidly on the tower next to me. People streamed in and out of the building and all around me. Wisps of cloud tumbled across the sky as the light blue behind it turned to a deep sapphire, and then dark indigo.

Lights inside the building and on the surrounding lampposts flickered to life. Pedestrian traffic was gone, except for a single girl walking out of the building. I walked towards her. I closed the distance between us until I could see her face. My sister Gemma!

I longed to talk to her, to hug her, and tell her I regretted everything. The intensity of my need to reach her jerked my vision self forward as Gemma turned in front of a grid of glass windows.

I followed behind as she marched along the dark concrete path until we reached a major well-lit road. Gemma had books clutched to her chest and more in the backpack sagging low on her back. She sped along the sidewalk at the time-advanced pace of my vision.

Gemma reached a brick building next to a large parking lot and an open grassy lawn. She pushed the front door open and the scene melted away. I was back in my hotel room.

I looked out the window at the barred shops across the street. Would I ever see Gemma again? She wouldn't know me if I did see her. I felt so tired and I ached with the weight of everything I had lost in the past few months.

I dropped onto my bed and curled up. Sadness washed over me. I let the tears come. Sobs wracked my body until all my energy left.

"Are you okay?" said Faith. She'd come several steps into our room, but I hadn't heard the door open.

"How long have you been standing there?" I dabbed at my eyes with the heels of my wrists.

"We heard you in the other room," Faith said softly.

"I saw my sister. She's the one who gave me the 8-ball keychain on my bag." I pointed at the bauble.

"I'm sorry. I can't imagine how hard it must be to lose your family. Don't forget, you've still got us. And Ilya. He's your family now." Faith's voice sounded uncharacteristically soft. Her eyes brimmed with sympathy.

"I didn't know you cared."

"Of course, I care. I know I've been bitchy lately. I don't have an excuse."

"You're still in love with Jonah. I get that. I can't help how I feel either." I swept more moisture from my eyelids with my fingertips.

"I'm getting over Jonah. I don't want to be the bitter bag who glares at you from the sidelines. I can't be with someone who doesn't want to be with me. It's embarrassing." Faith whipped her hair back with a nod and an eye roll.

"Ilya told me you were embarrassed while you were with him too. Don't let it eat you up." I sat up to face her.

"You and I both have to get our heads together."

"I'm glad you don't hate me." I took a calming breath.

"Likewise," Faith said confidently and smiled.

Chapter 5

"I'm going to UBC. I saw Gemma's dorm. I can find her from there," I announced as I walked into the guys' room the next morning. "It's probably a bad idea and a waste of time. I'm doing it anyway."

"I won't stop you, but I won't go with you," Ilya said.

"Don't forget, she's *your* sister too." I looked at Ilya and I saw realization flicker in his eyes.

"Go, but don't talk to your sister. If Rubin did his work well, and he always did, she won't know you." Cole stood at the kitchenette counter breaking up a pineapple with his bare hands. "You'll scare the hell out of her. She may even call the cops."

"Maybe she'll remember me if she sees me in person." I heard the desperation in my voice and saw pity on the faces of my friends. I waved away the chunk of pineapple Cole passed to me.

"We can't stop you from trying, but for what it's worth, I agree with Cole," said Faith.

"Go see her. Say goodbye somehow if you can. We'll be here for you when you get back," said Jonah from his bed.

Ilya nodded in agreement.

"Thanks. I won't make a scene, whatever happens," I said.

I returned to a bus stop I'd passed on East Hastings that had a UBC route listed on its signpost. A bus arrived a few minutes later. I swiped my temporary transit pass and walked to the back of the bus. I found an empty seat in the back row next to a window.

Vancouver's Downtown Eastside rolled along beside me. The crowds on the street gave way to boutiques and the lobbies of modern glass towers as we plowed back into the heart of the city. The bus turned onto the iconic Granville Street and the boutiques and eateries took on an edgy flavor. People with body piercings wearing ripped-up band shirts or skull-decorated tees and raggedy jeans flaunted studded bracelets, mohawks, and dyed hair. They walked the street mingling with tourists and business professionals. Windows populated with army boots and indie band posters existed alongside trendy clothing, pizza-by-the-slice, and tattoo parlors.

As the blocks of hard rock culture gave way to plain glass and metal towers again, the road took us out onto a bridge, like exiting through a gate and floating out onto open water.

We stopped on Granville Island. Nostalgia flowed over me as I remembered coming to the Island with Mom and Gemma. I looked at a yellow building with a rainbow archway behind the words Kid's Market. We'd visited Vancouver because Gemma had a science project in a provincial competition exhibited at Science World.

Mom took us shopping at the Market because Gemma's project had won a medal. She bought gifts for both of us to keep things fair. Gemma complained because she didn't want me to get a present for doing nothing. Mom still bought stuffed bears for both of us, but she also bought Gemma an expensive dollhouse, despite not being able to afford it after the cost of the trip itself.

I'd hated Gemma that day. I was jealous of her and ashamed I hadn't done anything special. I resented Mom for putting Gemma first, yet again. I remembered walking away from the Kid's Market and looking into the shop windows farther down the lane. Art supplies and finished works made me ache for the chance to make something myself. I badly wanted to believe I had the potential to create beauty.

For Christmas a few months later, Gemma's gift to me was a watercolor paint set. She'd remembered how I'd gushed over the arts community on Granville Island. She apologized for being a brat that day and told me she thought I would make a wonderful artist.

Over a decade later, Granville Island made me feel much the same way, inspired with a hint of resentment. I wanted to get off the bus and wander the artists' studios and gift shops, but I remembered where Gemma would be today and I stayed in my seat. Gemma was my only remaining connection to Mom.

The bus carried on through the hipster strip along West Broadway Avenue, passing upscale brands, designer consign-ment boutiques, and skateboard shops between bistros and brew pubs. Our route turned into a green space of carefully manicured lawns and lush forest. I saw a street sign for University Boulevard. We passed a golf clubhouse and entered a carefully crafted city inside the forest.

As the bus made a U-turn, I saw the library from my vision shining in the sun northward on the other side of an intersection. I hopped off the bus and walked briskly along Gemma's route home. I grabbed a copy of the student paper from a small self-serve newsstand.

I reached Gemma's building and kept walking past it, across the lawn and into the parking lot. I found a bench and got comfortable. I carefully positioned my newspaper so I could see over the top while concealing my face, allowing me to watch the door somewhat inconspicuously.

I waited. And waited. My stomach settled and my pulse slowed. I read a few articles in the paper while keeping one eyeball on the door. I lowered the paper, looked around, flipped the page, read more, and repeated the cycle. It occurred to me that I might become conspicuous simply by sitting on the bench too long. Had anyone exiting Gemma's building entered after I first sat down? My phone told me that over an hour had passed. Should I venture into the building and hope for a new vision?

I stared at the door, considering making a move when a man wearing a familiar pale blue shirt and metallic slate slacks exited the building. His face was covered in dark scabbing scrapes from his forehead to his chin in a ruinous swipe. The arm below his wounds had the sleeve rolled up to accommodate a plaster cast.

The injured man looked at his other wrist checking his watch as a woman in a black pantsuit joined him on the curb. I recognized her long dark ironed hair immediately. Tatiana! I knew the injured man before he turned to speak. The clean, unhurt side of Ivan's face bore an expression as cold and hard as ever. Ilya was right! Our father lived!

The pair paused on the corner in front of the building. Ivan surveyed the lawn and the parking lot while Tatiana examined her phone. Ivan pointed to the parking lot and stepped out onto the road.

Shit! Why had I come alone? Could Ivan hear me? Sense me? See me? Ivan kept walking into the parking lot and disappeared behind the frame of a SUV. Tatiana followed him, still looking at the screen in her hand.

My whole body flexed. I shifted in my seat, frantic for some sign of where Ivan and Tatiana had gone. Ivan's silver Audi rumbled into view behind the parked cars ahead of me. He turned at the end of the lot and drove around directly in front of me with Tatiana in the passenger seat.

Neither noticed the girl behind the paper on the bench next to them as they passed. I held my breath. I waited until the Audi drove out of sight. I waited some more.

Get up! Go! I shouted at myself. I stood and immediately flipped up the hood of my shirt. I tugged on the hood trying to pull it right over my face. I marched back to the bus loop.

What could the Krylovs want with Gemma? Leverage on me? Did she have a variation too? The parts of me not compelled forward with fear desperately wanted to turn back around and find my sister. I couldn't risk it though. What if the Krylovs came back? I'd have to get Ilya and return in disguise.

I paced inside a glass shelter until a number 14 bus reappeared and admitted the waiting passengers. I kept my hood up on the bus for the entire trip back to the Downtown Eastside.

I sped along Hastings to the Bella Maria, hood first, head down until I reached the safety of the hotel stairwell. I paused for a moment to catch my breath. I took deep, calming breaths. I had not been followed, I was sure of it. Nothing had happened, apart from sighting Ivan and Tatiana. If I could lie down for a moment, I would be able to tell the others without freaking out at the same time.

I slid my key card through the slot in my hotel room's door handle and pushed into the room. Ilya and Faith were entwined on her bed. They kept kissing for a beat until the sound of the door registered and they sensed me in the room.

I felt the look of shock frozen on my face. They both looked at me with similar expressions. I turned around and closed the door behind me. I crossed the hall and knocked on the guys' door.

"Use your card!" shouted Cole.

"It's Irina. Let me in!"

Chapter 6

"Back already?" Cole lounged in the room's only armchair, lazily clicking an old TV remote and working his way up and down the channels.

Jonah slept soundly in his bed.

"I saw Ivan and Tatiana," I said breathlessly.

"What!" Cole shouted. He paused for a beat. "Are you sure it was them?"

"One hundred percent. Ivan looks like he's got road rash on his face. His arm is hurt too. Tatiana is still perfect though."

Cole's features furrowed with concern. He massaged his face with both hands as though trying to erase my report from his memory.

Ilya and Faith came through the door to find Cole and me face-to-face in front of the kitchenette sink.

"This looks intense," said Faith, mildly amused.

Ilya looked anxious and said nothing.

"While I watched Gemma's building, I saw Ivan and Tatiana, not my sister." I shifted from one foot to the other, unable to stand still.

"What! How? Why?" blurted Faith, wide-eyed.

"What could they possibly want with your sister?" said Ilya. "I mean, our sister." He shoved a hand into his scruffy hair.

"I have no idea, but they came out of the building after I'd been watching for about an hour. I never saw Gemma, but they had to be in her room if they were there the whole time I was."

"Maybe they were spying on her too," said Cole. He frowned. Faith shoved his shoulder with no effect.

"Do you think they could have been looking for me? For us?" I asked.

"It's possible." Ilya looked out the window as though searching for something on the horizon.

"If he knows we're in Vancouver, he could also know we're on the Downtown Eastside. Either way, waiting for us at your sister's dorm room is a long shot," said Cole.

"Maybe your sister is a variant too and he wants her for research," said Faith.

"Don't make this worse than it is," said Cole with an eye-roll.

"Gemma is Irina's half-sister. It's not likely the girl has any variant genes," said Ilya. "The most sensible explanation is that my father wanted to check on Rubin's handiwork. He's probably making sure Gemma has no memory of Irina. It's a blessing you never made contact with her."

"Your aunt, I mean, our aunt, what exactly is her variation?" I asked Ilya.

"She isn't a variant, not as far as I know." Ilya shrugged his shoulders.

"How is that possible?"

"The magic of genetics," said Cole.

"Both our parents were freaks," said Faith gesturing between her and Cole with her thumb.

"Yeah, as far as I know, our mom was normal," I said, looking at Ilya.

"You can't be one hundred percent certain she had no variation whatsoever," said Ilya.

I sat at the small hotel dining table and stared out the window at the rundown walk-ups across the street. I tried to push away images of the world even worse off after Ivan's global 'renovation' came to pass.

"Since everyone is here again, it's a good time for me to give you guys the rundown on what I found on this Kingston guy's thumb drive." Faith addressed the room.

"I'm going for a walk," said Ilya, looking right past Faith. "I want to see if I can find our almost acquaintance from yesterday. The skin-changer I thought I heard. Whatever you guys think is useful, put it on the whiteboard."

Ilya picked up his wallet off the counter and left. I wondered if he heard my apocalyptic worries. Jonah stayed in a deep sleep.

"Well then, what's the scoop?" Cole clapped his hands and rubbed them with an inquisitive look. Jonah sat up in bed and I glared at Cole.

"Kingston had reports about his progress with variant plant strains. They were being cultivated alongside a strain of variant bees." Faith pulled a strip of fabric from her pocket and tied back her dreads.

"That tracks; he said something about bees," I leaned forward in my seat. "They were gone when Ilya and I got there, but I saw them in my vision. They were beautiful, covered in an oil-slick rainbow," I said.

"Well, Kingston didn't keep any data on the bees themselves, at least not in the files on his thumb drive." Faith leaned back against the dresser and gripped the top.

"They were probably designed to pollinate his variant plants," said Cole.

"Kingston *did* have a few quarterly reports from some guy named Doctor Peter Waynesburg. Kingston included a word processing file summarizing the reports," said Faith.

"Did you read any of it?" said Jonah, still blinking into wakefulness.

"I haven't picked through Waynesburg's report data, but I read Kingston's summary. It's an open letter to anyone who might get their hands on his thumb drive. The reason he's got Dr. Waynesburg's reports is because they were both being blackmailed and wanted to find a way to burn Ivan, especially if one or both of them got killed," said Faith.

"I'm sure Kingston didn't have Irina's gift, but to *know* you're working for a man that might kill you. And to have your fear realized. What a horrible way to go," said Jonah.

"Let's worry about feeling bad for this guy when we find out how they blackmailed him," said Cole.

"What matters is that Waynesburg owned a fracking company contracted with major energy players. According to Kingston, Waynesburg's reports include data on the success of ecological disruption. It looks like he intentionally polluted his work sites. There's also a separate report on seismic disruption potential. Waynesburg believed selective, strategic fracking could kick start another continental shift, bringing with it a whole new global climate, if they weren't careful about where and how their extractions were done. It seems pretty unlikely, but I know nothing about this stuff. Cole, you need to look at this guy's notes and see if it's even possible," said Faith, picking up speed and energy as she spoke.

"There's no way. Fracking operations don't necessarily align with fault lines. How could Ivan–," Cole's voice trailed off as he rubbed his jaw, deep in thought.

"Kingston's open letter also talked about '*The Compendium* men' as though Ivan was one of a group," said Faith. She retied the strip holding her dreadlocks back.

"Did he give any names?" I looked down to find my hands interlocked tightly.

"No, but we do have something good to go on since Waynesburg's reports are addressed to Innoviro's San Francisco office. The street address is the same one I pulled off the Victoria server when I hacked it."

"We've got to get the hell out of Vancouver now. Maybe we should keep heading to San Francisco. We were going to go eventually anyway," I said.

"Maybe it's time to get law enforcement involved. If we've got documentation – real evidence, don't we have something to hand over?" Jonah had become fully alert.

"On whom should we dump this fantastic disaster?" said Faith.

"Let's give it to the cops and start working with them," said Jonah.

I closed my eyes and rested my forehead on the table.

"Irina saw Ivan and Tatiana at UBC," said Faith.

"But, she wasn't seen and didn't make contact with her sister," said Cole.

"All the more reason to call the cops!" Jonah blurted.

"Screw the cops. I don't think we're in danger this instant, but we can't stay, not long enough to educate anyone about the variant world and the chances of Innoviro destroying the planet," said Faith.

"Well, I *do* think we're in danger." I propped my elbows on the table and massaged my temples. "What can the police do to help us? They wouldn't take any of this seriously over a thumb drive and our words. We're going to get killed and it's my fault." I swallowed hard and rubbed my eyes to cover the anxiety bubbling out of me.

"Nobody's getting killed. Irina, it's not your fault we're in trouble. We're in trouble because we all have a connection to Ivan and didn't stay on his bandwagon. Nobody thinks we're in this situation just because you were the first of us to find out about the real Innoviro." Jonah shifted in bed, trying to sit up straighter.

"We never blamed you. We had a harder time believing what Ivan was involved in because we ate his bullshit for longer," said Cole.

"If there is a Compendium plot, if Ivan wants to unmake the world as we know it, a lot of people will die. Eventually, if not soon." Faith sat in the other dining chair as her energy level dropped too.

"What are the chances all variants would make it?" I asked the group.

"Probably pretty fair that most of us would survive." Cole looked at Jonah's pale face as the latter rested against his headboard.

"If we let Ivan cause an apocalypse, whatever is left afterward would be hell on earth for the rest of our lives," said Faith.

"However long that might be," said Jonah.

"Hey, I've got a better idea than cops. Let's call the newspapers. Let's get a reporter involved. If we do some research and find the right person, we can bring him or her up here, show off our variations for proof, and hand over copies of everything we've got." Cole paced as he spoke. "Combine a little legit press with some or all of us outing ourselves on social media. That could be all it takes."

I started making notes on the whiteboard about what we *knew* and what we *wanted* to know. We knew about human testing, plant cultivation, bees, fracking, and pollution. The questions remaining disturbed me. Who were the missing Compendium players? How could Ivan and *The Compendium* be stopped? Our goal involved exposing the secrets of elusive and malicious ultra-wealthy people.

Faith leaned into my laptop researching potential reporters we could contact with our evidence. A sudden knock at the door startled all of us.

"Hey guys, it's me," said Ilya from outside the door. "I brought a friend."

"Come on in," said Cole. He crossed his arms and resumed pacing.

Ilya entered the room with a tall thin man at his side. The man had a receding hairline with long, fine hair hanging down his back. It hadn't been brushed in some time. A faint odor of sweaty feet and old skin oil filled the room.

"This is Donald," said Ilya gesturing at the tall man.

"Hey," said Donald sheepishly with a waist-high wave.

"Do any of you remember Josh Robertson?" said Ilya.

"Yeah," said Faith as she looked up.

"Sure," said Cole.

Jonah nodded.

"Donald is Josh's ex-roommate. He worked for Innoviro at the warehouse we found in North Van. And he helped move the seedlings out to Hope," said Ilya.

"You worked for Innoviro?" I said.

"I'd been a tree planter, so Josh got me a job with their silviculture project here in Van." Donald looked anywhere but our faces.

"Tell my friends what else Innoviro did here in Vancouver." Ilya looked encouragingly at Donald.

"There wasn't anything else. We raised crops the way the science guys told us. We were all let go when they closed the warehouse. I got a bonus for helping with the transfer to the site in Hope," said Donald.

"Are you sure Innoviro didn't have any corporate offices here in Vancouver?" Cole's muscular arms stood out crossed over his chest. Donald looked visibly uncomfortable.

"I'm sure. That business lady, Tatiana, had to work out of the warehouse when she came to Van. She was pretty pissed to be outside downtown," said Donald, still avoiding eye contact with anyone but Ilya.

"Thanks, man. That was all we needed to know." Ilya slapped a twenty-dollar bill into Donald's hand. He nodded at Ilya and backed out of the room.

We all stayed silent for a moment digesting the news. Vancouver had no secrets left to tell us.

"You didn't need to bring him here. We would have believed you," said Cole. "What if Ivan and Tatiana find him and he gives us away?"

"I seriously doubt that will happen. First, I'm sure they could care less about a warehouse grunt. And second, couldn't you smell him? That dude is living on the street," said Faith.

"She's right. The reason I found him is because I could hear him thinking about how great the Innoviro days were. He hadn't had a paycheck for years before then and not since," said Ilya.

"So if Innoviro tested on street variants here in Van too, this guy would have been one of them," said Faith. She wrote 'No Van Variant Testing' on the whiteboard and circled the text.

"He could have lied about it," said Cole.

"Not to Ilya," said Jonah, nodding at my brother. Ilya grinned.

"So I guess we should leave for San Francisco tomorrow." I stretched my arms up anticipating the discomfort of hours on the road.

"Not directly. We need a quick detour. Donald gave me Josh's address. He's living in Seattle now. Josh worked closely with my father before I was involved with the company. He might have information for us," said Ilya.

"Or he might still be working for Ivan," said Jonah.

"What would we have to gain from seeing Josh?" Cole paced again.

"He could be a decent person and feel the same way we do about Ivan and *The Compendium* people," I said.

"Hand me the address and I'll find it on a map," said Faith. She typed furiously on my laptop.

"Print it too. I don't want to rely on computers and phones once we cross the border," said Ilya.

"Getting to Josh isn't an emergency. And we won't get to San Francisco overnight. We can stick around Vancouver long enough to contact a reporter," said Cole.

"I've already got a few names. I'll try connecting with someone tonight. A decent reporter should be able to meet us inside a day," said Faith.

"We need better than decent. We need amazing," said Jonah.

Faith rolled her eyes with her chill-out-I've-got-this expression, nodding as she continued typing and staring intently at her screen.

We checked out of the Bella Maria shortly after eight o'clock in the morning. Faith had arranged to meet someone named David Wong at eight-thirty sharp in a downtown restaurant with a meeting room in the back. She'd given the man a fair chunk of verifiable information about us and Innoviro, along with the promise of corporate scandal. She left out any mention of variations. We all agreed to save that for our meeting in person.

"So what's the plan? Are we just going to throw a thumb drive at him, unveil our abilities, and hit the road?" said Ilya as we all followed Faith through the front door of a bistro outfitted with brushed steel and crisp laminate wood.

"Have you got something more elaborate in mind?" said Faith as she marched past the mousy blond woman eyeing us from behind the counter.

Faith pushed open a frosted glass door and we followed her into a room with a large round table and a dozen black task chairs perfectly spaced. Each setting had a notepad, mini pre-sharpened pencils, and an empty glass tumbler. A pitcher of water stood placid in the middle.

"Good morning," said the small slim man with black spiky hair and horn-rimmed glasses. His plain white T-shirt and dark blue jeans looked brand new.

"You must be Wong," said Faith briskly.

"What my charming sister means to say is, good. morning to you too." Cole stepped in front of Faith to shake David Wong's hand. Cole's beefy hand enveloped the reporter's.

"I don't want to rush this meeting, but we're leaving Vancouver. All we can do here is give you a rundown on what we're doing, hand over our evidence, and be on our way," I said as slowly and politely as I could manage through my nerves. I took a breath to steady myself.

"We have documentation connected to our former employer, a company called Innoviro Industries," said Jonah as he took a seat. His ashen face and heavy eyes suggested he hadn't slept, although I knew he had.

Everyone in the room followed Jonah's lead and sat. Cole frowned with concern looking at Jonah and he leaned forward to take over.

"We have reason to believe Innoviro was engaged in unethical human testing and malicious environmental sabotage," said Cole. He paused, considering David Wong's face. The reporter seemed attentive. "We still don't know how far-reaching the consequences will be, but we believe that Innoviro intended to effect global harm."

I sat speechless. Cole's physical presence - and personal style - made it easy to forget that he was well-educated.

"This is pretty serious stuff. And you've brought me hard evidence of this activity?" said Wong.

"Honestly we don't know the full extent of what we're handing you. This thumb drive is a copy of reports we haven't reviewed in detail," said Faith.

Faith, Cole, and Ilya took turns filling Wong in on what we had learned, from Kingston's files and our first-hand experiences. Wong took it all in with the best of poker faces.

"This is a wild story. I'm going to be honest. I don't see my editor – or my publisher – backing me on publication of any article connected to what you're saying," said Wong.

"Let's cut to the chase then." Glaring at Wong, Faith picked up a blank pad of notepaper off the table. She tore apiece off the top, and without breaking eye contact, she shot a flame from her fingertip at the crisp white sheet.

Wong instinctively jolted backward into his chair.

Jonah poured himself a glass of water. Instead of drinking it, he coaxed the liquid out of the glass, into the air, and back into the pitcher.

"Maybe you *should* drink that water," I said quietly to Jonah. In my peripheral vision, Wong's mouth gaped.

"And the rest of you?" he said with raw fascination.

"You'll have to take my word for it that I could crack this table in half without breaking a sweat," said Cole.

"Don't worry man, he believes you," said Ilya. He paused looking at Wong. "Yes, I can hear what you're thinking … six thousand seven hundred and fifty-two, no, fifty-three, dude, make up your mind."

Wong looked at me waiting for my story.

"I have visions," I said lamely. Wong looked confused and I felt heat rush to my cheeks.

"I mean, I can see the past, present, and future. I'm psychic, but it's hard to control. For the most part, I only get what comes to me. But I am getting better at seeing things I'm looking for," I said, fumbling to explain something I struggled to understand myself.

"And on that note, I think we're ready to go," said Ilya as he stood up. The rest of us rose as well.

"Wait, how can I reach you? This is huge. I still need your input. I need quotes. I need photos. You're willing to go on the record, right?" said Wong.

"We can't stick around, especially not to get roped into an investigation – by your paper or the cops," said Faith.

"You're joking! You can't drop a science fiction mega-story in my lap and run off!" said Wong.

"You've got my email. We'll be in touch," said Faith.

"We just won't be here," said Cole.

We left David Wong clutching our thumb drive and poking at a pile of ashes. None of us looked back. We walked calmly back to Cole's car and discreetly opened the doors.

Faith sat in the front passenger seat. Ilya sat between Jonah and me in the back. I had purposely stalled getting into the car, hoping not to sit next to Jonah. I didn't trust myself not to lean on his shoulder in my anxious state.

As we crossed the Granville Street Bridge, sailboats sprinkled the blue water of False Creek. The clear blue sky overhead completed the illusion of serenity all around us. I didn't feel at peace. Far from it. My stomach roiled, churning away with no more than a cup of coffee to process.

"When we get to the border, we'll need a cover story about where we're going and why," Ilya said as he looked around at each of us. "It should be something simple that doesn't contradict anything they can find with our passports."

"All we need to say is that we're going on vacation. We're

camping, so we don't have a destination address," said Faith.

"What if the border guards search us? They'll see we don't have any camping gear. They can scan the car now like they do with bags at the airport. They won't even have to ask to search us," said Cole.

"Why don't we tell the truth?" I said.

Everyone in the car turned to look at me. Cole eyed me in his rearview mirror.

"I don't mean the whole truth. We'll tell them the company we worked for folded and we're unemployed. So we're going on a summer road trip before we look for jobs."

"That could work. We tell the truth but leave out the part about looking for our ex-boss. We could give them Josh's address if they want to know where we're staying. What's the likelihood they'll call him to ask?" said Jonah.

"It's settled then. We're unemployed. Used to work for Innoviro. Road trip to see Josh and wander around Washington. I'm sure it goes without saying, but everybody, be cool when we get to the border." Ilya looked directly at Faith.

"What?" Faith smirked back at him. "I'll be good."

We cruised up to the Peace Arch border and took our place in the queue of cars waiting to cross. My heart pounded. I hadn't crossed the border for several years, and never without one of my parents taking the lead. Would I be convincing if I answered their questions? *I'm a crappy liar, even if I'm lying by omission. They'll see right through me.*

"You're going to be fine," said Ilya.

"We'll be in Seattle before you know it," said Jonah.

Our turn came at the customs window. I hoped I could keep my mouth closed. We had all given our passports to Cole so the customs officer could review them all at once. If Cole did all the talking, we would be fine.

"Passports please," said the officer.

Cole handed the booklets to the officer.

"Where are you headed?" asked the gruff barrel-chested man in the booth.

"Seattle." Cole's answer was cheerful but short. Good so far.

"What is the nature of your trip to Seattle?" said the officer. He examined each passport in turn, looking at our faces one by one. A fresh surge of anxiety rushed through my veins.

"We're visiting a friend. We're going on a road trip," said Cole.

The customs officer looked concerned.

"How long do you intend to travel through the US? What destinations will you be visiting?" said the officer.

"Um, we're going to Seattle and then we're driving down to San Francisco." The confidence in Cole's voice wavered.

"And your occupations?" said the officer.

"We're unemployed at the moment. Our employer recently went under," said Cole.

"That's not what I asked you," said the officer. "What do each of you do for a living? And who *was* your employer?"

"I'm, uh, a geologist. We worked for Innoviro Industries. And my friends are, uh–"

"We're a rock n' roll band!" Faith blurted out in a poorly rendered British accent.

"Okay. Sir, please pull the vehicle ahead and park in one of the stalls in front of our office." The officer pointed at empty parking spots and the building next to us. We should have been driving away into the stream of moving traffic! What the hell was Faith thinking?

A new customs officer exited the building to greet us. This

woman was tall and big-boned with a blond bob under her U.S. Customs and Border Protection ball cap.

"Women, come with me please," she said. "Men, remain in the vehicle and a male officer will be with you momentarily."

Obediently, I got out of the car and slung my backpack on my shoulder.

"Leave your bags. They will be subject to search along with your vehicle. You can take your wallet or anything containing relevant documentation," she said, directly to me.

"You've got to be kidding with this. I was joking." Faith rolled her eyes.

The female customs officer frowned at her. "Unless this is your first time crossing the Canada-United States border, you should know this is not the time or place to make jokes with officials."

We followed her, wallets in hand, into the small single-story office building. I ventured a glance back at the guys back in the car. They were talking, but all facing forward. *Stupid girl! What have you gotten us into?*

"Are you going to deny us entry to the U.S.?" I asked as calmly and politely as I could.

"Entry into the United States is not guaranteed. You need to cooperate fully and submit to a search," said the officer.

"You're searching the car with dogs, right?" said Faith.

Shut up! Please just shut up! I thought angrily.

As we followed the officer down a hallway, I suddenly realized why a woman had been sent to retrieve Faith and me separately. Her mention of a male officer for the guys should have alerted me to what was coming next. The officer gestured at a door with an icon of a gloved hand on it.

We entered the room to find a rectangular table and two

stacking chairs on either side. The walls were bare. The only other item in the room was a small camera mounted in the far corner.

"Remove your clothing down to your bras and underwear. Turn out your pockets and empty your shoes," said the officer.

My pulse throbbed and white noise squealed in my ears. I could barely breathe, but I followed instructions. I removed my socks. I looked over at Faith who seethed with rage. I expected the officer to produce a rubber glove and snap it onto her right hand.

She sifted through our clothing and patted both Faith and me around our breasts and backsides. She didn't ask us to remove anything else and neither of us volunteered.

"You can get dressed. Come back out front when you're ready." The officer abruptly left us staring at our piles of rumpled clothes.

"What the hell were you thinking with that stupid rock and roll thing!" I hissed at Faith.

"It was a joke. Everyone in the car knew it. The customs officer knew it. They've got badges so far up their asses, they can't handle the tiniest bit of humor," said Faith.

"This is the goddamn border, what did you expect them to do?" I said, raising my voice.

"Chill out honey. They're letting us go, aren't they? We haven't done anything, so they can't hold us," said Faith.

"I'm glad you're confident," I said scathingly. I fought my urge to say how stupid I thought she'd been.

We finished dressing and walked back down the hall to the main door. The officer was gone, so we left the building. The guys were nowhere to be seen, but the contents of Cole's car from dash to trunk had been unceremoniously emptied onto the ground.

Faith didn't say a word. She began repacking the trunk. I followed her lead and picked up the mess around the front of the car. I hoped she blamed herself as much as she blamed the customs officers. The guys returned as we finished repacking the car.

"Ready to go, now, Faith?" Ilya's eyes narrowed.

"Yeah, sorry, my bad," said Faith.

"Just get back in the car," said Cole.

"Let's get some food and forget about this," said Jonah.

We reached Blaine, Washington within an hour and Cole found a fast food drive-through for lunch. Jonah wanted some fresh air, so we headed for a city park with a picnic table instead of eating in the stuffy car.

"I feel like I just gained five pounds," said Ilya after finishing his burger and fries.

"I normally only eat this stuff if I'm hung over." Jonah crumpled his burger wrapper with a look of disdain.

"Me too." I looked at him and smiled.

"Want to go work it off on the swings?" said Jonah.

"It's better than getting right back in the car," I said.

Cole kept eating, working his way through his third burger. Faith had gone to the washroom. Ilya leaned back on one of the picnic table bench seats. I followed Jonah to the swings.

We sat on the swing set, pumping back and forth with our legs, passing each other in a blur, laughing.

"I couldn't tell you the last time I sat on a swing." I smiled, my nervousness melting away.

"We should all–" Jonah stopped short and fell out of his swing, crumpling like a rag doll. I turned back as my swing carried me forward in time to see Jonah's limp body hit the gravel with a crunch.

"JONAH!" I shrieked. I jumped out of my swing and dove down next to his body.

I heard footsteps and shouts behind me as I slapped Jonah's cheeks and shook his shoulders.

"Wake up! Don't do this, Jonah. Wake up! Wake up!" I chanted like a mantra.

"Try some water," said Cole, handing me a bottle.

I cracked the cap and tipped the liquid into Jonah's mouth. The water slid in as though pouring down a drain.

Jonah roused, grabbed my hand and the bottle together, sucking hard until he emptied the bottle. He was pale as a sheet. The rest of us were sweating in the heat, but Jonah's skin didn't release a drop of moisture.

"Take me to the ocean," said Jonah faintly.

We rushed to the car and headed west, not knowing the city streets, only the general direction of the Pacific. After passing through block after block of small-town America, we finally saw a pier ahead. And an endless sea wall with no beach.

"Look for a boat launch I can pull into," Cole said urgently.

Faith pointed out a ramp leading down into the sea next to the pier as we turned onto the main waterfront street. Cole drove right down to the ramp. Ilya and Faith quickly carried Jonah into the water.

He sat in the water for a moment. Frothy foam surged and swirled around his waist. Jonah leaned sideways into the water and floated, lounging peacefully. After several minutes, he stood, turned, and dove into the ocean.

We all stood on the boat ramp watching the surf, waiting for Jonah to resurface. I looked around to see if we had drawn a crowd with our friend's odd mid-day swim. A few pedestrians walked along the sidewalk behind us. One woman looked briefly in our direction. Nobody else cared about a young man plunging into the water fully clothed.

Jonah swam for a while before eventually coming back to us. He emerged from the water covered in dirt and seaweed, but looking more refreshed than I had seen him in weeks.

"Let's grab a flat of water before we get back on the road," said Jonah.

"Dude, whatever you need," said Cole.

Jonah peeled off his wet shirt revealing his pale muscular chest. He squeezed what water he could out of his shorts and we all got back into the car.

Chapter 8

The briny smell of sun-baked seaweed permeated Cole's car as we left Blaine, with a new flat of water in the trunk.

We passed outlet malls, resorts, and a casino, separated by woods and grasslands tinted yellow by the summer sun. Muggy heat stifled us. The only relief was the occasional gust of cool air through the car windows.

As we neared Seattle, software companies, research facilities, and corporate towers replaced brand-name clothing shops and chain restaurants. The highway poured onto a larger freeway. After many more miles, the great cement channel opened into an urban landscape. The Space Needle stood out in the distance as we drove onto a bridge.

"I have Josh's apartment, the name of the diner where he works, and his cell number," said Ilya as he consulted a piece of paper.

"We should text him first," said Jonah.

"Which of you guys knew him best?" said Faith.

"Probably me," said Ilya.

"Use my phone," I said, handing my precious digital treasure to my not-so-technically inclined brother. *Does mind-reading and the capacity to create illusions negate a need for technology? Or does he not like electronics?*

Ilya took the phone. "If you'd spent the last year living off-grid, you wouldn't be so excited about a phone."

I narrowed my eyes as I glared at him. *I never had gadgets or luxuries growing up. Mom and Darryl had less than half of what Ivan gave you.* Ilya rolled his eyes and turned his back to concentrate on my phone. I took a deep breath and looked up at the sky to stop myself from thinking anything else.

"David Wong emailed me already. He wanted to make sure he had my address right. Cole, I'm giving him your email too," said Ilya.

"Let's hit Pike Place Market before we meet up with Josh! Please! I've never been," said Faith.

"Oooo, that sounds like fun!" I wanted to see the Market, but paranoia filled my chest as I pictured the crowds inside. We would either blend in or be trapped.

"According to the map, we need to be downtown for Josh's work and apartment, so why not?" Ilya kept texting.

"We need something fun right now," said Jonah.

Ilya directed Cole to a parking lot down the street from Pike Place. The tiny lot was attended by an old man who wanted fifteen dollars per hour to park, the first hour upfront in cash. Jonah paid him and we left the car.

Pike Street overflowed with pedestrians. A sunny summer day brought hordes of tourists to blend with the already eclectic mix of bohemians, students, and business people. Suits and sarongs, bandanas and backpacks all churned in a sea of human traffic.

We found the entrance under the iconic PUBLIC MARKET CENTER neon sign. The huge clock told us it was nearly three. Josh returned Ilya's text and asked us to meet him at a nearby diner at five o'clock.

As we fell in with a stream of people flowing under the sign, I saw the famous fish market. Their workers were busy throwing fish and shouting, decked in rubber overalls as though they had just stepped off a fishing boat.

"Let's split up. I want to browse around," said Faith.

"How about we meet back here at quarter to five," said Ilya.

"Sweet!" Faith turned on her heel and veered into the nearest trinket shop.

"Has everyone got money?" asked Cole. We all nodded and he left.

"There's a record shop downstairs. I'll be there if anyone's looking for me." Ilya followed Cole.

Jonah and I were left to watch the fishmongers on our own. Neither of us said a word or moved to leave. My pulse quickened as our silence stretched on. Jonah gently took my hand. I squeezed it and released my grip.

"The incident at the park has me more worried than ever. About your health," I said softly, barely audible over the chatter.

Jonah leaned down and whispered in my ear. "I don't care anymore. If I'm going to die anyway, I'd rather be with you before it happens. What's an extra few days or months in the scope of someone's life?" His lips almost brushed my skin. The feel of his breath against me sent a tingle through my body. Anger replaced the attraction a heartbeat later.

"Don't talk like that." I threw Jonah's hand back at him and marched to the stairwell.

"We need to talk about it, so why not now?" Jonah caught up with me.

"Let's enjoy the Market. We'll talk later." *Good luck getting me alone after today*, I thought, vowing not to give Jonah the chance to corner me again. To change the subject, I said, "I think Faith and Ilya are getting back together."

"Really?" Jonah sounded surprised. "Good, I'm happy for them."

I exited the stairwell on the next floor down with Jonah next to me. I started browsing a table of leather goods in a room off the main hallway. "I walked in on them the other day. It surprised me too. Ilya *said* he still loved her, but he refused to make a move until he was sure she'd gotten over you."

"Faith probably started it then. She doesn't keep secrets or wait around when she wants something."

We moved on to a table of organic lavender and honey products. I turned away and headed back to the main hallway. "What's that supposed to mean?"

"Nothing. Sorry, I didn't mean it like that. I wish we had both been honest about how we feel before now. We could have been together for longer."

"I hate to keep saying this, but we're not together. Not until you're cured – or stable at a bare minimum," I said as we passed a window of glass sun-catchers.

"Can you let *me* worry about my health?"

"Let's agree to disagree for now." I walked into a small shop of handmade wool accessories. I lifted a price tag on a wool infinity scarf. "Three hundred dollars?" I blurted loudly. The proprietor sitting on a stool next to the cash register glowered at me.

"This *is* Pike Place Market," said Jonah. "If we ever go back to Vancouver, I'll take you to Granville Island. It's the same idea, an artists' market with cool handmade stuff we can't afford."

I followed Jonah back out into the hall. "I've been to Granville Island. Let's stick to window shopping from now on. It's less tempting. You know, if we all still worked for Innoviro, this stuff wouldn't be so impractical. It'd be a splurge. Why did I have to go digging and ruin everything?"

"Because you thought Ivan was doing something wrong. And he was. We didn't want to listen at first, but for my part, I think I'd known for a long time. I wanted my cure and I didn't want to get off the gravy train. It took someone new – who hadn't been sucked into the lifestyle yet – to question everything."

We emerged on another sub-level with a vaulted ceiling above two floors of open space. Inner windows from all the shops around us on the floor above displayed plants, clothes, books, posters, and more trinkets.

"Oh, I'd been sucked into the lifestyle. But I was naïve enough to think that asking a few questions might solve a problem. I didn't think I'd bring the whole place to a halt. Not at first." I craned my neck, looking around at each glass-enclosed shop.

"It needed to end. You should never question doing the right thing. We can't put the genie back in the bottle anyway."

"Good point. Hey, speaking of genies." I caught sight of a turban-topped antique mannequin in a glass and wood case with the word 'Swami' artfully painted on the front. The figure stood guard next to the entrance to a magic shop.

I stepped up to the swami and looked into his painted brown

eyes. *What do I have in common with this man? I wondered. How many real psychics have there ever been? Will there be more of us now?*

I stared and stared into the swami's eyes, thinking hard about Ivan, pondering where he might have gone with Tatiana in his silver Audi. The walls of the Pike Place basement dissolved like smoke and I stood in an apartment with a view of the Golden Gate Bridge. Fog covered the bay around it like a blanket of cotton batten. I turned to see the contents of the room.

Ivan and another man in a collared shirt were seated on an expensive-looking white couch. Ivan's face bore the scabby wounds I had seen outside Gemma's apartment at UBC. The other man had bright silver hair, although he looked to be no older than his early thirties. Two stainless steel coffee mugs floated on an almost invisible glass coffee table.

"I expect to view the site tomorrow. I didn't hop on a red-eye to amuse myself," said Ivan.

"You do understand, we're still weeks away from the earliest possible test date," said the silver-haired man.

"Listen, Waynesburg, *you* need to understand *me*. You're adapting to my timeline now. My son and daughter are on the loose with their friends stirring up trouble. My soft-hearted children have it in their heads that Compendium work needs to stop. I don't know how much they know, but I have to assume the worst. Tomorrow, we go back to the Island, and then, up to the test site."

The vision went black. In a blink, I snapped back to the Pike Place Magic Shop.

Jonah had his hand on my shoulder. He stood shielding me from the view of other shoppers. "What happened? What did you see?"

"Ivan and Waynesburg. They're in San Francisco, talking about a test and a site. Ivan is freaked out about the group of us poking into *The Compendium*. He pressured the other man for a tour of the site. I know the other man was Waynesburg because Ivan used his name," I said.

"Waynesburg was the guy working on controlled seismic activity. He must be getting ready to test a piece of equipment." Jonah's brow furrowed.

"You mean he's going to start an earthquake?" Disbelief came through in my shrill tone.

"The San Andreas fault line is a good place to trigger a seismic event. He can get right on top of it. The urban development in the area would be devastated though."

"No! We can't let this happen! In the vision, Ivan was cut up, exactly how he looked at UBC! That vision could have been the present, right now! Waynesburg said the test would happen in a few weeks. We have to get to San Francisco!" I put my hands over my face.

"Calm down, we've got time. It'll only take a few days to drive to San Francisco." Jonah followed me back the way we came.

"Let's find the others and go straight to this Josh guy. I'll tell him why we're early. We'll buy dinner and we'll be paying customers so he doesn't get into trouble."

When I explained my unexpected vision to my friends, they readily abandoned Pike Place. The streets were more crowded as we made our way back into the heart of Seattle. We went on foot, not expecting to find parking again near Josh's diner. By the time we found the hole-in-the-wall where Josh worked, he was already sitting on the step outside, phone in one hand, smoking a cigarette with the other.

Ilya approached Josh and the latter butted his cigarette on the ground. Josh wore his dark hair in messy short spikes. He had chiseled features that would have been handsome if not for the hint of menace in his dark eyes. Josh stood and the full impact of his frame hit me. He must have been at least six and a half feet tall. Ilya had to crane his neck up to look Josh in the eye. A flash of fear surged in me as the two moved to embrace. A clapped handshake transitioned to a hug and I wondered how the two had come to be such good friends.

Cole stepped up next and when his fist bumped into Josh's, I could have sworn I heard a deep metallic thud. Cole had unparalleled strength, but he wasn't made of steel. And then I realized what Josh had been at Innoviro. Security.

Chapter 9

Josh's apartment was a disordered collection of fast food bags, cardboard boxes, dirty laundry, and empty beer bottles. His few decorations consisted of war and action movie posters.

"So, can I get you guys some beers?" said Josh as we found seats by clearing trash off his couch and several folding chairs.

"We're good. We don't want to overstay our welcome." Jonah repressed his disgust as he looked around the apartment and shifted in his seat.

"As I said in my text, we're heading to San Francisco. We're tracking some dodgy stuff Innoviro set in motion. I assume you've heard the company went under?" Ilya happily picked through an open chip bag on Josh's kitchen table.

"Not in so many words, but I did get a message from the old receptionist, Melissa something-or-other." Josh took a sip from his beer.

"Stupid bitch. Wouldn't know right from wrong if it punched her in the face," said Faith. Cole glared at her.

"Melissa may or may not be on the wrong side of what's going on. Innoviro has plans to reconstruct the whole planet into a variant-only environment." Cole scratched his chin over his days-old beard.

"For a start, Ivan plans to set off an earthquake, on purpose, somewhere around San Francisco." I heard the desperation in my voice. I ran my hands through my loose hair, failing to soothe my nerves.

"They were doing genetic experiments in Victoria. And in Vancouver, they had a botanical lab engineering new plants, and insects too, we think," said Jonah, tugging on his shirt cuffs nervously.

"Okay, let me get this straight. You all are chasing Ivan and Tatiana Krylov over plants and insects. And you think he can start an earthquake down in California? I heard that Rubin's dead and Thorn's in charge now. Have you guys met Thorn?" said Josh calmly, looking at me over the rim of his beer bottle.

The image of that beast man's reflective cat-like eyes leaped into my mind. The rest of his face caught up, including every detail of his grimy skin, decayed fangs, and long matted locks.

"Yeah, we met Thorn," said Cole.

"And now he's dead too," Faith added darkly.

I saw Cole bound by webbing, followed instantly by Thorn's burned body.

"And you all still want to tangle with Ivan's people?" said Josh.

"We don't want a fight, but we all helped to further Innoviro's research and development. And now Innoviro is going to hurt people. A lot of people. We want to atone," said Jonah.

"Hurt people is putting it mildly. When my father unleashes

whatever he's got planned, we could be talking about billions of lives lost, the destruction of cities, and the end of human society the way we know it," said Ilya.

"Come on, man. This is a bit much, even for Ivan. You're blowing things way out of proportion. Just because Ivan plays things close to the chest doesn't mean he's trying to kick-start the apocalypse. If you do start some shit with him, be careful; there are more out there like Thorn." Josh crushed his beer bottle over the kitchen sink.

Josh's beefy hand sparkled with glass shards and dust, but not a drop of blood came out. He rinsed his large forearm under the tap and I saw it in the light as he dried it. His skin was flawless – completely impenetrable.

"We've got other reasons for chasing Ivan." I glanced over at Jonah, who looked weary.

"My variation isn't stable," Jonah said. "I'm dying and I think Ivan knows how to help me. He'd been giving me injections to stabilize my metabolism. If he was telling the truth, he was working on a permanent cure for my genetic malfunction. I think he already had it, only stringing me along to keep me working."

"We know something is deeply wrong with my father. I owe it to him to try to help," said Ilya.

Josh reached into the back of a cupboard above his range hood and pulled out a handgun. He set it down on the kitchen table between Ilya and Faith who both eyed the firearm with furrowed brows.

"If Ivan doesn't want you near him, you're not getting to him without a fight," Josh said. "You need to be prepared. You'll need weapons and you'll need to train. I can tell you that whoever else is working with Ivan's security team will not only be armed, with ranged and hand-to-hand weapons, they will each have a dangerous variation. Ivan trained his security people to use our variations with precision and deadly force. Before I worked for Innoviro, I worked for Darkwater, and before that, I was in the US Army. I wasn't the only guy at Innoviro with a military background."

The chaos of Rubin's attack on Ilya's Sombrio Beach settlement played out in my mind. It was sheer luck that some of us had gotten away. Most had been captured. It had all happened so fast. It wasn't simply a matter of Rubin's variants getting the jump on us. We outnumbered them ten to one, but Rubin's people had been assault experts.

"Then train us," said Ilya.

Josh stared at Ilya long and hard before looking around at each of us as though evaluating our potential. He picked up a gun harness off the back of the couch and put it on, along with his gun. "My parents have a farm out in North Bend. We can go there for space and privacy. My brother is there now with his girlfriend. They're both variants too."

"Thank you. You're doing the right thing." Ilya stood and shook Josh's hand.

North Bend was a little over an hour's drive east of Seattle. Josh and Ilya rode in Josh's black Jeep while the rest of us followed in Cole's car.

I felt a wave of déjà-vu as we drove through town. It didn't make sense. I hadn't seen it in a vision or a dream. Then we pulled up to an intersection in the middle of town. Behind a neon sign for "Twede's Café" the building on the corner advertised itself as "Home of Twin Peaks Cherry Pie" and I knew where I was. I had come to the middle of one of my Mom's favorite television shows.

"Hey, look at that! We're in Twin Peaks!" Faith craned her neck around as we passed the café.

"It's a little before our time," said Jonah.

"I think it came out the year I was born," said Cole.

"Haven't you seen the new episodes?" said Faith.

"My mom loved it. We used to watch re-runs over and over." I still couldn't remember Mom without a lump forming in my throat. The others must have sensed my emotions because none of them spoke. We drove until we followed Josh's Jeep down a long gravel drive to a large white farmhouse.

A carved wood sign announced "Foothills Glen Farm" on the front of the building. It looked like the sort of farmhouse I pictured when I thought of corn fields in Nebraska. The front of the house had a large veranda, complete with a bench swing. Surrounded by nondescript green fields, large rugged mountains rose in the distance, separated from the farm by a border of woodlands.

"Josh wasn't kidding about space, but this does not look private," Jonah said. He peered out the window at the landscape. "We're wide out in the open here."

Josh had one leg out the door of his Jeep when an equally large man stepped onto the veranda. Josh's brother had dark brown shoulder-length hair and similar facial features. His white T-shirt had copious dirt stains, as did his cargo shorts.

"Little brother!" said the large yet friendly man.

"Mad Max!" Josh grinned with surprising enthusiasm.

"These must be the kids you told me about," said Max.

"Holy crap! Between the two of you, who needs training?" Faith asked as she stepped out of the car.

"You'd think, but my brother is the hippie of the family. Not a huge fighter, this one, but he's got stealth covered," said Josh.

We looked at Josh and back at Max with confused expressions until Max touched the whitewashed wood paneling of the house and his arm disappeared. Max moved his arm back to his side and it looked like a section of the paneling had come off the house.

"Dude's a chameleon!" said Cole. He closed his car door and stretched his powerful arms.

"Perfect camouflage would come in handy," said Jonah.

"Did you know Hugo? Are you like him?" I eyed Max apprehensively.

"I'm not sure. Who's Hugo?" said Max.

"Who *was* he is the better question," Josh said to his brother. To us, Josh added, "No, Max can't disappear. He blends into the background."

The front screen door squeaked again and a familiar, willowy blonde girl stepped onto the porch.

"Camille!" I blurted with delight.

"Hello, everyone!"

"What are you doing here?" Ilya stepped over and hugged her while the rest of us smiled.

I felt so pleased to see a familiar person in good health and spirits.

"We're all so happy to see you," said Ilya.

"Coming from you, I'll take that literally." Camille returned all our smiles. "I'm here with my boyfriend, Max."

"A boyfriend?" Ilya paused to think. "Yeah, I can see it. You came to Josh after things went sideways in Victoria. And he brought you here. I'm glad you found a place on a farm. You're better suited to the quiet life than the big city."

Max frowned at Ilya. I didn't need telepathy to know jealousy when I saw it.

"Ilya was reading my thoughts. He's a telepath," Camille said to Max as she put her hand on his white wood arm. "And an old friend." Max's arm and face returned to normal.

"So what did you have in mind for training?" Jonah asked Josh.

"Did you want to wait until night, so we have some cover?" said Cole.

"The woods out behind the back fields have a clearing we can use." Josh lifted his arm to indicate a spot on the horizon.

"I'm not sure I should be training in the woods." Faith snapped a flame to life in her palm.

"I can keep tabs on any collateral damage," said Jonah.

"Are you sure you should be training too?" Cole asked.

"I'll sit down with him for another healing session tonight." Camille slipped her arm between Max's body and bicep, cuddling into him as she looked sympathetically at Jonah.

"I thought you couldn't fix him," I said.

"I can get him back to a baseline of health, even though I can't repair the genetic problem. As his condition worsens, his baseline will continue to drop," Camille answered me softly. To Jonah she said, "I can bring you back when you've overdone it, but I do suggest minimal exertion until you've got the underlying problem under control."

"What kind of irrigation system do you have?" asked Ilya as he scanned the ground around us.

"All forty acres behind the house have industrial grade above-ground PVC piping and impact sprinklers every two hundred feet," said Max, slicing the air in front of him at sample intervals.

"That should be more than enough to draw on if I need it," said Jonah.

"So, what do you want us to practice?" said Cole.

"As far as actual training exercises, let me think awhile. We should cover who can do what, exactly, along with range attacks, body combat, and defense strategies. Some of you will need to work more on defense than actual fighting. Not all variations are compatible with combat," said Josh. He loomed taller as he walked next to me.

"Makes sense. So when can we get started?" Cole cracked his knuckles with a POP-pop-pop and his muscles flexed.

"We'll start tomorrow morning. You all need a good night's sleep," said Josh.

We unpacked Cole's car and settled into guest rooms, but not the way we divided ourselves at the Bella Maria. The Foothills Glen Farm had six bedrooms. With Josh and Max's parents in Palm Springs for the season, Max and Camille took the master bedroom. Josh retreated to his old bedroom, leaving four rooms for the rest of us. Faith and Ilya took a room together. They said nothing but started acting like a couple again, holding hands and exchanging the odd kiss. Three bedrooms were left for Cole, Jonah, and myself. So naturally, I ended up on my own.

After we put our bags away, we met in the large dining room around the long thick oak table. Floor-to-ceiling windows flanked the table opposite the side where I sat. A painting depicting orcas at sea hung on the wall behind me. Near the kitchen, a large china cabinet was full of beautiful dishes with a floral pattern. I looked out the window at Josh's family's forty acres. Whatever they were growing, it must be a lucrative crop.

Camille and Max served us a hearty dinner; pork steaks, corn cobs, a berry spring mix salad, and buttermilk biscuits.

We had fresh apple pie with vanilla ice cream for dessert. I knew Camille and Max hadn't made all the food from scratch with supplies from the farm. But for a moment, I visualized a self-sufficient farm life, quiet and clean and safe. I knew I was romanticizing. It looked beautiful all the same.

The sky faded from soft lilac to deep cobalt behind the Cascade Mountains as we finished our dessert. We laughed. We drank wine. I almost forgot the next day would bring the start of training to use our 'mutant powers' in battle.

Chapter 10

J osh woke us at dawn. We had a simple breakfast of oatmeal, hard-boiled eggs, and milk. Minutes later we trudged through half-grown fields of what Josh told me were plain old potatoes. Our path followed one of the irrigation lines where no one could tread on the crops. Water rushed through the pipes as the sprinklers came to life. It wasn't glacier-fresh, but it would keep Jonah stable.

"When we reach the clearing, I'm going to put you in pairs. Faith, you're with me. Cole, you'll fight Max. Jonah, you'll fight Camille. Irina and Ilya, you'll fight each other," said Josh.

"No offense, but what are Irina and Ilya going to do? Punch each other?" said Cole. He grinned at me and I shook my head, wondering how the dig made my not-so-burly brother feel.

"We're starting with a form of capture-the-flag. We'll leave sparring for later." Josh rubbed his hands together with enthusiasm.

"Each pair gets a red flag and a blue flag." Josh pulled two flags from a side pocket of his shorts. "Your goal will be to capture your opponent's flag while keeping your own. For the first round, keep your flags visible and easily accessible, like a hip or chest pocket."

We reached the clearing and paired off as instructed. The field couldn't have been better for our purpose. The space was round with flat earth and the trees were twenty feet tall or more. Ankle-deep grass with a sprinkling of wildflowers gave the clearing an idyllic pastoral vibe.

Josh pushed out with his arms waving us all out of harm's way. "Faith and I will go first. Make a circle around us. Give us about a fifty-foot radius. I want you to see what we're doing, but I don't want anyone to get injured."

"Uh, speaking of injury, are you sure you can withstand fire?" Faith opened her palm and brought a small dense ball of flame to life.

"Worry more about what my offense is going to be."

Faith raised her eyebrows and rolled her eyes.

They squared off once we formed a ring around them. Faith wasted no time blasting Josh with a stream of vibrant orange flame. His clothes began to burn, including his flag. He walked forward, his body unhurt from the flames, and he reached for Faith's flag in the front pocket of her jeans. As Josh laid his hand on Faith's flag, he thrust one solid blow with the heel of his palm directly into Faith's solar plexus. The impact sent her flying, shutting off her fire and knocking the wind out of her as she hit the ground.

"Where did she go wrong?" Josh turned to us.

Faith gasped for air as she struggled to sit up.

"She destroyed your flag before she could take it." Cole stood with his arms crossed, not bothered by his sister being knocked to the ground.

"She didn't have a plan," said Jonah.

"She was over-confident. She unleashed hell because that usually works," I said.

Faith glared at me as she drew deep breaths.

"All good answers." Josh had flawless skin under the smoldering blackened remains of his clothing. "Brute force isn't a guaranteed strategy. And you might destroy something useful. Being powerful doesn't mean you're invulnerable. Cole and Max, you're up next." Faith returned to our circle. Josh peeled off his holey shirt and brushed ash from his sooty hair.

As Cole and Max reached the center of the ring, I decided they would have been evenly matched in a fist fight, if they were both normal men. Max towered at least half a foot taller than Cole, but the latter's sheer muscle mass would more than make up the difference. I had no idea how strength could defeat camouflage or vice versa. The pair stood sizing each other up until Josh gave the signal.

Cole crouched into a grappling stance and charged at Max, who easily sidestepped the attack, blending into the grass and trees. It wasn't until Max reappeared, holding Cole's red flag that anyone realized what happened.

"So, two for team Foothills. Jonah and Camille take your places," said Josh as Cole and Max reclaimed their spots in the outer ring.

"Are we sure this is a good idea?" I remembered the image of Camille shooting a molten golden substance from her fingertips into the sand at Sombrio Beach.

"If anything goes wrong, I'm the best person for Jonah to be around," said Camille.

"Give me some credit. I'm not made of glass," said Jonah,

irritated.

Jonah struck first, shooting a thin but powerful stream of water at Camille's hip. Her flag shot out onto the grass. Camille stepped to reach for her flag as Jonah bolted forward. Camille flung a handful of her stunning golden gel straight into Jonah's stomach as he dove for the flag.

He doubled over and I flinched. I fought the urge to run to him. As Jonah rolled on his side in the fetal position, I saw no visible damage to his stomach. He also had Camille's flag scrunched in his fist. Camille knelt and placed her hands on Jonah's stomach. He relaxed as she closed her eyes and pressed on his abdomen gently.

"Good work Jonah, but what's your next move? You're compromised. You sacrificed endurance for a quick win. In the field, you'd already be dead," said Josh.

Jonah stood up, still recovering his bearings. They both returned to the circle as Ilya and I reached the center. I stared at my male counterpart for a long moment. My twin brother was not a physical powerhouse like the other men around us. Even so, I knew he had tricks up his sleeve, developed over many years in the variant world. I stared at him, concentrating on seeing his next move, hoping to spark a spontaneous short-term vision.

Ilya took a step as two clones took steps to his right and left. Three identical brothers stared at me with my own amber eyes, all smirking in unison.

"Can't you tell us apart?" said the Ilya on the left. "How about the flags? Which one is real?" said the Ilya on the right.

I smiled and then pressed my lips together, eyeing each Ilya in turn, evaluating their features and subtle body language. I reached out hoping one of them would flinch and give away the game. Nothing changed and I retracted my hand. My frustration compounded as I circled the trio, careful not to get close enough for one of them to grab my flag. *What will his offense be? Can one of his illusions take my flag? What advantage does telepathy give him?*

I focused hard on each flag, looking for some distinguishing mark. I reached out again and to my amazement, the flag closest to me started to flap as though a breeze hit only Ilya's hip. The flapping flag wriggled free and darted straight into my hand.

"What the hell was that!" shouted Ilya as the center and farthest copies of him evaporated.

"Looked like telekinesis to me. Nicely done, Irina." Josh clapped slowly and I saw genuine respect on his face.

"I- I didn't do anything," I stammered. I looked down wide-eyed at the blue flag in my hand.

"You've got *his* telekinesis," said Ilya. I knew he meant Ivan.

"How? Why now?" I said.

"Innoviro's injections are complex formulas. Maybe this ability was dormant and your body is still processing the treatment," said Jonah.

"Maybe you need adrenaline to tap into this skill. The mind and body have a strong relationship when fight-or-flight kicks in," said Josh.

"So is this permanent?" I felt the flag in my hands, making sure I held the real thing.

"Who cares? Roll with it, honey!" Faith swiveled her hips triumphantly.

"You may have a combat skill now," said Cole.

"Try it again," said Max.

I held my arm up, palm first at Ilya, and tried to will him off the ground.

"Something smaller for now," said Josh.

I surveyed the ground around my feet. I spied a large dried maple leaf and reached for it, concentrating on guiding it up into the air. The leaf stirred and began to rise. I guided the leaf end over end, looping higher and higher above me.

"Excellent!" said Josh.

"Wild! This is going to be awesome!" Faith's purple tentacles of hair bounced as she hopped up and down in my peripheral vision.

"Well done," said Camille.

I broke eye contact with the leaf and looked around. All faces were trained on me as the leaf fluttered back to the ground.

"Okay, it's time for new partners. We've still got a lot to learn," said Josh.

The rest of the week passed slowly as grueling days followed exhausting nights. We all fought each other. Josh taught us basic blocking and attack moves. He gave us lengthy lessons in evading arm and leg attacks. He talked about avoiding blows from opponents when we didn't know their strengths.

I felt the bone-breaking force of Cole's fist in my ribs, barely softened by my new ability to keep his energy at bay. Faith burned my arm so badly once that Camille's healing took overnight to fully restore me. If I concentrated, I could sense Max while he was camouflaged, but I never moved fast enough to catch him. Whatever made up Josh's body, I couldn't lift him off the ground or anticipate his next move.

Finally, Jonah's fire hose-style attack knocked me down over and over. Surrounded by irrigation piping, Jonah was as strong as any of us in the clearing. I did not enjoy being

Chapter 10

knocked on my ass, but I felt reassured that he wasn't at death's door. I also considered that he could be faking his strength, ready to collapse at any moment. I pushed the thought away whenever it bubbled to the surface of my mind.

Chapter 11

I stood on an orange cliff under a purple sky. An unfamiliar canyon wound under the horizon on either side. I looked down to see a river of metallic sludge oozing along the canyon floor. Chunks of debris floated in the sludge. Steam intermittently wafted here and there. The sky darkened as I watched the river. Lights streaked across the sky, red and white, blinking. Black pellets fell from the lights, exploding in the distance as they hit the ground.

A figure walked through smoke from an explosion on the cliff directly opposite me. While the smoke cleared, Ivan reached the edge of the cliff. His face distorted with a ripple. He reached up with both arms, burying his hands in his hair. His fingertips pulled on his scalp. Ivan's expression melted. He peeled off his face in a downward motion taking the rest of his body with it. In Ivan's place stood a red-eyed humanoid reptile with giant curling horns. I'd seen this creature before, reflected in the window of Ivan's apartment.

The horned figure let out a ferocious roar. The ground shook. The landscape shivered until the canyon morphed into a green valley below dry sage-covered hills. Ivan seemed himself again, *smiling and tapping his wristwatch, strolling to me. I shuddered, shaking my head. The green grass floor trembled and a crack opened horizontally between us. Trembling turned to shaking. The crack ripped into the ground in both directions until a canyon separated us again.*

A hand brushed my cheek. I shouted and sat up. I whirled to find the source of the touch. I was in bed in the guest bedroom in Josh's farmhouse.

"Sorry, I didn't mean to scare you." Jonah sat on the bed beside me like a concerned nurse. The faint scent of his cologne, still clinging to his clothes after all this time, wafted over me as he placed his large hand on my shoulder.

"I had a nightmare."

"I know. You were talking in your sleep, saying 'no' and calling for help."

"I dreamed about Ivan. I think it was also about his earthquake test. Not everything in the dream made sense, but it ended with the ground ripping open between us. We need to get back on the road."

"Let's talk to the others at breakfast." Jonah stood to leave.

I wanted to reach for his hand and pull him back to me. Instead, I rose to follow him, changing into jeans and a T-shirt in swift fluid movements.

Everyone but Max sat at the dining table eating. Max emerged from the kitchen carrying a fresh plate of pancakes and a pitcher of orange juice.

"Morning, everyone. I had a dream about the earthquake test. It's time to get back on the road now." I picked up a plate and transferred a couple of pancakes to it.

"Good morning to you too," said Ilya.

"We're not ready yet," said Josh firmly.

"We don't have time to train to the level of Ivan's thugs. We have to work with what we've got." I glanced around the room at them, trying not to show my fear.

"We don't know who's still working for Innoviro or the full scope of Ivan's projects." Cole reached out to the plate of fresh pancakes and grabbed several with his bare hand.

"There might be nothing we can do to stop this test," said Faith.

"Can you all honestly tell me that if a giant earthquake hits California with no warning and kills thousands, you'll be okay with us having done nothing to stop it?" I said.

"I'm sure he's testing in the middle of nowhere for the first round. Sure it'll suck to let Ivan get one step closer to perfecting his tech. But the test itself probably won't do any harm." Faith gulped casually on her glass of orange juice.

"You could be right, but if you're wrong and he uses an urban area for testing, the effects could be a nightmare. It's not like he has to hide or face consequences. People will think it's a regular earthquake. Nobody will go looking for a perpetrator," I said.

"Do you have anything new to go on, apart from worries and the address of Innoviro's San Francisco office?" said Ilya.

"No, but we already have reason enough to act. If we go there, I'll have a new vision. I'm getting better at pulling a vision from physical contact," I said confidently.

"Fair enough. I know my father and if he wants something to happen, he won't stop pushing until he gets there," said Ilya.

"If we leave today, we'll be in San Francisco before the weekend," said Jonah.

"I can be good to go after breakfast," said Cole.

"Me too. It'll only take me a few minutes to pack," said Faith.

"So it's settled then? We're leaving after breakfast?" I asked, looking around to confirm consent.

"You should keep training as you go. Don't stop working on any of your abilities. Fine-tuning your mental and physical power is about more than chemistry. Your mind is a big part of what your body can do. The reverse is also true," said Josh.

"Thanks for everything you've done for us, Josh. We'll be sure to keep training on the road," said Cole.

"Josh, why don't you come with us," said Ilya.

"Yeah, we could use your help if you're willing," said Faith.

Josh and Max exchanged a raised eyebrow look.

"We need you here for harvest next month. It's not a good time for a road trip." Max's words had a surly undertone.

"You've got me now." Camille smiled and put her hand on Max's forearm.

"Let me think about it," said Josh. I expected he would want to talk to his brother in private before committing to join us. Josh had already done more for us than anyone not already involved with our cause. It was a wild and risky thing, taking on a corporate power with little more than a few brains and a few sets of hands.

"We'll pack while you think," said Ilya in his best conciliatory tone.

<h1 style="text-align:center">Chapter 12</h1>

The road to San Francisco included a detour to Spokane. Josh had joined us, with his Jeep, on the condition that we pick up his friend and fellow variant, Adelaide. She was a former employee of Innoviro's European sister company, Evonatura. When Ilya asked to ride with Josh, I volunteered too. I wanted to know everything Josh was willing to tell us about overseas variants.

"We'll need to spend the night at Adelaide's house. She's got a big place, like Foothills Glen, so there's room for all of us. If we don't piss her off too much. You'll piss her off if you stare," said Josh. He looked directly at me through his rear-view mirror.

I met Josh's stare. His dark beard stubble, army-green flak jacket, and sheer physical size would have intimidated me in any other circumstance.

"Why would we stare? Is her variation gross or something?"

"Don't say gross. She's one of us. But she does have a very noticeable variation. Like the angel sisters, she can't go out in public without a disguise," said Josh.

"You mean Rose and Sage? She's got wings?" said Ilya.

"No, she's got tentacles," said Josh.

"Did you mention this to the others?" said Ilya.

I quickly texted Faith. I smiled picturing her excitement at seeing such a cool variant. I hoped we'd all handle it well.

"I told Cole and asked him to discuss it, but it wouldn't hurt to remind them," said Josh.

"Already done. Just texted Faith," I said. "Anything you want me to add, Ilya," I said playfully. If he listened to my thoughts in the last twelve hours, he knew I was curious about their relationship. It took my mind off of Jonah's failing health. And the whole variant apocalypse thing.

Washington's highways took us from mountains and lush coastal forests to rolling grassy hills and wide flat plains. We passed through the towers of Spokane's core, over a river, and back into grasslands. Josh turned onto a long driveway that disappeared into a tunnel of trees. We emerged to find, not a farm, but an acreage stretching out around a large log cabin. The front door opened and a woman in a wheelchair navigated the porch to greet us.

"Hello, Josh! It's good to see you!" said the woman in the wheelchair. I detected a faint accent, but I couldn't place it. She smoothed the blanket covering her lap and legs.

"Hi Adelaide. How's it goin'?" Josh said, through his open door window. Cole's car pulled up next to us.

"Working from home again, so I can't complain." Adelaide wheeled forward a little with a welcoming smile on her face.

Her beauty struck me speechless. Ebony ringlets flowed from the top of her head, onto her chest and down her back.

Her skin was flawless. Green eyes shone under thick fringes of jet-black lashes.

"This is Irina. Over there is Ilya, Cole, Faith, and Jonah," said Josh, pointing fingers at each of us in turn.

"Come inside, everyone. Food is waiting." Adelaide wheeled back into the house and we all followed.

The entryway looked out on a spacious great room at least twenty feet high. A railing bordering the far corner of the living room suggested a lower level.

"Good to meet you." Ilya stuck out his hand. Adelaide shook it. Jonah, Cole, and Faith followed suit. I couldn't stop looking at the art on her walls. Huge canvases were covered in detailed elaborate scenes, fairies in a forest, a lively coral reef, a city in the clouds.

"You've got a lovely home," said Jonah.

"It keeps the rain off my head," said Adelaide.

"Are these yours?" I gestured to the paintings. "They're beautiful."

"Thank you. Painting has become my life's work, given that I do not work for Evonatura any longer," said Adelaide.

"You're among friends here, if you want to stand up," said Josh, beckoning her upwards with both his hands.

Adelaide sized each of us up. In response, Faith tossed a fireball between her hands. I floated my cup, doing my best impression of a funnel spin.

Adelaide slowly lifted her blanket to reveal a long row of fleshy tubes. Her simple yellow sweater turned out to be a dress, tailored to flare and flow like a skirt around her many legs. She slid upward onto eight s-curved tentacles, dotted with large pink suction cups on the underside of each. I wanted to ask if she had been born or made as she was. I wanted to ask about the nature of her work for Evonatura. I said nothing.

"Shall we eat?" said Adelaide.

We followed her through the kitchen, the only enclosed space on the ground level. Her dining table on the other side had a spread of cold cuts, fruits, vegetables, crackers, and slices of bread, all in generous proportions. Earthenware plates were stacked at either end of the table.

"Nice spread!" said Faith, picking up a plate. The combination of Faith's faded waffle shirt, weathered overalls, and purple dreadlocks looked as out of place as possible in Adelaide's elegant home.

"Thank you so much for having us." Jonah hung back. His heart-breaking fatigue had returned.

"I hope this isn't bad timing." Cole quickly followed his sister in creating a pile of food. His skater clothes looked only slightly more cultured than his sister's.

"So, Adelaide, did Josh tell you we're looking for companions to join our little road trip?" said Ilya.

"I said we were on the road, but I didn't say we were looking for recruits." Josh frowned at my brother's lack of tact.

"I think you'll find I'm not very helpful out in the world," said Adelaide.

"We're not going out in the world. We've got to stay under the radar. We need all the help we can get and I think you'd be a kickass asset," said Ilya.

"Sorry, Adelaide, we're not here to pressure you. I was going to wait until at least after our meal before starting this conversation." Josh glared at Ilya.

"I don't want to pry, but do you have any other abilities?" I asked.

"Apart from the obvious?" said Adelaide.

I blushed. "Yes, other than that. I mean, I'm psychic *and* telekinetic. I was thinking that maybe Evonatura gave their variants injections too." I looked away quickly.

Adelaide's tentacles pulsed as she lifted several into the air. Glowing blue rings appeared along the fleshy side of her tentacles. Adelaide opened her mouth. A slim tentacle with a beak on the end jabbed and snapped at me. Adelaide retracted the beak and rested all her legs back on the floor.

"One bite will kill a large person through respiratory paralysis within minutes. Evonatura had a biochemistry division and Adelaide was their toxicologist." Josh shoved his hands in his pockets and rolled back to the balls of his heels with a smug smile.

"You didn't think to mention THAT on the way here?" I asked him.

"Josh was being a gentleman. I am very choosy about the people who learn this much about me," said Adelaide.

"Irina is still relatively new to this life. She didn't mean to offend." Ilya brushed cracker crumb hands on his black T-shirt and I shook my head.

"Indeed. Life takes us all on different paths." Adelaide smiled at me. All trace of threat was gone.

"I'm asking you to come with us because we suspect that Innoviro Industries, possibly along with Evonatura, is involved in a conspiracy to remake the world and reseed it with variant life." Ilya pushed his shaggy cinnamon hair behind his ears. Over the last few weeks, I'd noticed this gesture was his main nervous tic.

"In a nutshell." Cole grinned bright teeth against his tanned skin. His eyes had a spark of mischievousness.

"Hmmm," said Adelaide, not alarmed in the least. "Sounds like something Ivan Krylov and Claude Mueller might cook up."

"Who is Claude Mueller?" I said.

"He's the CEO of Evonatura," said Josh.

"My former employer and fiancé." Adelaide's voice took on a hint of distaste.

"Currently, we're trying to stop Ivan from starting an earthquake in San Francisco. Will you help us?" Jonah asked softly. The bags under his eyes were darker than ever.

Adelaide looked at each of us and then stared out her back bay window for a long moment. I did not need telepathy to interpret her thoughts. A world where she could roam freely in society, and even fit in as normal, would have to be extremely appealing. Perhaps even telling her at all had been a huge mistake.

"Let me think about it." Adelaide crossed the great room in a rapid blur of limbs, climbed over the railing, and dropped into the opening. A moment later, a splash sounded in the distance.

"And now we wait." Josh popped a sausage and cracker stack in his mouth and chewed with a placid expression.

Chapter 13

We listened to Adelaide swim while we ate. I didn't want to spend the night in this home if our host wasn't going to join us. I didn't see any point in staying past our meal if her answer was no. But I knew better than to let impatience get the better of me.

"Hey Cole, did you ever hear from David Wong?" I asked as I pushed my plate away.

"Yeah, I figured he'd be harassing us by now. He emailed me a few hours after we left Vancouver. And then nothing." Faith had tied her dreads back as she always did when she wanted to concentrate.

"No, he hasn't contacted me. Maybe he lost interest," said Cole.

"I doubt Wong decided to drop the story. Not after the way he reacted," I said.

Faith had her phone out, tapping away.

"HOLY SHIT!" she shouted and clapped her hand over her mouth. "He's dead! They fucking killed him!"

"What?" Cole's brown eyes went black under his furrowed brow.

"How do you know?" said Jonah.

"I Googled his name. I was looking for his latest story. And there's this headline: 'Journalist Found Dead in North Vancouver Warehouse'. It's about Wong," said Faith, still staring at her phone with utter disbelief.

Ilya leaned in to see her screen and took the phone from her limp hand. "She's right. It says he was found beaten in an abandoned warehouse near the Lion's Gate Bridge."

"Oh God, he followed our story! We got him killed!" I gasped.

"We don't know that for sure. That was an unsecured dark building. If he went there at night, he could have been attacked by some random person," said Ilya.

"Are you kidding, man?" said Cole.

"If they were willing to kill Kingston, why not a reporter? It was probably Casey again," I said.

"Casey still works for Ivan?" said Josh. "Hmmmm. That's not going to bode well for us."

"I need some air," said Cole, running his hands through his short sandy hair. I watched his bulky frame disappear around the corner.

"I'll go see if I can float in Adelaide's pool for a while," said Jonah. I watched him remove his collared shirt leaving his usual white tee underneath as he walked away.

Ilya had his arm around Faith. Josh had slipped down a hallway muttering to someone on his phone. I felt the urge to pace and I didn't want to follow Josh or Jonah, so I went out onto the deck to find Cole.

"Mind if I hang out here?"

Cole turned around with a look of surprise. "Not at all."

"This is going to get worse before it gets better, isn't it? I guess I'd hoped we could contain this to us and them. Rebel variants versus evil Innoviro."

"I'm sure the rest of us weren't being that optimistic. But one death after another. It's getting real."

"Do you think she'll come? Adelaide, I mean. Seeing that someone else has died. She could get spooked." I stared straight ahead at the trees enclosing Adelaide's property.

"We couldn't blame her for staying out of this mess. She would be risking her life. And what *The Compendium* would create might be her dream world."

"I thought the same thing." I felt a pang of sympathy for Adelaide.

"It would be a difficult trip and a huge risk." Cole leaned on the deck railing, surveying Adelaide's acreage.

"We're all taking risks," I said.

"Does that include you and Jonah?" Cole kept his eyes locked on the horizon.

"Not right now. It still makes him sick to touch people. Or maybe it's only me. But whatever is happening to him isn't getting any better." Sadness closed my throat.

"We'll find a cure for him. Maybe Adelaide can help," said Cole.

"I doubt it. She'd be starting from scratch. It's Ivan who was working on a cure. I wish we could make him give it up. It's hard to justify that priority if he's on the verge of killing thousands, and eventually, millions of people." I swallowed and paused to keep my tears under control.

"I agree. But I hope you know that I want Jonah to get better as much as you do. He's still my best friend."

"Of course I know." I put my hand on Cole's rock-hard forearm. I left my hand there. I willed Jonah to look out the window and see me touching Cole. I wanted him to get angry and hate me. I wanted to feel a surge of attraction to Cole instead. The scrape of the sliding glass door startled me and I let go.

"She's in! She's coming!" whispered Faith excitedly.

We gathered around Adelaide's dining table once more.

"I have decided to assist you." Adelaide's wet ringlets bounced gently as she spoke. "I have some conditions. First, is that we, as a group, make a commitment not to end any variant lives."

"None of us wants to see variants hurt or killed," said Jonah. His hair was slicked back from the water and he wore a plush white robe. He looked marginally replenished.

"We certainly don't want to attract police attention either," said Ilya.

"Speaking of police, I don't know if you heard us all freakin' out, but we think a reporter we talked to … well, we think we got him killed," said Faith as she adjusted the straps of her overalls.

"You talked to a reporter?" said Adelaide angrily. She took a deep breath. "If he's no longer a problem, I won't worry about it, but there'll be no more publicity. My second condition is that any documentation or specimens we obtain are preserved, not destroyed. A good deal of hard work and money has gone into variant science, as some of you probably well know. We can neutralize a plot without erasing valuable knowledge."

Ilya leaned forward, elbows on the table with an intent frown. "Are you sure we should keep everything intact? We think Ivan developed some things built to harm or disrupt delicate ecosystems all over this planet. Some of what we'll find may have no positive use and nothing to teach us. Leaving those files or specimens intact would be a liability."

"I don't think so. Adelaide's right. Scientists don't destroy. We investigate," said Jonah.

"What about Innoviro's research for Jonah? Ivan claimed to be helping other variants too. Maybe it's all in one place. If other people are waiting on life-changing treatments, we should try to help, at some point," said Cole.

"Makes sense, if he wanted variants to take over, he'd have to make sure we're looked after," said Faith.

"I have one more condition you might find difficult. We must stay out of public areas as much as possible. I value the freedom I have in my home. I have to give up my freedom every time I go to a mall, a restaurant, a hotel, a downtown core." Adelaide lifted a towel to her hair and squeezed.

"So we go camping and take turns doing whatever shopping needs to be done," I said.

"Are you all in agreement?" said Adelaide.

Everyone nodded and said yes.

After spending the night in Adelaide's palatial modern 'cabin' I wasn't looking forward to camping. But a step closer to stopping Ivan felt worth it.

We added Adelaide's wheelchair-adapted van to our caravan and set out. I rode with Josh. Our next stop was Portland, this time for a connection of Faith's.

I spent the drive training myself in telekinetic control with a rotation of small objects in the car. I concentrated so hard that I didn't realize we were in Oregon until we entered Portland in time for rush hour traffic. We crossed an urban river and followed Cole's car down a tree-lined street to a little heritage home. The home's brown siding and early nineteenth-century design did not look like the home of a hacktivist, as Faith had promised.

Our group stood on the sidewalk, waiting nervously as Faith knocked on the front door. A skinny woman with stringy light brown hair, a narrow face, and thick glasses answered.

"Sorry, sorry, please make yourself at home. Bruno is working on a new simulation and I'm getting completely absorbed," said the skinny woman with a strong British accent. We followed the woman to the kitchen, passing the living room where an exceptionally hairy man sat hunched over a computer in the corner.

"Ralph is here too, but he's upstairs. Still doesn't like new people," said the woman.

"Guys, this is Nellie. She's the best network architect that Innoviro ever had," said Faith.

"Your email said Innoviro went under because Ivan did some dodgy crap. You guys aren't on the run, are you?" said Nellie.

"Not from the cops," said Faith.

"As far as we know," I added cautiously.

"Ivan doesn't have the resources to track us at the moment," said Ilya.

Nellie pushed her thick glasses up the bridge of her nose. Her fingernails flashed in the light. They looked like solid copper.

"Does anyone outside this house know you're here?" said Nellie.

"No," said Faith. Bruno appeared at the doorway to the kitchen. He grabbed the doorjamb with a hairy hand finished with dark brown claw-like fingernails.

"So these are the guys who want a hack," said Bruno. As he

spoke I glimpsed sharpened teeth in his mouth.

"We don't know for sure," I piped up.

"We want you to come with us in the event we find something we need help to hack. Faith is good, but she's the only IT-type among us," said Ilya.

"Where are you going again?" said Nellie.

"Our next stop is San Francisco at an Innoviro office," I said.

"We think Ivan is planning to test new tech that causes earthquakes," said Cole.

"We need to disable whatever he's working on, ideally securing it ourselves," said Jonah.

"From what these people told me yesterday, this is the beginning of a much larger endeavor," said Adelaide from her wheelchair.

"I can't say I want to get roped back into Innoviro's bullshit," said Bruno.

"It sounds like Innoviro is done," said Nellie.

"They're done as a research front. Ivan belongs to a group working on a project called *The Compendium Transmuto*. I'm sure Faith didn't put this in a text, but we're talking about ongoing and future pollution, genetic experiments, disease, and who knows what else," said Jonah.

From the looks on Bruno's and Nellie's faces, we were unwelcome and unwanted.

"We know it's a lot to ask, walking away from whatever jobs or gigs you've got going. This isn't going to make you any money or get you any legit credit," said Ilya.

"You think we do what we do for money?" said Nellie. I cast a glance around her kitchen. The sink was full of soapy food soup and partially submerged dishes. A stack of sticky plates rested on a crumb-covered counter. Paint peeled off the edges of the cupboards. Linoleum lifted from the floor in a few places.

"I'll tell you what. Convince Ralph to come, and we're with you too," said Bruno. He looked at Nellie for approval which she granted with a nod. He cleared his throat with a raspy growl.

"I'll make an argument. That's all any of us can do," I said.

"Hey, Ralph! Come downstairs. We need to talk. It's cool." Bruno directed his full volume up the stairwell between the kitchen and the living room.

A series of thump-bump-thump-bumps sounded on the ceiling above us. The thumps made their way down the stairs. The creature who appeared in the doorway almost defied belief.

The man appeared more reptile than humanoid. Thick green scales covered his visible body. Over that, a Metallica T-shirt and ripped jeans were the only suggestion of humanity. He had clawed hands and feet, a giant, body-length tail, and a muzzle full of serrated teeth. Ralph's lidless yellow eyes darted around the room. He startled us all when his forked tongue shot out and snatched a moth out of the air above us.

"What do you lot want?" Ralph's British accent and near-perfect enunciation seemed impossible through the tongue and teeth of a giant reptile, but there he stood.

"We need variants," I said plainly.

"To do what?" Ralph asked defiantly.

"Our father, Ilya's and mine, Ivan Krylov, CEO of Innoviro Industries is going to experiment with earthquake technology that could kill thousands. And we know he's got more in the works. He could destroy the world as we know it. Will you help us stop him?"

Ralph looked at me, he looked around the room and flicked his tongue. "No."

"No?" said Ilya.

"Did I stutter? I've never met any of you. From what Nellie tells me, you're a bunch of kids who drove their company under while playing around with conspiracy theories," said Ralph with slightly narrowed eyes.

"Don't you want to hear our side of the story?" said Cole, placing his hands on his hips.

"This isn't a whim or a suspicion," said Jonah with a plaintive expression.

"We can't force anyone to be a part of this," said Faith. Her dreads rustled as she gave a dismissive shake of her head.

"Of course not, but consider the consequences of letting Ivan run rampant transforming the planet. If he's willing to do it, he's lost touch with the last of his humanity." My voice rose, louder and louder. "Even if you place variant lives above everyone else, what if his master plan doesn't work? We could end up with a planet nobody can live on. Consider that for a moment!"

Ralph stared back at me. I looked over at Ilya. *What is he thinking? Tell me!*

"I got nothing. He's a brick wall," said Ilya as he threw his hands in the air.

Ralph looked around the room. His reptilian features revealed nothing of his thoughts or emotions.

"I have already asked them to commit to camping, and staying out of human society." Adelaide cast her blanket aside and stood. There was no reason for her to hide in a house where Ralph was a resident. His face remained void of emotion, as I could read it.

"Okay. We'll come with you to San Francisco. After the earthquake mechanism is destroyed, we come home." Ralph opened a door behind Nellie and disappeared down a stairwell into the basement.

"He's probably going for a walk. Our basement has a tunnel into the Portland sewer system. It's the only way Ralph can come and go." Bruno scratched his cheek with a dark-clawed hand.

"I know how he feels," said Adelaide.

Several hours later Ralph returned. Nellie and Bruno had packed for all of them. We waited until the night got dark enough to conceal Ralph. The Portland trio then joined Adelaide in her van. We drove for hours.

Josh followed Adelaide's van. Cole followed behind us. Wherever we were going was somewhere Adelaide knew. She wasn't sharing her route plans through texts, so we were blindly following her in the dark. We drove on and on, up a winding forest trail that barely qualified as a road. I had been on logging roads outside Prince George, but nothing this remote.

The forest gave way and we entered a large grass clearing. Moonlight poured into the space creating a bright, magical glow. Following Adelaide, Josh and Cole parked at the edge of the woods.

While Cole and Faith got a roaring fire started, Adelaide pulled a large black bag from the back of her van. In swift, fluid movements, she unpacked the bag and set up a large awning and fabric patio set.

More folding chairs came out of the back of Adelaide's van and Josh's Jeep. It struck me how ill-prepared my friends and I had been when we left Victoria, and then, Vancouver. We had expected to limp along from motel to motel. Camping shaped up to be a better option than I'd imagined.

I watched my friends and new companions form a ring around our campfire. They were all chatting, sipping sodas and beers. The clearing started to remind me of Sombrio Beach – a place for variants, far from the world, both protected and fragile.

And then I saw Jonah, tired, looking older than his twenty-four years. He lowered himself into one of the folding chairs. I wanted to put my hand on his shoulder. I wanted us to walk off into the woods, wrap our bodies together, and forget all the bad things from the last few months. I would have to settle for keeping him alive, which meant staying away.

Chapter 14

The scent of bacon drifted into my tent. The dim light of a morning sun still hidden behind the mountains lit the fabric walls around me. I heard unfamiliar voices. I couldn't make out the words of the conversation, but it reminded me how large our group had grown.

I closed my eyes and tried to picture a map, imagining where we might be on it, and how far that was from San Francisco. I tried to picture the San Andreas Fault and its crusty edges protruding from the earth in the photos I'd seen at Nellie and Bruno's house. I searched my memory for the face of Dr. Waynesburg.

As though I'd opened floodgates, images surged into my mind. My eyelids fluttered while the onslaught of information took my breath away. The images slowed like pages near the end of a book and I plucked a single picture out of the visual torrent.

A giant wood and glass door opened behind two looming pillars. My perspective retreated and the building became smaller, stretching behind a long slope of red brick stairs. Dr. Waynesburg walked out through the door and started down the steps with a manila envelope tucked under his arm.

I followed behind as he walked briskly along a pedestrian corridor full of people wearing backpacks and carrying armloads of books. Waynesburg had noticeably less white hair and more of a dark salt-and-pepper look. He walked by a wall enclosing four pay phones.

In the distance, I could see a large patina-green archway. A long castle-like square tower topped with a slim pyramid pierced the sky beside us. We passed a bulletin board titled BERKELEY CAMPUS SERVICES. Waynesburg reached a blue mailbox and promptly dropped the envelope through the slot. He made a 180-degree turn and started walking back towards me. Waynesburg strode mere paces from colliding with me when suddenly I was back in my tent in the mountains of Oregon.

I whipped off my long-sleeved knit shirt and sweatpants, tearing into a T-shirt and jeans. I unzipped my tent door and lunged out into the campsite.

"I just saw Waynesburg on the campus of Berkeley. Where is that?" I shouted to anyone who would listen.

"It's in California. The university is named after the city." Nellie pushed her glasses up the bridge of her nose.

"It's also on the eastern side of the San Francisco Bay Area," said Bruno.

"What was he doing?" asked Faith.

I scanned the campsite. Everyone was up and about except for Jonah. Adelaide cooked bacon and made coffee at the same time, while Ilya hovered next to her with ravenous eyes. His slim frame looked even slighter in his fitted jeans and black

T-shirt. Ralph lay curled up in the single patch of sun on the ground. Josh sat behind the campfire in his green flak jacket, frowning into his steaming metal mug.

"I saw Waynesburg come out of an academic-looking building and mail an envelope. That's all I saw, but it must mean something. It looked like it might have been a few years ago," I said earnestly.

Cole's sandy hair glinted gold in the early morning sun. "Berkeley has a research facility called the California Center for Earthquake Data. Maybe he was there."

"From what I saw in Kingston's documents, Waynesburg is working with fracking contractors, not university research facilities," said Faith, her words laced with confusion.

"Could be Waynesburg has expertise in both fracking and seismic studies. We should visit the CCED before we move on to San Francisco. We should also see a guy I know in Chico. He works for a fracking contractor. He's a buddy from UVic. He might know something about fracking in California," said Cole eagerly.

"Does he know about Innoviro? Or more relevantly, is he a variant?" Ilya glanced around the group as he sipped from a steaming cup.

"Not that I know of on either count. But I can visit him without taking the whole group. Which is probably for the best," said Cole.

"After what happened to the journalist, Wong, we should think carefully before we bring in more civilians," I said slowly.

"Cole, make sure your guy understands what Ivan and his buddies are capable of," said Faith.

"Not only this fracking guy, I mean people at Berkeley too. If the Compendium group is willing to kill a journalist, a few scientists they don't need won't give them pause," I said.

"So what does our route look like now?" said Ilya.

"If we go to Chico, we could pass through Berkeley on our way to San Francisco proper," said Cole.

"We're making good time, so I think we should stick around here and train today," said Ilya.

"Does everyone here know what each other's abilities are?" I called out, addressing the campsite.

Bruno stood up and roared. He took off his shirt and revealed an abnormally hairy chest. He picked up a fallen branch, broke it in half, and peeled the bark off with his fingernails.

"He's also an excellent programmer. And Ralph has paralytic venom in his teeth." Nellie stood up and stretched both arms at the intact half of Bruno's branch. An electric arc shot out of her copper fingernails and hit the branch with a deafening CRACK-BANG.

"Good thing we're out in the middle of nowhere," said Adelaide.

Jonah stumbled out of his tent. "What happened? Are we being attacked?"

"No, we're getting a demonstration. We can do a little sparring today if everyone's up for it," said Josh. Jonah looked confused but relieved.

"As much as I want to get back on the road, a bit more practice is probably a good idea," I said.

"Done deal then. Josh, what do you wanna do?" said Faith. She alternated snapping flames to life with either set of thumbs and middle fingers.

"Let's start with Adelaide and Ralph, then Nellie and Bruno. That should be educational," said Josh, flashing a rare smile.

"We're not fighters," said Nellie.

"Are you kidding me? Did you see what you just did to that branch? Do we even have to discuss your hubby there?" said Faith.

"Nobody fights who doesn't want to get their hands dirty." Cole stood with his hands out in a gesture of putting on brakes.

Faith glared at him through narrowed eyes. "We can't have people with us who won't jump in when something goes sideways. We don't know if or when that's gonna happen."

Jonah turned and went back into his tent. I glared at Faith, but she stared down Cole as though our latest companions had evaporated. I took a step in the direction of Jonah's tent but stopped myself. Without Camille in our midst to heal each of us, sparring took on more serious consequences.

"Not everyone is built to fight. It's a liability to have someone in combat who shouldn't be there," said Josh.

Faith scowled at Josh, and back at Cole again before she took a seat.

"Everyone, remember that Camille isn't here to heal anyone, so we should be careful. Why don't we take turns doing a demonstration for the group, and then we can practice individually? No hand-to-hand combat required." I paused to marvel at how far I had come from the streets of PG. If I'd known then, that I'd be using the phrase 'hand-to-hand combat' about something I planned to participate in, I'd have done a reality check.

"That sounds fair to me. I think Nellie and I have already gone. Ralph?" Bruno called out to his friend still curled peacefully in a patch of sun.

"Yeah, I'll do it. But I need a volunteer." Ralph stretched up to a standing position.

"You mean one of us?" I asked.

"I'll do it," said Josh.

"You're a braver man than I am," said Ilya.

"Everybody gather around. It's a pretty subtle thing," said Ralph.

Jonah must have been listening because he rejoined us. We formed a circle around Ralph and Josh, as the latter extended his forearm. We all peered in as Ralph bent down and opened his jaws wide around Josh's arm. He held his mouth open barring his teeth. Two fangs slid down alongside what would have been his eye teeth in a normal human mouth.

Ralph bit down on Josh's arm. Ralph glowered momentarily as he met the resistance offered by Josh's armor-like skin. When that didn't work, Ralph released his mouth and spit into his hand. He sprayed a fine mist on Josh's face.

Josh's expression revealed a brief shock and then he froze. Paralysis preserved his startled look perfectly. Not even his eyeballs moved. Ralph detached his grip on Josh's arm and gently pushed his shoulder. Josh fell backward and hit the ground, stiff as a statue.

"The effects usually last a few hours. Far too long if you're in a dangerous situation, but survivable if you're safe. It wears off completely." Ralph looked more pleased with himself than I'd seen yet.

"Impressive!" I said, feeling the corners of my mouth lifting.

"How many times have you used this venom?" asked Adelaide. I remembered her variation and wondered how often her beak had seen real-world use.

"On regular humans? There have been a few occasions, to give me time to get away from a bad scene," said Ralph.

"It sounds like a handy thing to have in your tool belt," said

Ilya.

"For best results, use with a memory wipe and you're golden." Ralph seemed pleased with himself, but it was still hard to tell.

My forehead furrowed. "So you've paired up with a variant that could wipe memories?"

Faith, Cole, Jonah, and Ilya all looked at me. "Did you ever work for Innoviro? With a variant named Rubin?" I said.

"Uh, no, I don't think so. I'm sure I'd remember that. I spent most of my life in the wild after my parents died." Ralph sounded sincere. I relaxed my face and my posture.

Adelaide abruptly diffused the tension with her aggressive display of blue-ringed spots, splayed tentacles, and the terrifying beaked second tongue.

Faith didn't wait for Adelaide to retract but turned to the campfire and commanded it to rise to bonfire height. As the blaze subsided Jonah noticed a clump of stray embers and conveyed a pot of wastewater to extinguish them.

Cole walked to the nearest tree. He hugged the trunk and jerked back, lifting the tree, roots and all, out of the ground.

Ilya broke into an ear-to-ear grin looking at Ralph. We turned to see what was so funny and Nellie screamed. Ralph had become a menacing black dragon, terrifying and triumphant. Ilya laughed and waved away the illusion.

"Sorry, Nellie. There's no need to call me a bastard though," said Ilya, smiling playfully.

"I, I didn't call you a bastard," said Nellie, still recovering.

"No but you thought it," said Ilya.

"I'll go next. I need a volunteer too," I said.

"You can try me," said Ralph, back to his plain old green lizard self.

I took a deep breath and reached out my hand and Ralph took it carefully. I looked into his reptilian eyes and the world around me melted away.

Ralph's body was much smaller. He wore only overalls, sitting on a stool in a laboratory setting. A woman in a crisp white lab coat turned and lifted Ralph's arm. She stuck an empty needle in his arm and began to draw blood. She removed the needle and set the syringe down on the counter. She caressed the back of his head and kissed his forehead lovingly.

"Your mother was a scientist. I saw you sitting in a lab in overalls. She seemed like a lovely woman," I said gently.

"Mother, parent, creator. It's all the same in my case. But yes, she was a lovely woman," said Ralph.

"And for my next trick." I picked up my backpack. "I'll demonstrate the hands-free shuffle." My body tingled with nervous energy. I didn't have much of an audience, but it would still suck to screw up.

I pulled my now infamous deck of tarot cards from the front pocket of my bag. I took them from their case and placed the stack in the palm of my left hand. With my right, I nursed cards upward one by one until the stack had separated into two equal piles. I guided the two piles together and visualized them shuffling. Miraculously, the cards obeyed. I coaxed the deck back down to my left palm. Everyone clapped and I blushed.

"I guess I'll go last." Josh must have recovered while all eyes were on my cards.

Josh walked over to the camp table where Adelaide had been cooking breakfast. He picked up a knife and stabbed his arm. We all gasped. Josh lifted the knife, displaying the 'C' curved shape of the once straight blade.

"I think that about covers it," said Ilya.

"Everyone pick a practice spot," Josh said. "Be sure to give yourself at least five feet in any direction. Irina made a good point about injuries. Let's not have any while we're an hour's drive from the nearest hospital."

Chapter 15

Having an extra ability proved interesting, even exciting, but it didn't make me physically stronger or less vulnerable. In a fight, telekinesis would be much more useful than seeing someone's past or future, so when I trained, it was all about moving objects with my mind.

I practiced levitating a branch and swinging it like a remote bat. I asked Cole to pose like a statue so that I could learn to lift a live opponent. I figured he didn't need much training himself. He was already built like a battering ram.

Josh had acquired a few training dummies somewhere between Spokane and our camp outside Portland. I watched Faith repeatedly torch her fire-retardant mannequin until it looked like a grotesque demon. Ilya and Jonah played a game of 'blast the illusion' in which Jonah shot fire-hose streams through Ilya's various apparitions, a bobcat, a bear, Thorn, and Ivan.

Watching Ilya on the side of the sparring ground reminded me that, as my twin, he wasn't much larger or stronger than me. Against individuals as deadly as Adelaide, Ralph, Nellie, and Bruno, Ilya had little more than his wits as weapons. He wasn't just my friend, he was my twin, and the more time I spent with him, the more he truly felt like my brother. Without Gemma, he remained my only family. I tried hard to picture Gemma's face. I visualized her dorm building, thinking about what she might be doing.

The field melted away and I stood in my parents' Prince George kitchen. The drapes were different, with a bright floral pattern. My mother looked almost as young as she had at the Roman ruins honeymooning with Ivan. This time, she stood over a high chair with a bright-eyed baby flailing in her direction – it must have been me! She placed pieces of chopped banana on the plastic tray in front of the baby, caressing her pregnant belly as she did so.

"It's strange how this pregnancy seems so much like the last one. You'd think I was having twins again!" Mom said to Darryl. Her face fell for a moment, but she looked at me and her smile returned. She grasped a small copper and glass pendant hanging around her neck and tucked it under her shirt as she leaned over to kiss my forehead.

"I hate onions and garlic again. I get the same twinge in my gut when I eat strawberries. I'm back to having those weird dizzy spells when I use any of the appliances. The doctor thinks I'm making it up, I can tell. I told him it was the same with my first pregnancy." My mother laughed.

I could still hear her throaty giggle when the Oregon wilderness materialized around me. I looked around to gauge how long my mind had been back in my parents' kitchen. My friends had stopped practicing and were tearing down our camp.

"Hey, space cadet! Get your ass over here and help pack! We've got about six hours ahead of us, not including getting back on the highway," said Faith from the back of Cole's car.

I retied my ponytail and ran back to my deflated tent. Jonah stood over it folding up elastic core tent rods.

"Thanks, but you don't have to do that." I heard forced cheerfulness in my voice.

"Contrary to what you might think, I am not on death's doorstep." Jonah's words dripped with bitterness. His pale teal eyes glared at me.

"Don't be like that. I don't want things to get weird with us," I said.

"Nothing is weird." Jonah hefted the bundle of tent rods and folded green fabric into the back of Josh's Jeep. "Keep riding with your new friend."

A lump quivered in my throat and subsided. Anger welled in my chest. *Fine, if that's how it's got to be.*

I looked up at Cole's car to find Faith and Ilya standing in front of the trunk, holding bags and staring at me. I frowned and they both turned away. A strong hand grabbed my shoulder and I jumped. Cole was behind me.

"We're on our way to Chico, California. Josh and Ilya agree that finding my buddy who works in the fracking industry could be a great lead."

"As long as we're still on our way to San Francisco, I want to check out the Berkeley campus, not just Innoviro's office."

"If you saw Berkeley in a vision, I'm sure it meant something. I trust what comes out of your head," said Cole.

Our convoy took over an hour to rumble back down to the interstate, which felt like floating on air after the rough logging roads.

Adelaide had requested that I ride with her privately. And I felt relieved not to be in Josh's Jeep after Jonah's jealous stab. So I sat shotgun in Adelaide's van with my backpack at my feet.

"What is it like to have a vision of the future? It must be different than a dream or a memory." Adelaide glanced away from the road for a beat to look me in the eye.

"Yes and no. I see the past too, and that can feel like a memory. Being in a vision is much crisper than a dream. It's like being in the real world but through a hazy filter," I felt energized as though talking about my mind's eye was like sharing a secret. "And once I've had a vision, it's not like a memory that fades. I can reference a vision in detail like replaying a video. If that makes any sense."

"In our world, all experiences make sense," Adelaide said calmly.

"I've only been in the variant world for about six months. I'm still getting used to it," I said.

"I hear your visions are extremely accurate," said Adelaide. She glanced at me again briefly.

"I trust the accuracy, it's the reasons that trouble me. I often don't understand the significance of a vision, or why I see what I see. It's like my sixth sense is smarter than I am, yet never loops me in afterward. I wish I knew for sure that the visions were given to me. You know, like a higher power. Deep down, I don't think it works that way though. My heart tells me it's more akin to tapping into knowledge that's simply part of the natural world." My thoughts tumbled out. I hadn't realized how much I wanted to talk about the process of second sight.

"That's a very mature and thoughtful way to look at it." Adelaide sounded confident and it made me feel good. "So have you surmised why I wanted some time alone with you?"

"It had occurred to me in the hour or so we spent bouncing down that old logging road that I was being retained for my services," I said with a smirk.

"You're funny. I like that in a girl." Adelaide looked at me with admiration in her emerald eyes.

"What would you like me to try to see for you? I've been improving at having visions on demand, but it's not like turning on a tap."

"Nothing specific. No pressure from me. I was mildly interested to see if you could peek into my future. I don't hold the belief that we are not meant to see the future, only that we lack the capacity. Apart from you, that is," said Adelaide.

"Can I ask … what is your accent? Where are you from? I've been fighting to place it. You sound like you might be French, but not. Or German, but not. I'm sorry if it's rude, but I'm dying to know now."

"I am Danish. Specifically, my mother was Danish and we lived in Denmark for the first few years of my life. I spent most of my time there in hiding." Adelaide paused and added, "But, I have lived all around the world. I identify more with my variant brothers and sisters than any particular country."

"It sounds like you've led an interesting life." I hoped I was treading as carefully as I thought. "You've certainly got an impressive variation."

"It feels less impressive when I have to confine myself to a wheelchair to go out in human society. What I want to know about the future is, will that ever change?" Adelaide extended one of her legs towards me. She kept both hands on the wheel and both eyes on the road.

I took the tentacle in my hand, holding the smooth side

gently. I closed my eyes. I felt Adelaide's muscles move inside the tentacle.

The car disappeared and I saw Adelaide and Ralph in a dirty urban alley. Adelaide sat in her wheelchair. Ralph wore a goofy sandwich board and a yellow fedora, holding a floating mylar balloon. Adelaide looked anxious.

Ralph's expression appeared as reptilian as ever. "He's not going to show."

"We don't know that. He responded to my text. They're still interested in us," said Adelaide, as calm as usual.

"Interested in using us," said Ralph, sounding irritated.

"Are we not also using them? Do you enjoy pretending to be in a costume to go out in public? I expect you are less amused than I am in my chair."

"Any human who looks at me closely will realize this isn't a costume. We should give up and go back." Ralph looked around, ready to bail.

"All the better reason to join them." Adelaide placed a hand on Ralph's forearm.

"We don't have time to wait." Ralph moved around behind Adelaide's chair and pushed her forward. They neared the end of the alley when a dark hooded figure rounded the corner to face them. The figure drew back its hood and the terrifying tangled brown visage of Thorn sneered at them.

I jolted in fear and dropped Adelaide's leg, transporting me back to the passenger seat of her van.

"What did you see?"

"Nothing. It didn't work. I must be tired. I think I just about fell asleep there."

Adelaide assessed me. If she could tell I lied, she didn't say.

"Why don't you climb into the back and find somewhere

soft to lie down? Get some sleep and we'll try again later. We've still got several hours before we reach Chico."

Chapter 16

The landscape of Butte County was all crispy yellow grass and clusters of sage bushes. Early August sun baked the earth. A hint of hazy smoke shrouded the horizon. Heat shimmered in waves floating above the pavement. Adelaide's van rounded a corner into a cute but dusty main street. Downtown Chico.

I rubbed sleep out of my eyes and glanced at the back of Adelaide's head. The image of her, Ralph, and Thorn flooded my mind. I picked up my phone and tapped furiously.

Ask Cole how close we are to his friend's house, I texted Faith.

She didn't leave me hanging. *He says not much further. After downtown, we turn and go around a hill. Follow us.*

I relayed Faith's simple directions and we hugged the edge of a rocky hillside. Cole's car turned up a meandering driveway. We drove where Cole had gone and the road leveled out in front of a lone mobile home. Cole was at the home's front door when we parked.

"I need to check something with Faith. I'll be right back," I said to Adelaide. My heart thudded hard inside my chest.

I hopped out and jogged to Cole's car, taking his spot in the driver's seat. I slammed the driver's side door.

"Adelaide and Ralph were working with Thorn. So, probably Ivan too. I saw it in a vision," I said breathlessly. "And if it wasn't the past, if I saw the future, that means Thorn is alive."

"Slow down. What's this now?" said Ilya.

"She asked me to look into her future, so I took her hand, I mean, one of her legs, and I saw them all in an alley," I said in a rush.

"An alley where?" said Jonah.

"Doesn't matter. Thorn is dead. I know when I've killed someone," said Faith.

"It matters if we can't trust them!" I blurted back. "In the vision, Adelaide was in her wheelchair and Ralph wore a sandwich board with a funny hat, so the rest of him would look like a costume," I explained.

"We need to know whether this is something we can prevent or something we have to deal with now," said Jonah.

"He's right, if they haven't done anything yet, we can't pounce on them." Ilya's amber eyes brimmed with unease, mirroring my own.

"We can at least confront them. They know Irina's for real. We can tell them point blank, that this is what she saw." Faith chopped her left palm with her right hand. "When they answer, Ilya will listen in and he'll know if they're telling the truth."

"It's not that simple. If it's far enough in the future, they'll say they don't know what she's talking about and they'll be telling the truth," said Ilya.

"So what can we do?" I said.

"Sit tight and keep an eye on them." Jonah adjusted his collar.

"Do either of them have phones? Could they be in touch with Ivan? We *did* just meet these people." Faith adjusted her eyebrow ring as she frowned.

"Relax. We'll keep an eye on them," said Ilya.

"I'm pretty sure neither of them has a phone," I said.

"Then it's settled," said Jonah.

Cole appeared outside the window next to me and rapped on the glass. "Come on out. We're having dinner with Parker tonight."

Adelaide and Ralph declined to come inside and the prospect of leaving them alone had me on edge. I counted on Ilya to keep an ear on their minds.

Parker was a very tall, skinny man with acne. His friendliness came across awkwardly and he joked about rarely hosting visitors. Parker didn't seem like a variant. His sparsely decorated mobile had a few bland watercolor paintings, a velvety floral sofa set, and a small laminate and chrome dining table with vinyl-padded chairs. It reminded me of Darryl's parents' house. But it was clean, except for maps and large rolled paper tubes scattered throughout his kitchen and living room.

"Parker, these are my friends Jonah, Faith, Ilya, Irina, Nellie, Bruno, and Josh. We appreciate you giving us a tour of the area. We've got a couple more out in the van, but they've got heat stroke, so they're out of commission for now," said Cole.

"Do they need to see a doctor? We've got a clinic in town here," said Parker.

"No, they need to rest. I trust their judgment," said Cole.

"Fair enough. So what are you up to while you're in town? Anything more than the facility tour?" said Parker.

"Our road trip is only for a few weeks. We need to be back

in Vancouver for Labor Day. We're headed to San Francisco, but we want to see some places a bit more off the beaten path before we get there," said Cole.

He had concocted a somewhat elaborate cover story about our background and our reasons for visiting California. *I wish I'd asked if this guy is a variant or a civilian. They must have talked about this while I rode with Adelaide. I better keep my mouth shut so the story stays straight.* Ilya looked at me and nodded.

"I hope you guys don't mind freezer burgers and fries for dinner. I've been so busy with work the last few months, I eat out most of the time. Can't keep a lot of perishable food in the house." Parker's voice had a slightly nasal tone, evoking sympathy in me.

"We're poor grad students, so we're happy to have whatever you've got." Ilya shoved his hands in his pockets and smiled cheerfully.

I copied his smile. In addition to knowing what would set Parker at ease, my brother already knew whatever cover story Cole had dreamed up.

"So when did you guys want to go for a drive? We should have light until around nine o'clock tonight. If you're staying around here, we could do it tomorrow. I can't offer you all beds, but you're welcome to crash on the property. Cole told me you're all doing a camping thing right now," said Parker.

"Could we take you up on both? We'd like to have a tour tonight, crash, and then get out of your hair in the morning," said Ilya.

"Whatever works for you. I'll fire up the barbecue," said Parker.

We dined on Parker's freezer fare and headed out for our tour directly. Jonah and Faith elected to stay in the van to keep an eye on Adelaide and Ralph. Since our rationale for not including them was heat stroke, it made sense to leave someone behind to care for them.

Josh took Bruno and Nellie while Cole had Parker in his front seat, Ilya and me in the back. I pushed worries about Adelaide and Ralph away by thinking of Jonah.

"He *is* jealous, but he's more embarrassed than anything else. He knows you're keeping your distance because you think he's weak," said Ilya.

I sighed. "I don't think he's weak." I palmed my face angrily, willing my brother to stay out of my head. "He has to know I'm not eyeing Josh. I don't know which idea is more ridiculous," I said.

"Then let's talk about fracking," Ilya said, raising his voice to address Parker.

Parker and Cole launched into a conversation I could hardly follow. Ilya smiled and I understood the idea was to keep Parker focused on geology, not on evaluating his guests.

We arrived at a field surrounding a slim tower of white pipes. Cole's car pulled up alongside a large brown pond behind signs that read: DANGER WATER HAZARD and RESTRICTED AREA. Josh parked beside us.

"There's not a great deal to see here, but I'll take you where the public is allowed to go. I've seen them do media tours." A thread of tension hung in Parker's apprehensive tone. My gut told me he was worried about getting in trouble with his employer.

"This is pretty impressive so far," said Cole.

I knew Cole was looking at a work of engineering. All I saw was a machine ripping into the earth.

"The structure in front of us here is the drill rig and well."

Parker pointed to the pipe tower.

"We don't have any fracking in the Lower Mainland around Vancouver, so I think this is the first time most of us have seen a well," said Cole.

"This one is small compared to what you'll see in Texas," said Parker. "And over here are the site generators." Parker gestured to two machine-like pieces alongside the tower. He started to walk and we all followed. "Over here, we have drilling mud tanks. The pond on our left is the waste pit for drilling mud."

"I recently read an article that some fracking operators in California are experimenting with inducing earthquakes. Have you heard anything about that?" said Ilya.

"My employer, Eco Energy, is not involved in anything remotely like that. Maybe try the CCED," said Parker.

"We are hoping to visit them too." Cole frowned at Ilya.

"Are we allowed to take pictures?" I asked.

"Sure, but please don't post them on social media," said Parker.

"We appreciate you bringing us down here." The casual authenticity of Cole's expression reassured Parker.

"No problem. I wish it was more interesting. We should probably head out soon. We *are* allowed to be here, but I'd rather not chat with security. They'll make the rounds sooner or later," said Parker.

We spent the night on Parker's bare dirt lot and rejoined him in his trailer for cereal in the morning. Luckily for us, we also had some groceries of our own left in the coolers in Adelaide's van. We shared eggs, bacon, milk, and orange juice to show our gratitude.

While I helped clear the little dining table and the living room floor, I suddenly noticed that Parker was missing. "Parker's been gone awhile. Do you think he's not feeling well?"

"I'll listen in on …. SHIT!" shouted Ilya.

"What?" said Faith. Cole, Josh, and Jonah looked up with anxious faces. Nellie and Bruno seemed less concerned.

"He's gone outside to check on Adelaide and Ralph. He wants to offer them some breakfast." Ilya rushed to extract himself from the corner behind the dining table.

Ilya ran outside and I followed with Cole at my heels. Parker reached the back of the van, knocked, and immediately opened the door.

"Sorry to bug you, but- UUGGGGLLLLE" said Parker as Adelaide's oral tentacle shot out, wrapping around his neck before her beak sunk into his chest.

"NOOOOOO!" yelled Cole running to his friend.

"WHY?" I shouted angrily.

We reached the van as Adelaide released her grip on Parker. He dropped to the ground like a bag of potatoes.

I rounded the corner to the open doors at the back of the van. Adelaide and Ralph were still entwined in a mess of tentacles and scaly green skin. Parker lay dead on the ground, his face tinted blue, his tongue bulging out of his mouth.

"I'm sorry! He startled us! It's a defense mechanism! Why did you let him come out here?" Adelaide untangled her tentacles from around Ralph.

"We need to get out of here," said Ilya.

"Can't you help him? Do something! FIX THIS!" shouted Cole. His eyes were wet with rage and grief.

"There's nothing anyone can do for him," said Adelaide.

"Cole," I said softly, putting my hand on his arm, "He's already gone."

Chapter 17

We left Chico in the dust after Cole moved Parker back into his home. Cole pocketed Parker's phone in the hopes there would be no other evidence of who the frac operator had interacted with in the days leading up to his death. Our schedule was straightforward; hit the road and don't stop until San Francisco. We would head to the Berkeley campus and regroup there.

Back in Josh's Jeep, I pulled my cards out of their pack. I hadn't touched them much since my time in Victoria. I hoped something of the serum that Ivan had coated them with remained. Nellie and Bruno sat quietly in the back seat. I closed my eyes. I concentrated on Ivan's face and the fracking tower. I prayed to the universe that wherever my visions came from, they would show me exactly what Ivan was doing in California.

Dust and diesel fumes blew past my face through the partially open window. Hot dry air whipped around my head. The cry of a hawk pierced the rumble of road noise and the darkness of my eyelids shifted into the interior of a cave.

My eyes strained to focus, but I discerned two figures and a cylindrical steel tube frame between them. The floor of the cave was sand. To my right, a bright archway promised escape in the distance.

"Will it drill deep enough? Fast enough?" Ivan smoothed his strawberry blond hair back and adjusted his cuffs.

"Of course, it'll drill deep enough! I've tested it! It's your compound inside that hasn't been proven in the field. The advantage of my technology is that it can drill faster than anything else on the market, with pinpoint accuracy," said Waynesburg.

I recognized their voices before their faces became clear. My eyes continued adjusting to the darkness. Ivan and Waynesburg's features resolved in front of me.

"When will we be ready?" Ivan examined his phone with his thumb. Waynesburg wasn't worthy of Ivan's undivided attention.

"Tomorrow. I'm more worried about our exit strategy. We won't have more than a few minutes from when the drill starts to when it reaches the fault. The detonator is on a timer. That's why I suggested an air retreat. Once you've secured a helicopter, we're good to go." Waynesburg pushed a button on the steel tube framework. BRRRRRRrrrrrowwww came from below the frame.

The sand on the ground shivered and the surface below the tube fell by a few inches. The machine settled into a grinding hum as it worked. Waynesburg switched it off, satisfied.

"My sister will be flying us. She is one day behind me," said Ivan

Waynesburg reached into the darkness behind him and

picked up the shell of an empty oil drum, open on one end. He lifted the drum shell and maneuvered it over the steel tube framework concealing it completely.

The vision ended with a CLA-BANG as Josh's Jeep hit a pothole. The hot fuming air of the desert highway hit me in a fresh gust.

"Josh!" I yelled out.

"Sorry. Did you see something?" said Josh.

"They're one day away from testing if I saw the present. Maybe it was the future. From the sounds of how serious this earthquake will be, we'd know if it had already happened."

"Where were they? If we don't stop, we'll be in San Francisco before dinner."

"They were in a cave. I have no idea where, but the floor was sandy and you could see the ocean in the distance outside the entrance. Waynesburg hid a drill with a fake oil drum."

"You knew for sure they were testing somewhere around San Francisco?" Nellie piped in from the back seat.

"The first time I saw Ivan and this Waynesburg guy talking about the test, they were in Innoviro's San Francisco office. Ivan wanted a tour of the test site. It sounded like they were talking about a location nearby."

Nellie pulled a tablet out of her bag and clicked it on. "How many caves can there possibly be around San Francisco?"

"Probably none," said Bruno.

Nellie started tapping on the screen of her tablet. I stared at the cars on the highway ahead of us while I waited for her. Travelers and families rolled along the road. Everything was so … normal.

I looked back at Nellie. She was frowning and tapping. "I'm looking for 'San Francisco' and 'cave', but I keep getting something called the Sutro Baths."

"What, like a bathhouse?" I said.

"When I search Sutro Baths, I get a seaside bathhouse. But all the cave imagery tagged with San Francisco is also tagged Sutro Baths. There must be a cave somewhere near or below the bathhouse."

"Josh, punch the Sutro Baths into your GPS. I'm going to tell Cole to do the same," I said, picking up my phone.

"What about Adelaide and Ralph? Neither of them has a phone," said Bruno.

I clenched my teeth and kept my mouth shut as I wrote to Faith with instructions for her car. I no longer cared if Adelaide and Ralph kept up with us.

"She'll be following wherever we go. I'm sure she's not going to freak out when we don't go straight to Berkeley." Nellie's tone sympathized with Adelaide.

We drove in silence. Josh kept his eyes on the road and Nellie tapped on her tablet while Bruno slept. I watched the rough dusty hills evolve into cultivated suburban developments, all under a clear cerulean sky. The landscape evolved into the concrete towers of a city. Towers shot up above us, looming steel and glass giants until we passed through and shot out onto the ocean.

The iconic Golden Gate Bridge hung majestically across two points of land on the other side of the San Francisco Bay. The bright red bridge gleamed in the sunlight in sharp contrast to the blue sky behind it. No trace of the infamous San Francisco Bay fog could be seen for miles. Summer sun beamed overhead.

Josh pulled into a parking lot overlooking a cliff bluff at the edge of the continental United States. The Pacific stretched endlessly into the distance. Not since my adventure at Sombrio Beach outside Victoria had the world seemed so limitless.

Cole and Adelaide each parked alongside us. Several other vehicles suggested summer tourists crowded the site. We grouped around the open door at the side of Adelaide's van where Ralph lay concealed in the back.

"We've got good timing. The tide is out, so we'll be able to walk around all the exposed ruins," said Jonah. I wanted to tell Jonah to hang back and take it easy, but I said nothing.

"It's not crazy busy here, but it looks like you've both got to stay behind," said Ilya to Adelaide and Ralph.

"Adelaide can take her chair. If there isn't a ramp, I'll carry her," said Cole.

We knew he meant chair and all. Jonah and Ilya eyed Cole carefully. Faith and I both had looks of pure surprise on our faces. I couldn't believe Cole volunteered to help his friend's killer mere hours after the incident, accident or not. I made a mental note to check with Ilya on how Cole processed the incident with Parker. I didn't want to ask in front of everyone and make things worse for Cole than they already were.

Adelaide activated the hydraulic lift that lowered her chair out of the back of the van. Once the coast was clear, she crawled from the front seat through the van, out the back, slipped into her chair, and positioned her blanket. Josh retrieved a flashlight from his Jeep. As he tucked the light into an inside pocket of his flak jacket, I saw his gun strapped in place. My confidence in Josh notwithstanding, the sight of his black metal weapon made my chest contract.

We reached the edge of the parking lot and evaluated the stairs down to the ruined foundations of the Sutro Baths. Sure enough, the steep stone steps were our only option. Cole picked up Adelaide's chair by the frame. I cringed even though I knew the weight was nothing for him. He walked effortlessly down the stairs.

Jonah led the way and we followed him single file with the ocean directly beneath us. A chorus of seagulls complained as we descended. The surf roared and crashed in the distance.

I directed a thought at my brother. *Ilya, hang back with me. I need to talk to you about Cole.* On cue, he bent down to re-tie a perfectly knotted shoelace and the others moved ahead.

"Are you sure Cole is okay around Adelaide right now?" I whispered, leaning into Ilya's shoulder.

"No, but he's not going to do anything stupid. The thought has crossed his mind a few times to rip that beak tendril out of her throat and leave the rest of her behind," said Ilya.

"WHAT! Then why are you letting us all head off together? He's carrying her for God's sake!" I hissed.

"When we find this cave, if *our* father is there with Waynesburg and maybe Thorn, what exactly will you do? Throw rocks with your mind? Concentrate on their future? I'm no better at fighting. I can distract people. I can perform tricks. I can't kill a man with one blow. We need her and him. We need to figure out how to keep her from changing sides."

I pressed my lips together as I thought. Fairness and justice were not on the agenda at the moment. Ivan was deadly, but adding Thorn, we didn't stand a chance. Not without people like Adelaide and Cole.

"If Cole understands how important she is, I guess that's enough," I whispered.

"Focus on what's at hand. Let's find this machine and shut it down for good. And then, when the time is right and not before, we'll gently probe Adelaide and Ralph about their level of commitment to our cause. Ralph can block me, but I can hear Adelaide. If he's confided anything in her – which from the looks of things this morning is highly possible – the info will come out in Adelaide's thoughts."

"I hope you're right. I've never managed to change the future. It makes me wonder if things *can* be changed. Maybe I'm only meant to be prepared."

"Screw destiny. Nothing is 'meant' to happen. We can stop it if we're smart."

Ilya and I reached the bottom of the stairs and caught up with the others. There was only one way to turn at the bottom of the stairs. We saw the mouth of the cave immediately.

"I'll go in first." Cole's square jaw locked with determination.

"No, I'd better go. If there's a nasty surprise in there, I can take the brunt of it." Josh pulled the flashlight from his vest and strolled inside the cave where blackness quickly swallowed him.

Chapter 18

Several people emerged from the cave before Josh reappeared. First came a young family, followed by a middle-aged couple. *More tourists will come. This is not the time or place for a variant fight*, I thought.

"You've got that right," said Ilya softly, standing at my side.

"We look like idiots standing here for no reason," said Faith. Ilya stepped away from me. He took Faith's hand with one of his and touched her cheek with his other. Faith rolled her dark eyes but smiled. Both her nose stud and eyebrow ring glinted in the sun.

"If we stay calm, everything will be fine," said Jonah.

Josh sauntered across the landing to join us. "There's no sign of Ivan or anyone suspicious. We can go in, but other people are dawdling in there."

"What about the oil drum? Did you see it?" I said.

"It's at the back of the cave. Nobody noticed it."

"If the drum is near the back of the cave and we get a few moments to ourselves, I can throw up an illusion to make it look like the cave ends before the drum. Should give us enough time to examine it properly," said Ilya.

"Sounds good to me." Cole took the flashlight from Josh and walked into the cave. We all followed.

The cave was a plain tunnel with a sandy floor just as I'd seen. In my vision, I hadn't noticed the handrail which extended along the side of one wall providing a lifeline from the darkness back into the light. The dull black air weighed heavily around me, but I kept moving. I reached out for the handrail, feeling for the cold metal tubing.

We walked until the darkness nearly swallowed us and only the flashlight remained. The oil drum was exactly as I'd seen it, nestled innocuously into the sand. I looked back at the entrance. The arch of daylight was empty.

"Ilya, throw up your wall now. The coast is clear," I said.

"Everybody quiet now. I need to concentrate," said Ilya.

We watched as Ilya examined the cave wall. He touched it, letting his fingers learn the surface of the rock. He closed his eyes and the walls grew together, closing us inside a tiny claustrophobic pocket.

"I can't stay in here much longer." Nellie hugged herself, rubbing her arms although the cave wasn't cold.

"Calm down hon, you're fine. I'm here," said Bruno. He cleared his throat with a growlish cough and put his arm around Nellie.

I stepped forward and put my hand on the top edge of the drum. The cave fell away and I stood in a grove of giant pines, with Ivan and Waynesburg again, this time at a campsite. They were dressed in simple jeans and T-shirts.

Waynesburg finished assembling a small nylon tent. I turned around to survey the rest of the campsite. A large pick-up truck and trailer were parked behind me. The trailer door opened and Tatiana stepped out, dressed in khaki shorts, a crisp white golf shirt, and brown hiking boots.

"How long are we going to be roughing it?" said Tatiana as she examined her expertly manicured nails.

"As long as it takes," said Ivan, looking past Tatiana into the trees.

"Think of it as a vacation." Waynesburg dusted his hands on his jeans.

"My vacations include five-star hotels and room service." Tatiana brushed debris from the soles of her boots.

"Have you retrieved a specimen from each of the test groups? This place will likely be underwater after tomorrow," said Ivan.

"Go in the trailer and see for yourself," said Tatiana.

Ivan went into the trailer and my mind followed. A mini fridge with a glass door took up most of the space on the counter. The racks inside were packed with jars containing small pieces of matter suspended in a liquid. A glass case full of rows of pinned insects sat on the opposing counter. Oil-slick bees had small tags on each pin. Below the bees, several rows of beetles were still partially camouflaged as leaves and grass.

Ivan finished his visual inventory with a quick flip through a clipboard on the trailer's dining table. I saw a receipt on the table from the Golden Gate National Recreation Area. Three adults had been admitted to Muir Woods National Monument.

I let go of the edge of the oil drum. The cave walls materialized around me.

"Ivan, Tatiana, and Waynesburg are nearby. They're retrieving specimens because that forest will be underwater tomorrow." I stepped back from the drum and rubbed my face to clear my mind.

Cole handed the flashlight back to Josh and lifted the drum up and off the small drilling rig.

"Can we pull it out of the ground?" Faith asked.

"I don't know!" I blurted.

Cole examined the machine. Nellie placed her hand on the drill's framework. Her copper nails reflected the glow of the flashlight.

"The circuit is rigged to ignite the detonator in the event of a short. If removing the drill damages a single wire, this thing will blow." Nellie let go of the drill.

"Can't you 'talk' to it somehow? Isn't that your specialty?" said Faith to Nellie.

"It's not a network or a piece of software. It's a drill rigged with a bomb," said Nellie.

"If this machine is designed to trigger an earthquake, setting it off above ground would collapse this cave," said Cole.

"Maybe if we find Waynesburg, we can force him to remove this thing properly," I said.

"It's possible. Or we could incapacitate him and Ivan to ensure they can't switch it on," said Josh. "That would buy Nellie and Cole time to figure out what to do with it."

"You said Ivan is nearby. Do you know where?" asked Jonah.

"The camper table had a receipt for Golden Gate National Park," I answered.

"That's north of here. I saw it on the map," said Bruno.

"Then we need to find them before they activate this thing," said Nellie.

"What if they're already on the way here? Or what if someone decides to mess with it before we get back?" said

Faith.

"We'll stay. Cole will guard the machine and I'll keep the wall up," said Ilya.

"I'll stay too. You'll need me if something goes wrong," said Adelaide.

I shot a look of panic at Ilya. My eyes darted to Cole and back to Ilya.

"It's okay. It's under control," said Ilya.

I relaxed. "We should go now."

"Nellie and I will go back and keep Ralph company," said Bruno.

"Take my tablet. It's better than a phone for looking at maps and photos," said Nellie.

The Golden Gate Bridge gleamed on the road ahead like an elegant red carpet stretching across the bay. The late afternoon sun gave the landscape a nostalgic yellow hue, making the bridge a fiery shade of vermilion.

I bounced in my seat and wrung my hands as we crossed amid rush hour traffic. "I'm not sure where their campsite is, but at some point, they were in the Muir Woods."

Faith launched a map on Nellie's tablet and passed it to me. I searched for images of campgrounds in the Golden Gate National Park. I scrolled through useless images of campsites and tents as we neared the end of the Golden Gate Bridge.

"This one!" I shouted out. "Hawk Camp. This is the one they're at!"

"How far is it?" said Josh.

"Stay on the 101 through Sausalito. Once we get to Marin City, we should see Exit 445B," I said.

I sat on the edge of my seat until we saw a sign for Exit 445B. The road took us straight to Hawk Campground. Dozens of cars and trucks were in the parking lot.

"All right. Now what?" Josh shut off the Jeep's engine.

"Now we follow Irina," said Jonah. "Just like Sombrio, remember?" Jonah added to me.

"But at Sombrio we weren't looking for someone who wanted to kill us," I said, widening my eyes as I held Jonah's gaze.

Faith snapped a wad of gum I hadn't realized she was chewing.

"Ivan probably has security you didn't see in your vision," Josh said to me as he touched his gun. I thought I saw him switch off the safety.

"I didn't see Thorn in my vision. It was a quaint little campground. They just happened to have a trailer full of specimens. I didn't see any security."

"Then you missed something," said Josh.

"So we'll go carefully," said Jonah.

"Are you sure you wouldn't rather wait here?" I said to Jonah. I heard the concern in my voice. I remembered Ilya's comment about Jonah feeling ashamed.

"Agreed, Irina and I should go by ourselves," Josh said decisively to Jonah and Faith.

"I'm fine! How many times do I have to say it?" Jonah blurted angrily.

"Maybe we should hang back. Fewer people means less noise. Irina still has to find them. Josh is a soldier who is literally bulletproof." Faith held up her hands in a shielding gesture.

Josh retrieved a hunting knife and another gun from his glove compartment, adding them to the contents of his vest. "Provided we don't run into anyone, we'll be there and back before the sun sets," he said.

"And we'll stay here." Faith looked at Jonah sternly. He glared back at her and me.

"Let's go. Irina, you lead." Josh got out of the Jeep and I followed obediently.

I didn't look back as we headed along a dirt trail into the campground. I led the way along a dirt path flanking a zig-zag fence made of weathered rough-cut pieces of lumber. I still didn't recognize the area and my stomach started to twist.

Every campsite we passed was occupied. I met the gaze of several campers, a mom, a young girl, and a grandfather. I couldn't allow a fight to break out around here. I kept marching with Josh alongside. "I still don't see the right spot. I'm hoping this is the wrong place. Too many civilians in the line of fire."

"That's why we're scouting now, not going in hot. As soon as you catch sight of something familiar, let me know and I'll handle our approach."

We neared the edge of the campsite and the trail headed off into a dense forest. The chatter of the campers faded behind us as we reached the tree line.

"They were in a grove of tall trees. I won't know if this is it until we're inside," I whispered to Josh.

"Okay, this is good. We can use the forest for cover. I'll lead now."

We left the trail and skirted the tree line until Josh became satisfied we had a good spot to enter the forest. He gestured with a finger to his lips indicating silence. I followed him, crouching and ducking behind trees as he did.

We made slow progress, but my nerves weren't in a hurry to discover our quarry. Josh caught sight of something and his arm shot out to block my next step. He pointed at his eye, and then to a white spot between the trees ahead. The trailer!

Josh gestured for me to stay put. He went on alone. I let the professional scout do his job without argument. I crouched down in a patch of ferns to wait. My heartbeat pounded a frantic rhythm.

Rustles and snaps sounded in the trees around me. Birds chirped. A woodpecker hammered a trunk. I flinched as something scuffled through the brush. A whoosh overhead sent adrenaline through my veins. I sighed in relief. It was only a bird.

Josh eventually returned, shockingly silent as he walked through the underbrush. He gestured at his lips for continued silence and I followed him back out of the woods. Once we were back on the trail towards the campsites, Josh finally opened his mouth in a whisper. "It's them. Their perimeter has a trip wire. Probably alarmed."

"Can we get in?"

"I'll come back at night on my own. I might not be able to get anything from them without using deadly force. I won't know until I'm in it."

"Should we go back to the Sutro Baths first?"

"We should watch the park entrance so we know if they leave. Don't worry. This is what I'm trained to handle."

Chapter 19

A weight lifted off my chest in the parking lot as I saw Faith and Jonah right where we left them, sitting comfortably in the back of Josh's Jeep. Twilight took hold. I squinted to see the outlines of Faith and Jonah's heads. I smiled, remembering a time when I would have felt gut-wrenching anxiety at seeing Faith and Jonah tucked in a back seat together. With disaster on the horizon, their feelings were the least of my worries.

"I'll move the Jeep farther down the road before I head out again," said Josh. I hopped up to the front passenger seat.

"We found Ivan, Tatiana, and Waynesburg. Josh is going into their campsite," I said.

"We still need that Waynesburg guy to get his drill out of the ground," said Faith.

"But Ivan and Tatiana … it's not like they'll be arrested and prosecuted," said Jonah.

"We don't know that. We can destroy his work. And we could expose him on social media or through the news." I said, adding quietly. "We can find a new reporter."

"Going the destruction of science route, how will we know when we've got it all? Even if we find the Compendium documents you saw, let's be realistic. The only way to end this once and for all is Ivan's death. Probably Tatiana's too," said Jonah. Faith nodded.

Josh stopped the Jeep at what looked like a park maintenance trail. He got out and we followed his lead.

"So what are you going to do? Is the plan to 'secure' Ivan and Waynesburg," I said, using air quotes, hoping Josh wasn't just going to shoot on sight.

"Shouldn't we do this together? I really can help." Jonah's eyebrows arched with eagerness.

"Yeah, now that you've scouted the place, you can use us for something," said Faith.

"California doesn't exactly need more forest fires," I said.

"I work best alone anyway. I'll disarm the trip wire, sneak into the campsite, capture and detain," Josh held a handful of zip ties up and pocketed them again. "Don't worry about me. If Ivan wants to take me out, it's going to take time and planning," said Josh.

"So if you're caught, run. If he shoots, so what?" said Jonah.

"He doesn't want to lead them back to us," I said.

Josh smirked. "It's going to be fine. I know what I'm doing."

"So, we just wait here then," I shrugged my shoulders.

Faith and Jonah found tree stumps to sit on and I paced as Josh jogged back in Ivan's direction. I watched his silhouette blend into the trees. In the failing light, I thought I saw another figure. I strained to make out features. Thorn!

I shrieked as the horrible decayed mouth and tangled mane came into focus. Thorn was on us in a flash. He grabbed a fistful of Jonah's shirt, yanking him off the ground as I screamed Josh's name. Someone had a hold of Faith. The tattooed girl from Victoria held Faith with a crushing hug. The girl flexed her biceps, bringing life to her tarantula, falcon, and bright yellow snake tattoos.

The spider raced from its owner's flesh, onto the ground, and jumped at my chest. I lost track of her other ink creatures.

"Get it off! Get it off!" I screamed. I felt hot jabs as the creature's fangs sank into my skin. The forest disappeared.

I blinked and my skull throbbed. My jaw clenched as I lurched groggily back to consciousness in front of a campfire. My arms were pinned behind me. My vision regained clarity slowly, blink after blink, heartbeat after heartbeat.

I sensed bodies around me. Josh's dark beard stubble, Jonah's glossy black hair, and Faith's springy dreads glowed in the firelight.

Each of us was secured to tent chairs with Thorn's sticky silken webbing wrapped around us like grotesque cocoons. Jonah remained unconscious, his head drooped listlessly forward. Josh jolted awake, gained his bearings, and squinted at something behind me. Faith roused slowly.

I looked down at my chest to evaluate my cocoon. The revolting material had the consistency of a spider's nest with the strength of fishing twine. I could move only enough to flex my arms and suck air into my lungs.

"Wake up kids," said a woman's voice I didn't recognize.

"Welcome to California!" said a more familiar voice.

I looked up to see the white-haired man from my vision. Waynesburg.

I turned my head to see the tattooed woman standing next

to me. My nerves seized and relaxed again. I noted her crossed arms and placid face. I saw no sign of Thorn, Ivan, or Tatiana.

I tried to levitate myself. Nothing happened. Faith concentrated on the campfire. Nothing happened.

"Thank you for coming to visit us tonight," Waynesburg said. "I've been waiting for years to implement real-world geological engineering. Admittedly, I have my reservations about hitting the button a little early."

"You can't!" I croaked. I whipped my head around looking for Ivan, Tatiana, and Thorn. They were all gone. I knew without asking they were on their way to the Sutro Baths cave.

"The city! Those people!" blurted Faith.

"Why is Ivan risking exposure here?" said Josh.

"There's no risk, you idiot. California has earthquakes all the time. No one's going to go looking for a cause. We will be at a safe distance. I can't say the same for whoever you left to guard the drill."

Scathing hate filled Faith's voice. "People like you make my skin crawl. You're so selfish. You think nothing of ruining an entire planet for billions of people."

"That's the plan," said Waynesburg.

"What makes you think you can remake the world with any measure of control?" snapped Josh.

"Science. You kids aren't too bright, are you?" Waynesburg shook his head.

"Okay, you've had years to plan. Say your science is right on the money. How can you justify it?" I asked bitterly.

"I don't have to justify myself to you. Any of you." Waynesburg looked around at us.

"Ivan is nuts, so let's write him off entirely. But you, you're a human being with a conscience. Are you even a variant? How can you be sure Ivan will let you join his club in the new world order?" I asked.

"Why don't you let me worry about my fate, sweetie?" Waynesburg turned his back on me.

"What do you want us to do with them until morning?" said the tattooed girl.

"My friend needs water. He'll die if he doesn't stay hydrated," I said.

Waynesburg ignored me again. "Split them up. Have Rose and Sage carry them up to those hills. Make sure they're all a long way from civilization."

"Rose and Sage?" said Faith.

"Are you listening? Jonah could die! He needs water." I raised my voice.

Our pale-winged friends stepped out of the darkness. The orange light hid the blue hue of their skin. Their platinum hair shone like spun gold. They wore identical pale pink dresses and tailored dark brown leather jackets with the same texture as their wings.

They flexed and closed their wings in unison. Faint snaps and cracks popped from a far-off point in the forest. I seemed to be the only one who heard the sounds. I tried my best version of a poker face as the twins eyed me.

"What are you doing with these assholes?" yelled Faith.

"You can't be on their side!" I shouted.

I glared at Rose and Sage while I strained to hear sound from the trees.

"Have you never considered what our lives are like? Living around human society, but never *in* it," said Rose.

"Everyone but us gets to have a life. We're sick of it," said

Sage.

"Why do you suddenly get to put yourselves before every other person on this planet?" I said. If help was coming, I wanted an argument with the twins drowning out any footsteps in the forest.

"Dr. Waynesburg is right. We don't have to justify ourselves to you," said Rose.

"No, let's talk justification. Ivan is your father. Both you and Ilya are betraying your *own* blood. For them." Sage gestured aimlessly at the world around her.

"I *am* them," I said.

"Well we're NOT!" shouted Sage. Crackling underbrush echoed somewhere close.

A visceral animal snarl like something from an enraged wild cat erupted in the dark, somewhere right outside the campsite. Was Thorn still around, lurking out of sight? The snarl rumbled into a deep growl and stopped.

"Shut up! There's something out there," said the tattooed girl.

"Thorn went with the Krylovs," said Rose as she looked around cautiously.

A swooping WHOOOMP cut through the air. A tree trunk whizzed over our heads knocking Sage, Rose, and Waynesburg to the ground. The treetop grazed the trailer scratching the siding with an ear-piercing SQUEEEEEE.

Sage and Rose scrambled to their feet and flew away, disappearing into the night. Waynesburg lay unconscious on the ground, bleeding profusely from a head wound. Reflected firelight danced on the growing pool of blood beneath him. The tattooed girl was nowhere in sight.

"Is everyone all right?" Cole stepped into the campsite.

"You are the best big brother a girl ever had." Faith smiled at him.

"How about getting this foul crap off us?" said Josh.

Cole ripped away the back of Josh's cocoon. He flicked it off his hand with disgust.

"Jonah's still out cold," I said. "The girl with the living tattoos had a spider that bit me. I don't know what knocked him out."

Cole freed me and moved on to Faith. I ran to the picnic table and grabbed a bottle of water. I cracked it and gently tipped it into Jonah's sleeping mouth.

"It was the girl. She got all of us except Josh," said Faith. "I think they gassed him."

Cole reached Jonah and removed his cocoon, placing him on the ground. I resumed trying to get Jonah to drink. A few moments later his eyes flickered open. I hugged him.

Ilya stepped into the campsite and I realized the snarl we'd heard had been one of his illusions.

"Speaking of the world's greatest brother! How did you know?" I said.

"When you screamed for something to get off you, it caught my attention. You come in louder than most, even from fifty miles away," said Ilya, tapping his temple.

Suddenly my chair started quivering. The trailer began to tinkle and crack. The plates on the picnic table rattled. Nausea surged up inside me. The ground, the air, and everything around me vibrated. Cole shielded Faith as a branch fell from a tall pine.

"Oh shit!" Faith covered her nose and mouth with both hands.

"Was that what I think it was?" I said, frowning as I tried to listen for something, anything.

"That was an earthquake," said Cole, hanging his head, dejected.

"It wasn't so bad," I said.

"Here, no," said Ilya.

"Damage in rural areas is often minor, even when the epicenter is close. It's the urban areas that usually suffer. The shaking didn't last for even a full minute, so the damage shouldn't be that bad. Let's pray there are no aftershocks," said Cole.

"We should go back to the cave for the others," said Faith.

"We need to get Jonah to a hospital," I said.

"No, I'm fine."

"He'll have to wait in line behind people with life-threatening injuries. They can't offer him any useful treatment. We're better off to keep hydrating him ourselves," said Josh.

"Can we even get back into San Francisco?" I asked.

"We should at least try," said Ilya.

"What do we do now? We've failed," I said.

"We'll pick up Nellie, Bruno, Ralph, and Adelaide," said Josh.

"We should still go to the CCED at Berkeley. If we can get our hands on some of Waynesburg's research ... maybe he has a copy of Ivan's *Compendium*," said Cole.

"I don't know if I can face the city. What if buildings came down? Real people could be dying, trapped in rubble ... and we could have stopped it. What if a tsunami is coming?" I fought a lump in my throat.

"Like I said, the damage won't be that bad with such a short quake. Worry when the shaking lasts more than four minutes. That's when you'll get an epic wave," said Cole.

"We still need to move quickly. Now!" Ilya gestured at the

trail.

I helped Jonah to his feet, hanging on to his waist.

"Follow me. I left quite the path. I'm parked next to Josh's Jeep," said Cole.

Chapter 20

City lights twinkled in the distance and the Bay Area appeared stable. I rode in the back of CCEDCole's car, cradling Jonah's head, barely conscious, in my lap.

I pulled out my phone and searched 'San Francisco' and 'earthquake' and tapped 'News' in the results. The region had suffered a six-point-five earthquake. No risk of a tsunami. Authorities continued to assess the damages, but the public was ordered to shelter in place.

We didn't have the luxury of staying put. We headed back the way we'd come, south on Highway 101 through Sausalito. Glancing around at the moonlit landscape, San Francisco didn't look much different. Until we hit traffic backed up at Lime Point.

"The Golden Gate Bridge is packed to the gills with gridlock," said Cole as the tip of the Bridge came into view on the horizon. Jonah sat up.

"Why are these people lined up here, waiting?" said Jonah.

"I don't know, but turn around now. Before we get trapped. Josh will follow." I tried to imagine what Faith and Ilya were saying in Josh's Jeep. As the thought entered my mind, I concentrated on the traffic jam, thinking hard at Ilya, holding the picture in my mind. My phone jingled. Faith wrote. *What the hell is this?*

I tapped back, *Earthquake panic probably. We're turning back. There's another bridge to the north. Have you heard back from Nellie?*

Faith replied, *No, nothing yet.*

I wrote furiously. *Tell them to meet us at Berkeley. Cole wants to go to CCED. He thinks we can get our hands on some of Waynesburg's research. Maybe even Compendium docs.*

Faith answered, *Will do. Josh says we'll follow you north. It's called the Richmond-San Rafael Bridge. Check to make sure it's moving! I can't find anything on it yet.*

I replied, *Keep going anyway. If it's blocked, we'll deal with it then.*

"Faith says the bridge to the north is the Richmond-San Rafael. She can't find anything online saying it's open or closed," I said.

"We might as well go anyway. It's not like we've got any choice." The tension in Cole's voice ratcheted up my anxiety. If we got bogged down in San Francisco, how could we hope to catch Ivan?

"How far do you think Ivan and Tatiana got?" I asked.

"You said they were waiting on Tatiana because she could fly them out on a helicopter, right?" said Jonah.

"Looks like they didn't need to run that fast after all. They must have expected to rip a hole in the earth," said Cole.

"They know the concept works. I'm sure they do better next

time. I bet that helicopter went as far as it could take them on a single tank of fuel," I said, and added, mostly to myself. "Wait, let me try my cards. That'll help me focus."

I fished my cards out of my backpack and eased them out of the pack. I took the first card off the top and ran my fingers across the faded diamond pattern on the back. I flipped it over and frowned at the image.

The Sun. It displayed upside down, so I rotated it for a better look. A personified pale yellow sun looked at me sternly, overseeing an androgynous naked human on horseback. The artistry of the cards still caught me off guard at times. I ran my fingertips firmly across the surface, thinking more about serum than strange old art. I thought about Ivan's face, and the cast on his arm, and then the fresh image of Thorn's frightening visage popped into my mind.

Cole's car fell away around me and I stood in a dusty desert at night. Ivan and Tatiana were camping again, alone. As I watched, they toasted with opaque camp mugs, smirking at each other. I wanted to slap them both. Thorn walked into view, dressed in greasy overalls and a dingy brown T-shirt, his matted hair pulled back into something resembling a ponytail. His arms hung savagely at his sides, claws as filthy as ever. Instinctively repelled, I dropped the cards and Cole's car reappeared around me.

"They're in a desert. It looks like they had a campsite all prepared and waiting for them," I said.

"Probably the Mojave or the Sonoran. They couldn't have gone much farther," said Cole.

"Nevermind Ivan for now. Try to see Nellie and the others. If she's not answering Faith they could be in trouble. They could be trapped in the Sutro cave. Or worse," said Jonah.

"Of course. Sorry," I said, fumbling my cards back into my hand.

I repeated the strategy, fingering and flipping cards over in my hands. I came to rest on an image of a compass with strange characters, hoisted into the clouds by a pair of angels. The Wheel of Fortune.

I touched it and flashed to the parking lot above the Sutro Baths. Adelaide's van remained where she'd left it. She sat behind the wheel, with Nellie in the passenger seat. I concentrated on shifting my view and floated around in front of the windshield. Sure enough, Ralph and Bruno were in the back of the van.

"Is it charged yet?" said Bruno.

Nellie picked up a phone, connected by a cord to Adelaide's console. "You'll be the first to know when it's got enough juice."

I concentrated again to float high above Adelaide's van for a view of the Baths. The ruins had been demolished. Only rubble remained. They couldn't possibly have been in the cave when the earthquake hit. In a lucky turn, it looked like most of the drill's damage had been above ground in its immediate vicinity.

I dropped my cards again and texted Faith. *They're all right. They're in Adelaide's van above the Baths. They've got a phone; I think it's Bruno's. Keep going to Berkeley and tell Nellie to follow as soon as you hear from her.*

We reached the Richmond-San Rafael Bridge and hit more gridlock. We had no choice but to push through. It took us an hour of tedious, mind-numbing stops and starts to get to Berkeley.

We found University Avenue and made our way to the

campus. Josh's Jeep kept up behind us. The gate I recognized from my vision was perfectly intact.

"It's down this street here." I pointed at the next turn. "The entrance has Roman-style pillars on either side."

"Nobody will be there at this time of night. Especially in an emergency," said Jonah. Cole parked across the street from the building I'd seen in my vision. He felt certain that the place I saw Waynesburg and the CCED were the same office. Josh parked behind us. I sized up the brick and pillar structure while my friends poured out of both vehicles.

"Nothing about the CCED should inspire a lot of security. It's an academic office. I'd expect to get in easily," said Cole.

"Irina, do you have any idea what might find? A thumb drive? A binder full of paper?" said Jonah.

"He had a manila envelope and dropped it in a blue mailbox. But it was not a recent vision. He looked younger, so it could have been years ago," I said.

"If there's nothing here, we could go to the local Innoviro office. If they were expecting the building to collapse in an earthquake, they might have been careless about leaving evidence," said Jonah. "San Francisco was the only other office working on genetics, as far as I knew," he added.

I quickly picked up his meaning. The cure for his genetic degeneration might be there. "Then we have to try," I squeezed his hand.

"I'm starving. We need food," said Faith.

"I'm hungry too," I said.

"It's three o'clock in the morning," said Jonah, looking at his phone. "We'll have to hit a gas station."

"Food has to wait. We can't split up. The city is too unpredictable right now," said Josh. "Cole, Irina, and I will go into the building. Everyone else, wait here. We'll find provisions after."

"I'm so glad you're here to guide us all," Faith glared at Josh.

He opened his mouth to respond at the exact moment a handful of windows on the second floor of the CCED exploded in a blast of fire that sprayed us with hot glass.

An alarm wailed into the night. Sprinklers rained on ruined black rooms.

"Shit!" yelled Cole.

"Time to go!" shouted Josh.

Nobody wasted time piling back into our vehicles. Cole shot away from the curb and Josh stayed on his bumper. I looked out the back window of Cole's car and watched helplessly as smoke billowed out of a charred building.

Chapter 21

Outside the Berkeley campus, the streets rumbled with anger. A handful of people were yelling around an ambulance and fire truck at the scene of a fresh car crash.

A convenience store in the other direction had a line spilling outside the door. Several apartment buildings nearby were completely dark. I felt foolish for thinking that *some* lights on a city's waterfront meant everything was fine.

"I hate being two steps behind these assholes!" I yelled at no one in particular.

"Don't yell at us," said Cole.

"She's venting. I'm angry too," said Jonah.

Cole blew out a long breath and pulled over. He glared at the chaos around us.

"Is this what you do in the middle of the night after an earthquake? Run down to the corner store to panic shop?" Cole sliced the air over his steering wheel, jabbing at the people outside. Josh parked behind him, but we stayed in our vehicles.

"People are stupid when they're scared," said Jonah.

"What should I text Faith?" I said.

"Maybe it's time to leave town. We won't starve. We can get out of the worst of this mess to regroup," said Cole.

"No!" Jonah and I blurted at the same time.

"We shouldn't leave Nellie and the others behind," Jonah said quickly.

"I'm not leaving until I know there's nothing for us at the Innoviro office. That was a better shot than Berkeley anyway," I said.

Cole sighed.

"We can't try that without resting and eating. We passed a closed supermarket. I can get in and out before anyone catches us. Text that to my sister," said Cole.

"You won't be able to carry enough by yourself. To make it worthwhile, we all need to go in," I said. Nerves prickled my already angry stomach. I wasn't bothered by the idea of stealing from a corporately owned supermarket chain. What bugged me was the chance of being caught. The time Faith and I got locked up in Victoria was enough jail for a lifetime.

We backtracked to the supermarket. A large plastic and florescent sign over the entrance flickered and the building was dark. We all filed out of the cars again.

"Looks like the power is out. The alarm is probably down too then," said Faith.

"Let's hope so." Ilya evaluated the building's exterior.

The prospect of a supermarket roof collapsing on my head nearly nailed my feet to the ground. I forced one foot in front of the other watching Ilya and Faith ahead of me.

My eyes adjusted to the dark as we searched for the dry

goods aisle. Ilya found a flashlight and batteries. He ripped open the packages and popped the batteries into the back of the flashlight.

"We should look for food that doesn't spoil easily and doesn't need cooking. The lighter and smaller, the better," said Ilya.

"I keep forgetting how long you spent out on Sombrio Beach." Faith smiled and grabbed Ilya's hand.

"I told myself all that self-reliance would come in handy one day," said Ilya.

"What, specifically, should we get?" I asked.

"Crackers, dried fruit, nuts, granola or cereal, beef jerky, Gatorade powder," he answered.

I picked a box of cookies off the shelf and put it in my backpack. I took a package of fruit gummies next. It hadn't taken much to dissolve the social barrier that would normally prevent me from walking into a supermarket and brazenly taking things.

Here we were, scavenging in a supermarket in the middle of the night after an earthquake. It felt like a post-apocalyptic movie. Little did the already panicked San Franciscans outside know, that the end of the world was on the horizon if we couldn't stop my ex-boss, and worse, my father, from completing his *Compendium* projects.

We stuffed our bags as quickly as we could and jogged back to our cars.

"Where are we going from here?" asked Josh. "I'm not pretending to be in charge. We should decide together," he added, looking at Faith.

"Irina doesn't want to leave San Francisco until we find the Innoviro Office," said Cole.

"Have we given up on our Portland friends?" asked Jonah.

"I texted them but got no reply. I like the idea of trying to find a new reporter," said Faith.

"We can't do this alone, not anymore. It's not up to us to save the world. We could send everything we gave Wong to a new reporter," said Jonah.

"but what did he have? Our actual evidence is thin," I said.

"Journalists will take time. They will fact-check. And while they do, Ivan is going to set off his next disaster," said Josh.

"Even if we roll into a newspaper and demonstrate our abilities for someone else, all that proves is that we're variants. We need proof that this earthquake was Ivan," I said.

"I can see a news story being all about the existence of variants. And the terraforming part getting lost in the mix. It's too wild a story to believe without seeing what we've seen," said Cole.

"We need *The Compendium* to figure out what disaster comes next," said Ilya.

"I want to know who else is helping Ivan. He can't carry this all out by himself. There has to be a network," said Cole.

"So what's our next move then?" said Josh.

"It has to be the Innoviro office here in San Francisco. They had working computers and hard copy files and specimens the last time I saw it in a vision. And Jonah knows they did genetic research here," I said.

"The city is still reeling and that might work for us. An alarm can be passed off as a malfunction. Police and rent-a-cops will have their hands full by now," said Josh.

"How long should we give Nellie and the rest to reply?" asked Faith.

"Remember my vision of Adelaide and Ralph with Thorn? What if that's how he found us? If they're a package deal, it might be safer to keep going without them," I said.

"You saw what?" said Josh, alarmed.

"It doesn't matter. We're not ditching anyone. Nellie is my friend. I vouched for all of us to get her to come," said Faith. On cue, her phone chimed and she fished it out of her bag. "Nellie's got service. They're on their way here now."

Ilya looked at Faith, then at me.

Did you 'hear' anything? Did my vision of Adelaide and Ralph with Thorn already happen? I thought at my brother. He shrugged his shoulders wearily.

Faint light returned to the sky. It was almost dawn and I felt exhaustion weighing on me. "We all need to sleep," I said.

"Let's find somewhere we can camp, somewhere Ralph and Adelaide can walk around. If they're playing both sides, I want to look them in the eye when I ask," said Josh.

Faith tapped, swiped, and tapped her phone. "Nellie's going to a garage between us and the Bay. She sent a map link. Can I say we'll meet them there?"

"Underground spaces might not be safe right now. After-shocks could still happen," said Cole.

"We'll have to take our chances. It'll be an express meet-up, then we'll find somewhere to camp," said Josh.

The parking garage mocked us with a CLOSED sign when we got there. A yellow and black barrier arm blocked the entrance.

We waited until Adelaide's van rounded the corner. Josh waved to get her attention. Cole got out of his car and discreetly pulled up the arm. I heard the hinge mechanism inside the arm's joint squeeeeeee and then CRACK. I looked up and down the street. We hadn't drawn any attention.

Cole drove through, followed by Josh and Adelaide. Ilya ran back to the arm and pulled it down behind us. I hoped the closed sign would work in our favor long enough to let us plan our path to Innoviro and then out of the city.

Josh found a secluded section of the bottom level. No sooner than we shut off our engines, the ground began to vibrate. The sounds of glass tinkling and car alarms wailing drifted down from the surface. The world continued to rumble and rumble and rumble. Cole's words about the duration of an earthquake rang in my ears. The shaking kept going and my chest constricted. Acid swirled in my guts. Fear wrapped around my throat. And the shaking kept going. I ran between Cole's car and Josh's Jeep as the ceiling ahead of me began to rain dust and crumbs of concrete. Suddenly a giant slab of the roof came down with a BANG between our corner and the path back out of the parking garage. More pieces of concrete trickled down through the dust.

"In the corner! NOW! Everyone!" shouted Cole.

I stood for a moment, watching the dust clear, watching the wall of rubble take shape in front of me. We were trapped. I snapped out of it and ran to the corner where my friends huddled, disoriented and terrified.

Chapter 22

Concrete dust permeated the air. Darryl had told me it was dangerous, so I pulled my shirt over my nose. White noise rang in my ears.

"Don't breathe in the dust! Concrete dust is like asbestos or something!" I yelled to Faith and Jonah who were huddled next to me. I waved furiously at everyone else to get their attention, alternately pointing to my shirt between waves.

Through the horrible fog, I looked at each of my companions in a clumsy cluster against the wall. I heard coughing and the light taps of small particles crumbling and settling. I wanted to escape the dust so badly that my muscles ached from head to toe. Claustrophobia crushed my chest.

Energy bubbled up through my abdomen and pulled me to my feet. A force passed out of me and through the air, screening the dust like a fine invisible fabric. I could breathe. Slowly each of my friends uncurled from their positions.

"Where the hell did *that* come from?" said Faith.

"I think it was me," I said.

"Well done!" said Ilya.

"Don't get excited yet. That was a long earthquake," said Cole.

"We need to dig our way out of here. Now!" said Josh.

Panic coursed through me.

"Everyone, listen. We don't have time to dig ourselves out. A tsunami will hit us in ten to fifteen minutes," said Cole.

"How do you know? Are we safe?" cried Faith.

"Irina, can you 'hold' the walls up?" said Josh.

"I can keep the water out," said Jonah.

"I can't hold up walls!" I blurted.

"What about the rest of the San Francisco?" shrieked Faith.

"Does anybody have a wireless connection?" asked Bruno.

"You know better than that," said Nellie. Faith and I checked our phones anyway.

"So we sit here assuming a flash flood is coming above," I said.

"It won't be a flash flood. It'll be a raging wall of cars, concrete, street lights, mail boxes ..." Cole trailed off looking at the ceiling.

"Anything loose above is ammunition for the wave as it scrapes the surface of the coast," Ilya added as he eyed Cole and extracted his thoughts.

"We can't seriously just sit here while millions of people die! We have to do something!" shouted Faith.

"Even if we manage to dig ourselves out before the wave hits, we can't survive it. No combination of telekinesis and aquakinesis will keep a tsunami at bay," said Adelaide.

Our concrete cave grew silent. White noise and the crackling of loose pebbles gave way to a rumbling sound that raced towards us, getting louder as the rumbling intensified. I grabbed Jonah's hand. His eyes were as full of fear as mine.

"Are you strong enough?"

"I'll have to be. We'll do it together."

Jonah kissed me and I let him. He pulled away quickly and closed his eyes to concentrate. I did the same.

I pictured our disaster-made cave as an impenetrable bubble. I focused on keeping the air where it was, holding the walls in place with sheer willpower. I felt the crushing weight of the ocean overhead.

Chunks of rubble popped off the ceiling and out from the cave-in beside us. Water hissed in through cracks. But our pocket held. The rumbling finally stopped.

"It's gone," said Jonah.

"Along with most of San Francisco," said Nellie.

"Cole. With me," said Josh as he gestured at the rubble wall.

Josh and Cole began to dig, carefully picking through the concrete chunks. As they hit the surface, water rushed in. Then silence.

"Where do we go from here?" said Bruno.

"Should we still try to find the Innoviro office?" said Faith.

"There won't be anything left at Innoviro worth digging up, even if we still could," said Nellie.

"We won't know unless we try. I doubt we'll get out of the city quickly anyway. Not in our cars," I said.

"If we can get the van out, Adelaide and I could leave from here and meet you in the desert. You don't need us at Innoviro," said Ralph.

"There's no point in discussing this until we know what the rest of San Francisco looks like," said Josh.

"We'll keep digging, but we have to be careful. For now, we only need enough room for bodies to crawl through safely."

Cole walked over to the wall of rubble and beckoned for Josh to join him.

"What are Ralph and I going to do if we leave on foot? If the terrain is bad out there, my chair will be useless," said Adelaide.

"If you stay close to me, I should be able to disguise both of you," said Ilya.

"You can do that?" said Ralph.

"It'll only work if you stay close to me," said Ilya.

Ilya closed his eyes and took a deep breath. He squared his shoulders, breathing deeply. The air around Adelaide and Ralph grew hazy, but not like the concrete dust. Their bodies blurred while the world around them remained crisp and clear to the naked eye.

Adelaide flickered back to reality first. She appeared to be herself, only completely human wearing a pair of faded light blue jeans. She looked down at her legs and touched them, bewildered at what she saw.

Ralph took shape as a lean man in a collared shirt and khaki slacks. He could have been one of the teachers walking around Berkeley. Was this what Ralph would have looked like if he had been human and not variant?

Ralph looked down at his hands and surveyed the rest of his body. He touched his face, slowly reading his new features with his fingertips. Then he turned to stand in front of the van's tinted back window. Ralph took in his new face bit by bit, looking at his reflection, prodding his eyes and lips. He turned to his right and left for the profile on each side.

"And this is an illusion? I'll be myself again if you break it or if I go too far from you?" Ralph asked Ilya. Disbelief tempered the look of wonder in his eyes.

"I would have offered this earlier, but there hasn't been a good time. I knew we'd split up and you'd lose the illusion, possibly at a bad time," said Ilya.

Adelaide walked over to Ralph and kissed him passionately, wrapping a single human leg around his waist. He kissed her back, but only for a moment before he gently pushed her away.

"You could have done this back in Portland when we first met," said Ralph.

"Yes, but keep in mind, you're still you. And when you break the connection with me, you'll instantly be your old self. You haven't changed. Either of you." Ilya turned his attention to Adelaide. "I've simply changed how you see yourself and how the world sees you."

"Why don't we dig into some of the food we scored at the supermarket?" said Faith.

"Cole, Josh, stop working and come eat," said Jonah.

Faith, Ilya, and I unpacked our bags while Jonah, Nellie, and Bruno reassembled our makeshift campsite. Ralph and Adelaide continued sizing each other up while the rest of us ate cautiously.

When we were done, Cole and Josh resumed work on the wall while the rest of us sat and waited.

"So here's what's been eating at me," Faith said to Adelaide, "How did Ivan's thugs find us in the woods? Has he got a sixth sense?" She turned to Ralph, eyes narrowed, "That beast-man is downright feral. Not much of a creative thinker."

The hair on my arms stood up as I waited for either of them to answer. I badly wanted to ask these questions, but I was afraid - of both variants and the disaster around me.

"Thorn must have a heightened sense of smell. He's probably a brilliant tracker," said Jonah.

"No, I think it was something else," I said, looking at Adelaide too.

"What are you two saying?" Nellie looked at me intently.

If she considered Ralph to be family, she wasn't going to take my vision at face value. She'd make even more excuses than my friends had.

"Nevermind. It's probably nothing," I said.

"Can I talk to you alone?" Ilya held up the keys to Cole's car.

"Of course." I got up and followed Ilya.

Once sealed in Cole's car, Ilya said, "When I created Ralph's illusion, I finally saw something inside his head. Well, a lot of things, but there's only one thing worth mentioning. Ralph knew Rubin! They worked together. I don't know if Ralph's lying about having nothing to do with Innoviro, but he knew Rubin, that's for sure. You should have a look at his past, as soon as you get a chance," said Ilya.

A knock on the glass startled both of us.

Jonah peered in through the driver's side window, glaring at me past Ilya. "Can I have a turn in the confession booth?"

"Seat's all yours," said Ilya. I felt envy that my brother could hear Jonah's thoughts, but I never would.

"I know this is a shitty time to be selfish. But I want you to use your vision to see if the Innoviro office is still standing. I am almost certain that Ivan had a serum, here in San Francisco, that was meant for me." Jonah held my hand.

"Trying to stay alive isn't selfish," I squeezed his hand and released it quickly. I tried not to think about how much time he had left.

"It's selfish when the fate of the planet is at stake," he said.

"It sounds so bizarre to say that out loud. I have moments where I can't believe it's real. I have to keep remembering the things I've seen in my visions. But none of you have seen what I've seen. Except maybe Ilya, poking around in my head." I looked at Jonah's blue eyes, pale as I'd ever seen them. "You know, it's hard for me to see you like this. I want to be near you, but I can't stand the idea of hurting you so that *I* can feel good."

"That's how I felt after the first time we kissed," he said as he took my hand. "So you should know that I mean it when I tell you that I don't care if you drain me."

He tried to kiss me and I jerked away. I threw his hand back at him.

"Why am I supposed to be alright with watching the person I love writhing in pain?" My mouth hung open. The words had spilled out too quickly.

"You love me?" Jonah smiled with a cheeky playfulness. "Good, because I love you too. And I'll leave you alone until I get better, but I *will* get better. Don't doubt that. You might be the one who started this war with Innoviro and Ivan, but we're all in it now. I'm every bit as angry as you are, and just as ready to fight. And I'm not so damn fragile!" Jonah slammed his fist on the edge of the steering wheel. He seemed strong for a moment and I wanted to believe him.

"Okay. It's a deal." I leaned over and kissed him quickly on the cheek. I pulled away before he could kiss me back.

Jonah paused, considered me, and got out of the car. I followed him, afraid someone else might corner me.

Josh and Cole were making progress with the wall of rubble. Ralph and Adelaide had rejoined our circle. I decided to seize my opportunity before it passed.

"Hey, I've got a game you guys might find fun." I hoped my lighthearted tone sounded authentic.

"It's not a great time for a game," said Ilya, frowning. I shot him a wide-eyed glare. *Just play along. This is how I'll get into Ralph's past!*

"I'm in!" Faith grinned.

"Don't you want to know the game first?" I said.

"You're going to tell us our futures!" blurted Ilya.

I glared again. "Now, you've ruined the surprise."

"I'll go first!" said Faith. I sighed, impatient and nervous. *After this, suggest that Ralph go next*, I thought in Ilya's direction.

"Okay, give me your hand." I reached out to Faith. She placed her hand in mine and I closed my eyes to concentrate. I saw her and Ilya under a three-story wall of neon advertising. It was nighttime. It looked like something from New York or Tokyo or London – I couldn't be sure since I'd never been to any of those cities in person.

"You and Ilya go on your honeymoon somewhere with giant neon billboards." I had no idea if they were on their honeymoon or not, but it was probably the future. So why not make it a happy one?

"Nice!" said Faith.

"Do me next," said Adelaide.

I took her hand and concentrated on the image of her and Ralph with Thorn in the alley. In a flash, I returned to the alley. Ralph was his reptilian self, with his hat and sign as a costume. Adelaide was in her chair. Nothing about the vision seemed different, but this time I looked for landmarks. Out on the street cars rolled past the gap between the brick walls.

On the other side of the street, a gas station housed cars waiting behind occupied pumps. I looked up. Fire escapes zigzagged up the side of the building in front of me. At the end of the alley, a grimy dumpster overflowed with trash bags.

There was no sign of where they were. Thorn left the alley and I dropped Adelaide's hand.

I stood looking at Adelaide as I frantically tried to think of a story to tell.

"You and Ralph have a happy future ahead. You go back to your home together, so we must get out of this." I forced a laugh.

"I knew it!" Adelaide looked lustfully at Ralph.

I felt a sharp pang of remorse. They deserved to be together, both happy, for once. I was sure they'd had unimaginably hard lives. I still didn't know at what point they would betray us. I had to hope it hadn't happened yet. It made sense to interpret their presence with us - aside from being trapped in rubble - to mean they were still on our side.

Nellie and Bruno both waved a passing gesture. Ralph came next. Perfect!

I took his smooth human hand in mine. I turned it over and looked at his palm, not to feign reading it, but to marvel at my brother's handiwork. I looked at Ralph's plain brown eyes and mouse-brown hair. He had a pale complexion and a bit of beard stubble. If I hadn't seen Ralph's true self, I never would have believed the man in front of me was a giant lizard.

I closed my eyes and wiped my mind. I pictured Rubin's face. My body tensed at the image and I gripped Ralph's hand tighter.

My mind's eye transported me to the lobby of an apartment building where Rubin and Ralph stood. It was pitch black and seemed to be the middle of the night.

"When we get the girl, bite her quickly. We can't afford any noise in here," said Rubin.

"We're in a student dorm. I don't want to tangle with

security or police any more than you do," said Ralph.

I looked around the lobby. It was hard to be sure in the dark, but I thought the layout of the space was familiar. The furniture, the elevator – it was like déjà vu.

The elevator door opened and light spilled out. Someone stepped forward, lit briefly by the elevator's florescent roof. Gemma stared drowsily at my position. Rubin must have woken her telepathically! This was how he got to her to wipe her memory!

I hung on to Ralph's hand for another few beats. He must have yanked it back from me. I slid back to the caved-in parking garage. I felt the frown on my face.

"Wow, how bad is it? You were saying, 'No, no, no,'" said Ralph. The human version of him blinked at me with doe-eyed confusion.

"Nothing. A block, I guess. Sometimes it doesn't work," I lied.

I forced myself to take a deep breath. I needed to think before I came down on Ralph. I had to talk to Ilya and evaluate this properly.

Chapter 23

Cole and Josh neared the end of their tunnel through the wet rubble. My whole body vibrated with stress. I sensed tension in everyone. We knew what waited for us above would be total madness.

I had to remind myself over and over that whatever we saw above was not our fault. Not the destruction from the earthquake or the loss from the tsunami. I would regret forever that we hadn't prevented it, mostly because I felt so stupid for thinking the initial shaking was the worst it would get. Had Waynesburg somehow engineered a delayed reaction, a mild foreshock, and a violent main quake?

Gemma's face shoved its way back into my mind. I could still save her from further harm. Understanding why she'd been looped into the variant world would go a long way – if I could get Ralph to share. I had to find a way to get Ilya aside, preferably without arousing suspicion. Then again, what is a mind-reading brother for if you can't communicate with your thoughts? I stood next to him and linked my arm into his at the elbow. I rested my head on his shoulder.

You need to see what I saw in Ralph's past. You were right about him knowing Rubin. They worked together. He was in on Gemma's memory wipe! Can we do anything? Should we? I still don't know how and when Ralph and Adelaide will turn on us. I feel like Ralph following Rubin's orders makes it almost certain that they've been working for Ivan the whole time.

Ilya stood still for a moment and I gave him time to pick through the images in my mind before I sent more thoughts at him.

"So when we get out of here, we're going straight on to Innoviro and then getting out of town, right? Anyone got other plans?" said Ilya casually, probing to see if Ralph or Adelaide would try to stall or break away.

What if the meeting has already taken place? Don't we want to get rid of them? They could be feeding our every move to Ivan and Thorn.

"Sounds good to me," said Bruno.

"Yeah, the sooner we put miles between us and this catastrophe, the better as far as I'm concerned," said Faith.

"We should consider our safest route out. We won't be able to get a signal for any of our devices until we get farther away. There's simply no way to know what's going on out there," said Nellie.

"The damage will be widespread, possibly far past the Bay Area," said Jonah.

"If anyone wants out of this little crusade, now is the time to say something. We won't think any less of anybody who bows out. It'll only get more dangerous from here on in," said Ilya.

I looked around at my comrades while I processed Ilya's

words.

"If anything, we're in this thing even more than before," said Bruno.

"I agree. You need us. Who else could you ask?" said Nellie.

"Us too," said Ralph. He squeezed Adelaide's hand. She smiled at him, and then around the room at the rest of us.

"Okay, I'm going to be straight with you," I said to Ralph as I stepped forward. Ilya reached for my arm and I brushed him aside.

"I've seen you and Adelaide in a vision, meeting with Thorn in an alley. You were talking about them being 'interested' in the pair of you. You were going to join him," I said. Nervous energy tingled in my gut and my limbs. Confrontation was not my strong suit.

"I don't know what you're talking about," said Ralph, offended.

"We would never do that. Neither of us would ever join that lunatic," said Adelaide.

"You were talking about how you didn't like hiding from regular people," I said, trying to urge the truth from their lips.

"I don't like it, but I can blend in," said Adelaide.

"I've been on the outside my whole life. I'm used to it," said Ralph.

"You had Thorn's phone number," I said to Adelaide.

"I don't know what you saw, but I don't have a connection to anyone named Thorn," Adelaide said darkly.

"It would explain how they got the jump on us at the campsite outside the Golden Gate Park," said Faith.

"Isn't it possible you saw something in the future, something that hasn't happened yet?" said Ralph.

"That's possible. But, I've seen it twice now," I said.

"But now we know, so we can change it," Ralph said. "We won't make contact with this man."

"Is he telling the truth?" I asked my brother.

"They both are, but you're making them uncomfortable," said Ilya.

"Of course, we're fucking uncomfortable!" Adelaide took her hands off her hips and crossed her arms angrily.

"I'm not trying to start a fight. I'm trying to protect my friends," I said.

"And we're not your friends?" said Adelaide.

"I hope you are. I care about you both. That's why I'm warning you about this guy," I said.

"You're *warning* me?" Adelaide's words dripped with bitterness and I remembered the sharp beak poised and waiting in her throat. I wondered if it would still come out while Ilya's illusion held. Would I see it coming if she did strike?

"This isn't helping anyone," said Jonah.

Cole and Josh came back to the group wiping their hands on their pants.

"So far there's only room to make it out on foot," said Josh.

"If we're still trying to find Innoviro before we leave the city, a group should go now while some of us stay behind to keep digging," said Cole.

"We shouldn't split up," Ilya said.

"Are we leaving the cars behind?" said Faith.

"I'm not leaving my Jeep," said Josh.

"I'm not leaving my van. A wheelchair-adapted van and my chair itself were expensive. Despite what you think based on my house, I'm not made of money. I can't leave them in the rubble," said Adelaide.

"Look, I don't want to leave my car either, but this parking garage isn't safe and there's nothing we can do about that," said Cole.

"Why don't we find some abandoned cars above?" I asked.

"Anything up there will have flooded engines at a bare minimum," said Nellie.

"It could take days to find enough working vehicles to transport us all," said Bruno.

"So we need our cars," said Josh.

"You're both our strongest fighters. If we run into something while you're back here digging out cars, we could be in serious trouble," I said.

"I doubt you'll run into any Innoviro thugs in this mess. I'll be surprised if you see anyone," said Josh with darkness in his last few words. A sudden picture of limp bodies on the street sent chills down my spine.

"Where's our next stop? After Innoviro, I mean," said Faith.

"Ivan and Tatiana are somewhere in a nearby desert, but I have no idea where. They might already have moved on," I said.

"If we're going to split up, we should agree on a rendezvous point," said Nellie.

"I picked up a couple of maps back at the supermarket," said Ilya.

"Perfect. Get them out and we'll mark where we are now and where we're going," said Nellie.

"I've already memorized the location of Innoviro." Faith accepted the pair of folded paper maps from Ilya. She circled 'Bay Farm Island' on each map and made a dot on an intersection near the water.

"I remember the Google Maps page well enough to mark our current location." Nellie stepped forward, accepted Faith's pen, and marked an 'X' between Berkeley and the Bay on both maps.

"It's settled. Cole and I will stay behind to dig out the vehicles while everyone else moves on to Innoviro," said Josh.

"We'll catch up with you at Innoviro. A couple of us will have to double back for the van, but it shouldn't be a problem. Once we're mobile again things will move more quickly," said Cole.

"Grab whatever gear you don't want to be without for the next day," said Jonah.

We each slung a bag on our backs. One by one, we crept through the tunnel that Cole and Josh had carefully hollowed in the rubble.

Out in the sunshine, I blinked for about a minute adjusting to the brightness of the early afternoon sun. Once my eyes had regained focus, I saw the full extent of the aftershock's impact.

San Francisco lay in utter ruin all around me, soaked as though a monsoon had fallen. An office tower directly across the street looked as though it had split and folded in on itself like wet cardboard. Down the road, another building had collapsed. A wall of half hexagonal façade melted into its supporting structure like a deflated soufflé.

Buildings as far as the eye could see had caved in like children's block towers. Huge slabs of former walls and sporadic piles of rock spilled into the street in both directions. A few buildings hadn't collapsed entirely but reached part way to their former height like jagged stumps left where an unseen force had snapped off their tops. Our group stood in a cluster, scanning around, up and down, looking at the destruction around us, evaluating the glistening wreckage. No cars moved.

A handful parked on the street suffered irreparable damage from chunks of concrete and tipped-over street lights. The intersection ahead was mostly clear, but it would be slow going.

"Does anyone else here have any hiking experience?" said Ralph. Adelaide raised her hand, followed by Bruno, Nellie, and Ilya.

"Are you talking weekend hiking trails or rough wilderness?" said Ilya.

"I'm talking about wilderness. I mean rationed food and no power. Maybe wildlife too," said Ralph.

"You think we're going to run into wild animals on our way to Bay Farm Island?" said Faith.

"He's saying you never know what a disaster like this can shake loose," said Adelaide.

"We should also stay alert for more aftershocks. No more going underground or into buildings unless we have no choice," said Jonah.

"We're not making any progress standing here. Does anyone know which way is south?" I said.

"I've got a compass. I always carry one," said Ralph.

"Lucky for us," said Faith. Adelaide glared at Faith who returned the look with an indignant expression. "What? I meant it."

"New rule. No more talk about back alley deals or who is friends with whom. We're together now and that's what matters," said Jonah.

Adelaide looked at the ground.

"Ralph, you lead the way." Ilya handed his map to Ralph.

My stomach turned. The more I considered the destruction around me, the more I thought my vision of Ralph and

Adelaide with Thorn in an alley couldn't possibly be anywhere in the Bay Area in its current state. Either my vision had been a more distant future, or it had already happened. I clenched and unclenched my fists as I walked. I would have to attempt another vision as soon as possible next time we stopped to rest.

We walked in silence through the flooded streets. I kept my gaze level with the remaining skyline, avoiding scanning the street for fear of seeing bodies. Everyone but Ralph and Adelaide appeared to be doing the same. I looked over at Jonah's pale skin and sunken eyes. I'd hoped the moisture would give him a hit of vitality, but he looked stricken.

The sun blazed mercilessly, dehydrating us in the midst of muddy puddles. We stopped every few blocks to sip from our water bottles. I checked the time on my phone. We had been walking for an hour and we hadn't made nearly enough progress. The worst of the tsunami damage lay behind us, but we were still in the midst of a war zone.

"We need to find some shade and get a break from the sun," I called out to Ralph. He continued walking and the rest of us kept pace.

"At this rate, we're going to camp at least once, maybe twice before we get to Innoviro," said Ralph.

"That'll give Cole and Josh a chance to catch up with us," said Faith.

"Why did we start ahead if we were going to wait for those guys?" said Bruno.

"We don't know how long it's going to take for them to dig the cars out." Jonah wiped at the layer of sweat and mud on his forehead.

"We've come this far. Let's keep going," said Nellie.

"If we can go for another hour, we should be in good shape to camp and make it to Innoviro early tomorrow morning," said Ralph.

Ralph turned a corner around a brick building and stopped. As we caught up with him, I saw what had stopped him in his tracks. Another group of people trekking through the destruction were resting and snacking. They had set up a makeshift campsite against the building, shaded by a tarp tied to the racks of an SUV.

"Hey." Ralph's alarm was obvious, to me, if not to the campers on the sidewalk in front of us.

"Hey to you too," said a girl with a long brown braid. She stirred a pot of soup over a camp stove. She wore a sack dress with a beach landscape across the mid-section and sky drifting up her back.

"I thought we were the only ones stupid enough to be making our way across the city in this mess." Ilya stepped in front of Ralph. I hoped he was listening to the campers.

"Do you mind if we share your stove?" Faith asked brightly.

"When you're all finished with it of course." Ilya frowned at Faith.

"Sure, you bet. Pull up a rock and hang out," said the bearded boy next to the braided girl. His full beard and fitted knit cap had to be warm in the California sun, but he seemed unaffected.

"Are you staying here overnight?" I asked.

"We are. We were back in town to start school at Berkeley, but we're all pretty sure that's out of the question now. We're trying to get out of the city. I'm Brian, by the way. And this is my girlfriend, Meadow," said the bearded boy. Meadow waved around at us.

"This is Alex, Sam, Hollis, and Becky," said Brian as he pointed at his friends in turn. I worried that their modest yet trendy clothes and unassuming dispositions made my friends look out of place. And then I remembered that even if they found us suspicious, they weren't in any better position to call for help.

"Y'all are welcome to chill with us for the night. We won't bite if you don't." Hollis flashed a bright white grin. His thick Southern U.S. accent was the first I'd ever heard in person. It made me grin too and I dropped my bag to the ground.

"That's what we wanted to hear." Jonah set his bag next to mine and sat in the shade of the building's ruined wall.

I tucked in next to him. I put my hand on Jonah's shoulder and offered him the rest of my water. He took the bottle and drained it in a few gulps. We had a tough twenty-four hours ahead.

Chapter 24

Gemma's plain brick dorm looked safe and innocuous as I watched from across the road under a dim pre-dawn sky. And then a scruffy man in overalls with matted hair tied behind his neck carried a tan laundry bag out through the front door.

He had been substantially cleaned and scrubbed, but it was Thorn nevertheless. His presence - with a human-sized bag - only went unchallenged because the early morning hour offered no witnesses. Except for my mind's eye, helplessly documenting the situation. Thorn moved quickly into the parking lot and stopped at a large white van.

I concentrated on the back of the van. My perspective shifted. I slid forward through the air and turned to face the doors as Thorn opened them. Ivan and Tatiana were waiting in the back of the van which had several layers of blankets. Thorn heaved the bag into the back of the van and shut the door.

I had to focus harder, willing my mind to go through the

steel doors. I slipped inside the van with Ivan and Tatiana and the bag. Ivan loosened the drawstring at the top and wiggled the fabric down around Gemma's head.

My sister fell forward, limp and unconscious. I heard the sound of the van's driver and passenger side doors opening and closing. Thorn took the driver's seat and the tattooed girl sat in the passenger seat. She reached into the glove compartment and passed a small cork-stopped glass bottle of something milky-white to Ivan. He uncorked the bottle and tipped the milk into Gemma's mouth.

"We should not be bothering with this girl," said Tatiana.

"She is one of us," said Ivan.

"She's not yours by blood," said Tatiana.

"That's not what I meant and you know it," said Ivan.

"I don't care. She is useless to us and poses no threat. Not like Irina," said Tatiana.

"Don't be so sure. Her memory came back. So she is not useless. She must have healed herself when Rubin died. Only a healer could undo his work. And maybe, if we win her over, she'll bring my children back into the fold," said Ivan.

"*My* turn is coming, don't forget. I'm your sister. You share more blood with me than those offspring you created," said Tatiana coldly.

Chills danced up the back of my neck as I wondered what Tatiana meant by her turn. I closed in on Gemma's face, focusing only on her. The scene shimmered and I was transported to the kitchen space of a small, dark trailer. My feet felt unsteady. I looked to my right and saw an empty bench seat behind a dining table. On my left, past the wood-paneled bathroom door, I could see a lump in the bed. I took a step forward and the sleeper rolled towards me. I mentally leaned in over the body. Gemma stayed unconscious. Vibration and the sound of tires crunching on gravel accompanied the scene. I imagined myself staring down at the moving trailer.

My perspective popped up through the roof and I watched a green pickup, the same pickup from Ivan's campsite at the Golden Gate Park, pull the same trailer forward into the desert. I saw a small brown sign by the side of the road in the distance. I focused on the sign as though squinting in my mind's eye and my mental self zoomed to the sign. It read: Mojave Desert Joshua Tree Road Scenic Backway.

A siren wailing in the distance snapped me out of sleep. The glow of my tent walls meant the sun was up. I picked up my phone. It read 9:53 AM. My gut told me my sister slept in the trailer at this very moment, bumping her way down a gravel road somewhere in the Mojave Desert. I sat up and rubbed my eyes. I grabbed my brush and ran it through my hair until I could pull it back into a ponytail neatly.

I was torn. I could continue picking through the rubble of San Francisco making my way to the Innoviro office to the south, or I could relate the vision of Gemma to Ilya and the others, making an argument for veering east to the Mojave. I had a spot on a map to go on now. If we tracked Ivan, we might him before the sands of the desert erased any trace of him.

Based on what I knew, I conceded that Gemma would be safe, at least temporarily, with Ivan and Tatiana. If they were right and she had variant DNA, he would hang on to her and keep her alive if she didn't give him too much trouble. The chance was slim, but Innoviro's San Francisco office might still hold treatment for Jonah.

I unzipped my tent and stepped outside to find the Berkeley

students breaking up their end of the campsite. Ilya and Bruno were doing the same.

"What, were you guys going to let me sleep and leave me behind?" I said.

"You've got great timing. I was tellin' your friend Bruno here that we're headed in the same direction," said Hollis. He looked identical to the day before, not the least bit disheveled from sleep.

"Really?" I said.

"Hollis and Brian heard that there's far less damage to the south side of the city," said Bruno. The advantage of being as hairy as Bruno was that you looked the same whether you had just rolled out of bed or spent an hour grooming.

"That's great news. We're headed to Bay Farm Island. The company we work for has an office there." I wanted to say as little as possible. I couldn't work out whether having civilian companions would work for or against us. As long as Ilya stayed near Ralph and Adelaide, the Berkeley kids shouldn't be a problem. I hoped.

"We were thinking of traveling together and pooling our resources," said Brian as he scratched the back of his head.

"One more day of trekkin' out of this wreckage should do it," said Hollis.

"I think so too," said Ilya.

Meadow appeared on the sidewalk carrying three stacked donut boxes. Her sculpted braid had transformed into a neat bun on top of her head, looking far too elegant for first thing in the morning.

"Hey, guys. Guess what?" said Meadow.

"You found a bunch of Red Cross aid workers?" said Hollis.

"Better. I found a bakery around the corner and it wasn't

too badly damaged. I've got breakfast," she answered with a broad smile.

"Sweet! You rule!" said Faith as she stepped out of her tent, her frizzy purple dreadlocks looking like an unkempt muppet's.

Jonah's tousled morning look always made for an endearing improvement in his normally manicured appearance. Nellie frowned, rubbed her eyes under her glasses, and made her way to Bruno's side. Ralph and Adelaide looked the same as Ilya had made them the day before. Within minutes of my waking, our entire group sat on camp chairs or the curb, ravenously eating stale donuts and muffins.

It struck me that our number counted mostly couples. Ilya and Faith, hip to hip on the curb. Nellie and Bruno in side-by-side camp chairs. Becky and Alex on the bumper of the latter's SUV. Brian and Meadow leaning against their truck. I sat down next to Jonah, feeling optimistic at the possibility of medication for him on the horizon.

We all finished our donuts and took turns at Brian's keg of wash water. Nobody wanted to waste bottled drinking water on hand washing. I couldn't say anything about Jonah's needs in front of our new friends.

"Are you sure there's room for all of us to squeeze into these vehicles?" said Ilya to Brian.

"We're going to have to put a few of you in the bed of my truck, but I don't think anyone's going to give us a ticket," said Brian.

"Good point," said Ilya. To the rest of us, he asked, "Any volunteers for riding in the back of a pickup?"

"We'll do it," said Bruno with a wave.

"Us too then," said Ralph, answering for Adelaide as well.

"That puts Faith and Ilya in the back of Alex and Becky's Suburban. Irina and Jonah, you come with me and Sam," said Hollis.

We drove single file slowly navigating heaves in the concrete and debris on the road. Our drive lasted about a quarter of an hour before Hollis' sedan stopped behind the truck and SUV ahead.

"Is that what I think it is?" said Hollis.

"Dude, that's one fucking big hole!" said Sam.

I peered out the car window, but I couldn't see more than a black puddle in front of Brian's truck. I got out of the car.

"Irina, it's not safe! Get back here!" shouted Jonah.

I walked towards the black patch ahead, ignoring Jonah, watching the puddle turn into a canyon in the concrete. I stood in awe of a giant crack in the earth that stretched for miles in either direction, perfectly perpendicular to our path. We would have to back up and go around it.

While I contemplated the total distance of the canyon a CREEAAAAK sound of tearing metal screeched at me from the other side. I saw half a basement visible near the surface, partially concealed by collapsed concrete. Debris tumbled forward into the giant pit.

Rocks tumbled down into the canyon and echoed back up as they hit walls of earth. I didn't dare risk one more step forward.

"What the hell are you thinking?" Jonah grabbed my arm and yanked me backward.

"We'll have to go around this. For miles," I said.

The rest of our group vacated their vehicles to stare alongside me at the pit.

"Can anyone see a safe crossing in either direction?" said

Brian.

"I think it goes for about twenty blocks both ways," said Alex. He and Brian both craned their necks searching the landscape.

"We should go east to look for a crossing. Even if there is ground connecting south on the western side, anything closer to the ocean is less likely to be stable," said Jonah.

"Should we go on at all? People will be evacuated sooner than later. If it's this dangerous, we might want to think about staying put," said Brian.

"Hangin' worked out real well after Katrina," said Hollis.

"That was different," said Meadow.

"Why, because it was the South?" said Hollis.

"Don't be like that," said Becky.

"Listen, guys, I appreciate if this is getting too hairy for you, but we can't afford to wait," I said.

"What's more important than staying alive?" said Meadow.

"Jonah needs medical treatment – from our office on Bay Farm Island," I said.

"We don't know for sure there's anything there. I can't ask people to risk their lives to get to that office," said Jonah.

"It's worth the risk!" I shouted. I forced myself to calm down and took a deep breath.

"We were on foot before, we can do it again," said Ilya.

"And who knows what fresh disasters we'll find," said Faith.

"Why don't we be democratic and put it to a vote?" said Brian.

"All in favor of staying here?" said Ilya. Brian and Meadow raised their hands.

"All in favor of going on foot?" Ilya said wearily. I raised my hand. I looked around at each of my friends' faces. Bruno and Faith eventually raised their hands.

"And all in favor of driving east?" Ilya said, with a hint of optimism in his voice. The rest of the group raised their hands. Democracy worked.

"Okay, who else has got a working GPS?" said Hollis.

Our convoy started heading east. We drove even more slowly. I wished for a moment I sat next to Ilya so I could ask him if everyone else radiated as much fear as me. I wanted to hold Jonah's hand, but I couldn't risk draining him, especially not with civilians in the front seats.

"It's been almost two days now. Where's the aid? Where's the government? Why aren't there choppers overhead lifting people out? Can't the army swoop in and start helping?" said Sam to Hollis.

"Maybe they can't get in here. Maybe there's worse hit areas and that's where they are. Sometimes it takes a few days. Then again, maybe not enough people are willing to risk their lives right now," said Hollis.

"We could still be in for another aftershock. Or two. Maybe 'they' are waiting on the proverbial dust to settle," said Jonah.

"I feel bad saying this, but I'm glad we don't live here. I wish we'd been able to–" I caught myself and stopped short before sharing that we could have prevented the earthquake. Hollis and Sam didn't notice my misstep, but Jonah looked at me sympathetically.

"I know," he said.

Hollis checked his GPS a few times as we followed Brian and Alex through the streets. We had to re-calibrate our path eastward several times to drive around blocked streets while staying parallel to the concrete canyon.

Brian's truck pulled over next to a baseball field. In the ruin around us, the green lawn shone like a tropical oasis.

"I think we're making camp again," said Hollis as he parked too.

"I guess we're not on a ticking clock as much as we were before," I said quietly to Jonah.

"We don't know what Ivan's next stop will be," said Jonah.

Hollis and Sam got out of the car leaving Jonah and me to talk.

"I still think he's in the Mojave Desert. Correction, I know he is. And he's got my sister with him," I said.

"What? Then screw the Innoviro office. We can grab a car and head for the desert!" said Jonah.

"I think she'll be safe. It sounds like she's a variant too, although she may not know it. Ivan won't hurt her. Twisted as he is, he values variant lives," I said.

"So you still want to go to Bay Farm Island, even on the tiny chance we'll find a vial of something or a piece of paperwork or something on a disk?" said Jonah.

"Don't you value your own life? I sure as hell do!" I said.

Jonah looked out the window thoughtfully. "We'll get there faster if we stick to vehicles."

"So if they want to make camp, we'll make camp." I got out of the car before Jonah could argue.

Our progress had been a pitiful ten blocks when the sunset shut us down. Even so, we were exhausted and acknowledged the danger of moving at night. We couldn't see our surroundings, including potential assailants. So, nobody protested when Brian and Hollis started setting up camp. Ilya's illusions on Ralph and Adelaide held without so much as a flicker. Hanging around civilians in a social capacity was like taking a break from being a variant; I assumed the feeling was much more intense for Ralph and Adelaide. I prayed silently to the universe that we had changed their minds - and all of our fates.

As I looked around the random urban park we'd chosen for camp, it occurred to me that I had traveled farther from my Prince George home than I had ever been in my life. And the amount of growing up I'd done was immeasurable. My childhood memories seem like they belonged to someone else, from another reality. The real world around me was a ruined San Francisco street.

Hollis built a makeshift fire pit with bricks from the adjacent street and he had a roaring fire going shortly afterwards. A few cars crept by in both directions, but for the most part, the ball field and surrounding neighborhood were deserted. I wondered how many people were hiding at home, how many had already left, and how many were injured, waiting for help which seemed less likely to arrive with every passing minute.

Meadow walked around filming and taking photos. Brian asked her if she planned to post her videos and she said that she would, when her phone had service again. I wondered what social platform she preferred. It felt like years since I had used social media, though it had only been a handful of months. Anxiety slid over me as I contemplated what it would be like for myself and each of my friends to showcase our abilities in shareable videos. Would exposing ourselves solve our problems? Or would users think we were no more than special effects artists?

Sam and Alex distributed beer to each of us. I accepted reluctantly. I hadn't developed a taste for beer, but I did think it was a good idea to lubricate an evening of socializing with relative strangers.

"So what will you guys do this year, now that you can't go back to Berkeley?" I settled into a camp chair.

"After we get the hell out of this city? I guess I'll go home to Louisiana and work for a year. Probably not the worst idea, money-wise," said Hollis. The novelty of his accent still hadn't gotten old.

"This is going to sound stupid, but I have to say it. Your accent is awesome! We don't have many accents in Canada, apart from Newfoundlanders and English-speaking Francophones. Where I'm from in Northern BC, you don't hear much other than plain vanilla Canadian," I said.

"You sound different to us too," said Brian.

"What? Get out," said Faith.

"They don't sound so different to us. But we're from Oregon," said Ralph.

"She's not from Oregon." Meadow gestured at Adelaide.

"I'm originally from Denmark." Adelaide cracked her can of beer and crossed her legs, looking extremely odd in contrast to the woman I'd first met in Washington State. I tried to picture how she was actually sitting that made us see a pair of crossed human legs.

"But the rest of you are all Canadian?" asked Brian.

"Nellie and I are from Oregon too," said Bruno.

"I'm from Seattle," said Josh.

"How is it y'all work for the same company?" said Hollis.

"We worked at different offices, in Victoria, Vancouver and Seattle," I said quickly.

"Some of us were thinking about transferring to San Francisco, well, Alameda technically. Our Oregon friends are former employees." Ilya made a much more convincing con artist than me.

"So what's the plan instead of San Francisco?" said Hollis.

"I've always wanted to see the Mojave Desert." I shot a knowing look at Ilya. I tried thinking at him, but he wasn't paying attention.

"Maybe we'll just keep going where the road takes us," said Faith.

"Spoken like a true hippie." Ilya nudged her arm playfully. She slapped his arm in return.

"Easy, you two." Jonah grinned.

Heat rushed to my cheeks at I savored Jonah's smile. As silly as I felt openly gawking at my handsome would-be boyfriend, a little vindication slipped into my heart, after a little voice in my head reminded me that Jonah felt the same desire for me.

"There's nothing wrong with being a hippie," said Meadow.

"We know *your* parents are – or were – pretty free thinkers to name you after a field of flowers," said Brian. "Dear, sweetie, light of my life." He held her hand and she let him. I frowned at him anyway.

"I like my name. It's unusual," said Meadow.

"I think your name is pretty. Take Irina for example. People know I'm part Russian, but that's it."

"Try having a name that makes people assume you're religious," said Faith.

Firelight made Faith's purple dreadlocks look bright pink above orange-hued skin. Ralph and Adelaide sat next to each other, hands clasped with fingers interlocked where the arms of their camp chairs came together. Everyone looked warm and happy in spite of the chaos and ruin around us. Not being able to talk about our Compendium worries forced us to be normal, even if only for an afternoon.

Ralph got up and walked to the public bathroom behind the dugout. The structure's simple cinderblock construction had survived the earthquake. It made our campsite on the ball field an even better choice. I seized my opportunity to talk to him and followed. As Ralph came out of the building, still his professor self, I met him. He looked startled at first.

"I need to talk to you about something, away from the others," I said quietly.

"Look, I think we said everything we had to say. Adelaide and I are on your side," said Ralph.

"That's not it. I need to ask you about a man named Rubin."

I met Ralph's gaze and his face fell.

"How do *you* know Rubin?" Ralph dropped his volume to match mine.

"He worked security for Innoviro back in Victoria. He wiped my sister's memory as part of my boss's plans to rope me into long term commitment," I said. As I spoke, Ralph looked down at the ground. "Do you remember taking a girl from a dorm room in Vancouver?"

"Rubin told me she needed rehabilitation and wasn't co-operating. We were only supposed to wipe her memory temporarily, so she could get the treatment she needed."

"Did you help Rubin with any other memory wipes? Did you go up to Prince George?" I felt grief wrapping its cold fingers around my throat. I swallowed again and again to push the feeling away, down into my stomach.

"No, most of the work I did for Rubin was in Seattle. It wasn't much. Nellie connected us. I take it the girl from Vancouver is your sister?"

I nodded. I felt tears welling in my eyes.

"I'm so sorry. I didn't know," said Ralph.

I nodded again and waved him away.

While Ralph returned to the fire pit, I took a moment to collect myself. I wiped my face and retied my ponytail. When I got back to the group, everyone was laughing.

Adelaide focused intently on her phone. I couldn't say whether she had picked one up or borrowed it from someone at camp. When Adelaide and I had traveled in her van, she didn't have a phone, which made me uneasy watching her. I wanted to ask what she was doing or how she had service, but I kept my mouth closed.

Hours passed with more beers and more stories. I watched

more than I talked. The unease of Adelaide's surfing wore off as time passed and I finished my third beer. Sirens wailed again in the distance. Closer to us a CRAAACK, SLAP and rumble signaled another collapse. I shuddered and rubbed my sleeves.

"Ow, hey! UHHHHHH," cried Ilya. I whipped around to see my brother slumped in his camp chair. Faith had sprung up.

"What is THAT?" shrieked Faith. A familiar giant spider skittered across Ilya's lap and jumped across to Bruno. A bright yellow snake slithered on the ground.

"What the–" spat Bruno before he too slumped in his chair.

"AIIIIIEEEEE!" screamed Meadow as the yellow tattoo snake struck her.

"Get in the truck!" yelled Brian.

The cry of a falcon screeched above us.

"Damn it!" shouted Faith as she shot a stream of fire at the spider in mid-air. She missed and the spider landed on her face, muffling her scream. A moment later Faith fell silently to the ground.

"Holy shit man!" said Hollis. He looked at a spot behind my head. I turned to see Thorn, mouth open, shooting his thick sticky webbing at me. The noxious threads I thought I'd never see again wrapped around and around cocooning me.

"NOOOOO!" shouted Jonah. Thorn punched Jonah in the face with a loud THOCK and sprayed him with webbing as well.

I fought against the wrapping around my body. I heard the sound of Thorn clearing his throat behind me. Jonah lurched and lay on the ground, not moving, covered by webbing from head to toe. All our training in Washington had been useless in an ambush at night.

A sticky dart shot over my head and hit Hollis in the chest. Alex picked up a section of pipe he had propped up against his chair. He'd been the only one of us to think of arming himself.

"Hit him!" shouted Becky. Alex shifted from one foot to the other, holding the pipe like a baseball bat, ready to swing, but hesitating. My head snapped up at the flapping of giant leather wings.

Rose snatched the pipe from Alex's hands and hit him over the head in two smooth movements. Becky let out a near-sonic squeal. A gust from wings over my head knocked me down as a metal thunk silenced Becky's scream.

"What the hell ARE you?" shouted Sam. I saw Adelaide's legs flicking and twirling on the ground ahead. Ralph's green body crossed in front of me. Adelaide stepped in front of Sam and he dropped to the ground.

"Noel, they're all secure," said Adelaide.

"Ivan wants his kids," said Sage.

"Leave the variants alive. Make sure all the humans are dead," said the voice of the tattooed girl who must be Noel. I heard Thorn's throat a few more times.

"There isn't room for us in your van. We'll meet you at the farm," said Rose. I heard the twins' wings as they took flight.

"You promised Adelaide nobody would be hurt! We had no reason to kill these college kids. They were on their way back home!" yelled Ralph.

"What did you think was going to happen? We'd shake their hands and ask them nicely not to mention this to anyone?" said Noel.

"We would have been long gone by the time these kids could get to anyone who'd care!" said Ralph.

"Haven't you learned not to trust humans? If we want to

stop hiding, this is how it had to go," said Adelaide quietly to Ralph.

I felt the sharp sting of Noel's favorite hairy-legged tattoo. The voices faded and sleep took me.

I woke up across from my unconscious brother who lay crumpled on the floor of a rumbling van. It was dark, still night. Streetlights flashed intermittently through the windows in the back doors of the van. Noel sat next to Ilya. She noticed me awake and flexed her forearm releasing her spider. I took a breath to scream and I felt a stab in my ankle. The world went black.

When I woke the next time, I was in a field, lying on a quilt. The grass beneath my blanket felt soft and mossy. The sky beamed bright blue with a scattering of fluffy white clouds. My Mom sat on the other side of the quilt. Plates of fried chicken, fries, salad, and a giant bowl of fruit were laid out between us.

"Mom, you're alive! Are you alive? Are you real?" I sat up. My bonds were gone. I hugged Mom. Her muscle, bone, and hair felt real. She smelled like the apple perfume she always used to wear. I felt tears coming and I let them roll down my cheeks as I held Mom.

"What happened to Ilya? Where are Jonah and Faith?"

Mom smiled. She picked up a paper plate and filled it with food. She set the plate down in front of me.

"You've had a long day, sweetie. You need to eat," said Mom.

"Where is this place?" I said.

"This place is just a plane of existence. Think of it as a visiting room. A place between our worlds," Mom explained as though she were showing me a photo in a book.

"I must be having a wild dream from the spider venom." I grabbed my head as a sharp pain intruded.

"Unfortunately, you had to get here through trauma, but you can train yourself to come back." Mom reached out and put her hand on my arm. Her touch felt so real. And then the visiting room disappeared and I was in the back of an old van.

Ilya slept on. I expected Thorn to keep him out cold to stop him from creating an illusion or listening to their thoughts. I blinked and risked a look around the back of the van. We were alone. A thick brown canvas curtain hung between us and the front seats. Panic energized me despite my splitting headache.

I cursed myself for letting my guard down at the ball field campsite. I cursed each of my friends in turn. The only two of us with the instincts of fighters were digging our cars out of a parking garage. What were the chances Cole and Josh could find us now?

Chapter 26

Road noise rumbled below me. We hit a pothole and my head bounced off the thin carpet on the floor of Thorn's van. The vibration around me felt like a high speed. We did not stop and start as we had done picking our way to Bay Farm Island. Those two variables added up to driving away from San Francisco.

"Time to stop for food," said a deep male voice from behind the curtain.

"I'll text the others," said Noel.

About ten minutes later the van slowed to a stop.

"Make sure they're still asleep," said the deep voice.

"Ralph and Adelaide want to talk to them," said Noel.

"The girl, fine. The boy stays asleep. Five minutes," said the deep voice.

Another handful of minutes passed and I heard the click-cluck of the back door being opened. I sat up and squinted into the bright light.

"Talk fast. Irina only. Thorn's orders," said Noel. I wished with all my might for Ilya to wake. I tried to will away however much extra toxin Noel had pumped into his body.

"Irina?" Adelaide's figure resolved before me as my eyes adjusted to the sun. Gravel crunched as Noel walked away.

"We wanted to tell you we're sorry and that this is all going to turn out well," said Ralph.

"What he means is that you're being taken to your father. You're safe," said Adelaide.

"Why would I want to see that man?" I asked.

"Hopefully you'll come to understand how important family can be," said Ralph.

"So, I was right about the two of you. Tell me, when did you meet with Thorn? Give me that much at least," I said bitterly.

"He found us at the Sutro Bath ruins and we slipped away to talk while you were down in the cave. Didn't you realize such a sensitive site would be under surveillance?" said Adelaide.

"How did you fool Ilya?"

"We spend our lives lying. You think we can't keep it going in our heads?" said Adelaide.

"Why did you wait so long before turning us in?"

"Because we struggled with it!" said Ralph.

"As sweet as those college kids were, they never would have accepted Ralph or me as we truly are. You take your whole life for granted, Irina. Think of every simple little thing you can do that we can't. You go shopping, you walk in the park, you ride the bus. You think those things are boring because you can do whatever you like, whenever you like, and nobody would scream or shoot you or lock you away. In Ivan's world, we will fit in with everyone else. There is a better future for us if *The Compendium* is completed," said Adelaide, pointing between her, Ralph, Ilya, and me.

"You make it sound like I live the life of a spoiled brat. I don't. My life is hard too. Even if I had it easy and your life proved near impossible, you don't have the right to take out the rest of the human race." My voice rose in volume as my anger accumulated.

"There's no point in debating this. The decision has been made and we all have to live with it," said Ralph. Gravel crunched behind him.

"Time's up," said Noel.

She dropped a wrapped sandwich in front of me and reached behind me to untie the rag tightly bound around my wrists. Ralph and Adelaide walked away and Noel closed the van's back doors one after the other.

I kicked at Ilya over and over until I worried I'd broken the bones in his calf. I untied his wrists as well and shook his shoulders. He flopped like a rag doll. I gave in and unwrapped my sandwich. As I ate, muffled voices rose and fell outside the van. I couldn't distinguish the words, but I heard Thorn's voice. A sudden slam against the side of the van startled me and I jumped in my seat, dropping my sandwich. Lettuce sprayed onto the grubby floor.

"Don't make a mess in here. You'll stink up the place." Ilya sat up groggily.

"What do you MEAN there isn't a spare?" roared Thorn from outside the van.

"You're awake! Finally! Thank God!" I whispered.

"He thinks we've got a flat tire." Ilya smiled wearily.

"You did that in your sleep?" I said in disbelief.

"It was tricky because someone kept kicking me." Ilya glanced at his calf.

"I was trying to wake you! We've got to get out of here! They killed the Berkeley kids and they're taking us to Ivan. He still wants to use us," I hissed desperately at my brother.

"Shit. Noel's snake got me before I could do anything." Ilya massaged his temples.

"I'm sure that's why they attacked you and Faith first. Nellie and Bruno too. Anyone who could defend themselves." I felt a lump in my throat as I considered how defenseless the Berkeley kids were.

"You keep forgetting to use your telekinesis when the need arises," said Ilya, frowning at me.

"Damn, you're right. Damn it!" I rammed the heels of my hands into my eyes as I felt tears forming.

"Do you know where we are? I can send an image to Cole or Jonah. It'll be hard with this venom in my head, but I know their minds. I can pick them out from hours away."

"We're in the middle of nowhere, that's where we are! On our way to Ivan, remember!" I said.

"Pick up your sandwich. Touch the wrapper and see if you can get a vision of where they bought it." Ilya nodded at my lunch

"You're a genius!" I grabbed my sub. "Now get inside my head so you can see what I see."

My partially unwrapped sandwich had a wrapper. I closed my eyes. The paper felt smooth and slightly waxy against my fingertips as I turned it over, passing from hand to hand as I concentrated on the sandwich being made. The blackness of my eyelids disappeared and I stood next to Noel in a small shop.

"Lettuce on all of them. No hot peppers," said Noel. I scanned my surroundings in the shop. Nothing gave away our location. I focused trying to back myself out of the building.

I felt a light pull as my perspective drifted backward, up and out of the sandwich shop, hovering above a sign for Sage Hills Shopping Center. I dropped the sandwich.

"They were somewhere called Sage Hills. I saw the outside of the mall, but I didn't recognize the area. I'm sure Nellie can find the mall if you show it to Cole."

"Good. But there's no telling how long ago they bought these sandwiches. We need to know where we are now, and ideally, where we're headed." Mostly talking to himself, Ilya closed his eyes as though listening. Voices murmured angrily outside and stopped.

"Thorn is leaving. They don't want to risk calling a tow truck and getting a third party involved. He's angry because he has to run back to a town called Pleasanton. We're supposed to make Bakersfield by sundown and we won't at this rate. He mentioned the 'I-5' which must be this highway, but he keeps thinking of it as a 'freeway,'" said Ilya.

"No wonder Ivan wants us back; a psychic and a telepathic illusionist make a great team," I said.

"I'll send the images to Cole and hope for the best. You might be impressed now, but if you remember, interpreting what I send – especially over long distances – isn't exactly conversational," said Ilya.

I remembered seeing his apparition outside a culvert in Victoria's Inner Harbour and my heart sank. Cole could easily misunderstand where we were and what happened to us.

"There's not much else we can do." I took a bite of my sandwich and passed my brother's unopened sub to him.

The back door of the van clacked open and Noel peered through the opening. She frowned at both of us and thrust out her forearms. Her spider and snake tattoos swelled up and off her arms, leaping to me and Ilya.

"No! You don't have to–" I stopped short to turn my head away from the repulsive arachnid as it leaped at me. Fangs pierced my neck and sleep smothered me.

We were rolling down the road again when I awoke. Ilya slept. Noel sat in the back with us, scratching away at a Sudoku book.

"You're a stubborn one." Noel didn't look up from her book.

"I'm not trying to be," I said.

A loud CRACK hit the back of the van and we all slid as a pile into the doors.

"Sonofabitch!" Noel threw her book down and knelt in front of the back window. "Assholes," she said to herself as she watched something pass around beside us.

The van stopped hard with a SQUEEEEEEE sending us all flying to the front. Noel tumbled and slid halfway through the curtains. Ilya and I hit the driver and passenger seats.

"Fuckin' hell!" Noel untangled herself from the curtains and crawled into the front passenger seat. A rumbling growl came from the driver's seat. The door opened and shut. Noel scrambled out through the passenger side.

Somehow Ilya stayed asleep. I wriggled back out of the cloth strips binding my wrists. I untied Ilya and crept to the back door. I ventured a glance outside the window. We were stopped on the side of a highway. Jonah's face came around the corner and I let out a cry of shock.

A surge of flame whooshed beside us as Jonah opened the door. "Are you guys alright?"

I grabbed him and kissed him hard on the lips. "Stay with Ilya. He's still asleep." I pushed past Jonah and hopped out onto the road. I scanned the ditch across from me for a huge rock. It was full of trash and weeds in either direction.

Cars veered around Faith and Noel. Streaks of flame shot here and there at the bird, spider, and snake trio guarding their master.

I looked farther up the road in time to see Josh deflect one of Thorn's darts. Cole was nowhere in sight. I had to act.

Desperate, I searched the hillside and finally found what I wanted; a head-sized piece of loose bedrock.

I willed the rock into the air, guiding it with my hands. I knew I could do it with my mind alone, but my arms helped me to focus. I flung it at Thorn's head. He dodged effortlessly.

I retrieved the rock remotely and this time sent it into the back of Noel's head as hard as I could. The blow knocked her forward, face-first onto the road. Her animals fell to the ground too. As blood pooled out of the back of Noel's head, her animals deflated, losing all their color until they were no more than puddles of skin on the pavement.

Faith gawked at me, eyes full of shock. I turned around to see Cole wielding a road sign like an axe. He struck Thorn in the gut, severing the man in two. Blood gushed out onto the road. Cars streamed past while rubber-necked passengers stared in disbelief.

"Is everyone all right?" said Cole.

"We've got to go. Now! We're going to have cops on our tail fast!" I blurted. Jonah was suddenly next to me holding Ilya like a sleeping child.

"Put Ilya in the back of my car. Faith, go with them. Nellie and Bruno are in the Jeep," said Cole.

"I'll go in the Jeep," I said to Jonah. He looked drained, but I kissed his cheek anyway.

"Double back to Pleasanton and head into that park," Josh

said to Cole as they ran for their respective vehicles.

I ran to Josh's Jeep and hopped into the front passenger seat. I looked back at Nellie and Bruno. I smiled at them.

"You look chipper for a recent kidnapping victim," said Nellie.

"What can I say? Blasting evil bitches with rocks makes me feel good," I said as I clicked the buckle on my seatbelt.

Chapter 27

"How did you make sense of the images Ilya sent?" I asked Josh as we sped northward on the I-5 freeway.

"We got service on a phone and tablet, so all we had to do was a couple of image searches," said Josh. "Ilya knew what he was doing."

"He got the images from me, you know," I said.

"Are we competing for credit now?" said Josh. He smirked at me and added, "Ilya showed us the ball field where you camped too. We hit the same ravine inside the road that you did on our way to Bay Farm Island. We had already detoured to the east when Cole saw something from Ilya."

"They were with us by the time we woke up," said Nellie.

"Did any of the Berkeley kids make it?" I asked.

"Brian, Meadow, Sam, and Alex were already dead when we regained consciousness. Hollis and Becky died minutes later," said Nellie.

"We had to take out Thorn's darts. We can't leave variant evidence behind if we can help it," said Bruno from the back seat. I turned around and saw the pained look on his and Nellie's faces.

"So it looks like they got mugged in the ball field?" I said.

"It won't stand up to much scrutiny as a straight-up mugging, but they won't figure mutated people were involved," said Bruno.

"Maybe we shouldn't be hiding evidence of variants? If we could 'come out' so to speak, it could take some power away from the argument Ivan and his buddies make when they recruit people. If variants like Ralph and Adelaide can live normal lives, there's no way they'd side with *The Compendium*," said Josh.

I remembered my daydream of exposing variant abilities on social media. My stomach flipped anxiously and I reminded myself it wasn't happening. Yet.

"We should have ditched Ralph and Adelaide when we had the chance." I wanted Bruno and Nellie to feel guilt for bringing Ralph. We should have left him in Portland to roam the sewers. Better still, we should have skipped Portland and Spokane. I turned to Josh and glared at his profile.

"If variants 'come out' to the public, how long will it take before people accept us? Won't there always be someone out to get us? Maybe people will want to kill us. Maybe they'll lock us up for testing, same as Ivan. But I'd rather rip off the bandage and let the aftermath run its course than solve the problem with a mass extinction. That's the solution we all agreed to when we started." I let a silence hang in the air before I resumed my rant. "What we should have done in the first place was go straight from Seattle to San Francisco. It was foreseeable that Adelaide and Ralph would want Ivan's new world order. Without them, we might have stopped the earthquake. We might already have Jonah's serum. And those Berkeley kids would be alive!" I heard the accusation in my voice. It tasted like blood and vindication.

"That's a lot of speculation. Maybe this, maybe that. There's no way to know how things could have gone differently. And there's no changing the past. We've got to work with what we have. Cole and I spotted some park space west of Pleasanton. We'll fall back to that point, regroup, and go straight to Bay Farm Island. The city is still a mess. We won't get in and out quickly, but we won't dawdle," said Josh.

"If we don't find a serum for Jonah, I don't know what I'll do," I said.

"All we can do is try. He deserves a chance," said Josh.

"Thank you for saying that. I need some optimism right now," I said.

"On the bright side, we don't have to go back to the parking garage for Adelaide's van. She can take it or leave it on her own now," said Josh.

"Yeah, *that's* the bright side." I laughed a little.

Less than an hour had passed when we saw a sign for the Pleasanton Ridge Regional Park. Josh turned into a dry and dusty clearing.

In the parking lot Cole's car waited for us. Jonah sat on the ground against the door on the shady side, gulping water from a plastic bottle. Two empty bottles lay on the ground next to him.

I got out after Josh parked and went to Jonah. "Are you all right?"

"Getting there. That spider venom knocks you on your ass," said Jonah.

"I think I'm having some kind of reaction to it. The last time she dosed me, I had a weird vision of my mom and sister. It was nice actually," I said.

"Too bad Noel is gone," said Jonah.

"I wouldn't go that far." I surveyed the parking lot.

I paced around our cars, thinking, and centering myself. Strong afternoon sun beamed down on the tired faces around me.

"We still need to go back to San Francisco, guys. It's for Jonah. This is non-negotiable as far as I'm concerned. Anyone who feels differently should go their own way from here." I had Nellie and Bruno in mind, but I genuinely didn't want to be dragging any reluctant travelers any longer. I was ready to walk back to Bay Farm Island alone and empty-handed.

"We're with you," said Nellie.

"Ralph was our friend—is our friend. But, we're not taking his path," said Bruno.

"We'll have our strength back if we rest here overnight," said Nellie.

"I second that," said Faith.

"Josh and I weren't bitten by anything, so we're ready to go," said Cole.

"True, but we shouldn't split up again, especially over such a long distance. If something is waiting for us on Bay Farm Island, it'll still be there tomorrow," said Josh.

"I wish I had your confidence," I said.

"I should have the final word." Jonah stood up, sweating in the sun. "I'm sick of wondering and waiting. I'm trying to be strong and put it out of my mind. But I can't stop thinking about how often I feel like I'm dying. Every time someone catches up to us and we have to fight, I have to worry not just about getting killed, but about getting one of *you* killed."

"Nobody thinks of you as a liability," said Cole.

"Bullshit. Now listen, if we get there and there's no serum and no lead on one, then you leave me. Go out to the Mojave and put an end to this," said Jonah.

"You make it sound so simple," I said.

"It can be. Let's get on with it. We'll go back to Innoviro and then down to the Desert. If we don't screw around, we'll have it done by this time tomorrow," said Faith.

"Anyone opposed?" Josh looked around at each of us.

Nobody raised a hand.

"Okay then, back in the cars. Cole, follow me," said Josh.

The traffic into the Bay Area was light and the roads had been cleared. The highway brimmed with congestion coming out, but only a few other cars were stupid enough to try getting back into such a devastated disaster zone.

A helicopter hovered over the exit to the Oakland International Airport. Traffic died altogether as we breezed past the airport into the light industrial buildings of Bay Farm Island.

We passed several collapsed buildings. Josh slowed looking for Unit 15 at 2595 on the Harbor Bay Parkway. Energy danced through my veins when we saw that the building was still partially intact. We had come a long way to find that we had a real chance to save the man I loved, and the rest of the world with him.

"Ilya and I should go in first. Noel and Rose and Sage were told not to harm us. If anyone's in there, they might've been told the same thing," I said quietly to Josh while Jonah slept curled up in the back of the Jeep.

I'm not leaving this place empty-handed. Please, whatever it takes, help me. For Jonah, I thought at my brother when Cole's car parked next to us.

"All right, but text me if you get into trouble," said Josh.

I stepped out of the Jeep and Ilya waited for me. *Let's get this over with*, I said, in my head.

The door was unlocked and the hall was silent as we entered at the door nearest to us on the structurally sound end of the building. Fluorescent lights flickered behind plastic panels above us. My pulse knocked inside my ears and my lungs constricted. I remembered the rabid scorpion dog in Victoria. I pictured Thorn's face. I thought of Hugo's crushing arms. With each step, a fresh horror entered my mind.

Ilya put his hand on my shoulder from behind and I jumped. "Relax. There's nothing monstrous or dangerous here. It's deserted, I promise."

I took a deep breath and paused. I breathed deeply. "Here's Unit Fifteen."

I reached out and turned the doorknob. The space in front of me looked like a hybrid between a warehouse office and a science lab. At the back of the room, two rows of islands had sinks and outlets on the surface. Bunsen burners dotted the counter alongside empty beakers.

Nearest to me, a handful of desks had computers on them, all dark. Along the wall, several familiar-looking specimen fridges were lit. The lab hadn't been gutted, not entirely.

"I can't believe this place still has power," said Ilya.

"It's almost like they meant to come back, but didn't get the chance. Hadn't they planned to abandon this place?" I asked.

"Maybe they just don't care about what they left behind. It probably doesn't matter to our father if Jonah recovers. Or if any of these other experiments go unfinished, not if his other plans are still rolling ahead," said Ilya.

"So, he won't kill variants if he doesn't have to, but he won't help anyone who isn't on his side?" I asked.

"He's methodical and apathetic. I know it makes sense, in his head," said Ilya.

I walked over to the specimen fridge and opened the door. Unlike Victoria, these shelves were all small liquid vials. No organic matter. Each of the liquid vials had a serial number. Some were blue, some yellow, others clear. Some swirled with a metallic pearlescence that shimmered in the light. All had identification numbers.

"How can we tell what's what in each?" I said.

"Turn on one of these computers. We'll start searching the local drives and whatever network we can access." Ilya knelt and pushed the power button on one of the towers before he took a seat in the chair. He pulled a thumb drive out of his pocket and plugged it into the tower.

"That'll be like finding a needle in a haystack. We need a strategy." I stared at the dark screen nearest to me. I opened one of the fridges and picked up a vial of blue liquid. I ran my fingertips over the hand-written number. I felt the ink on the rough paper and closed my eyes.

The lab came to life around me. The lighting glowed soft white and steady. Two men in lab coats were measuring something in beakers next to each other at a sink.

A young girl with a large black bun on her head clacked away at a computer. "Burt, can you remind me where Tatiana said to save the catalog file?"

From behind the sink, one of the men responded, "The root of the Admin folder on the C Drive."

"Thank you," she said brightly.

The lab melted back into the empty flickering present. I met Ilya's gaze and smiled.

"There's something in the root of the Admin folder on the C Drive," I said.

"I need a user account," said Ilya.

I plucked a sticky note off the desk behind him. "Try this one," I said, passing him the note.

"I'm in," he said.

I watched behind Ilya's shoulder as he clicked on the Start menu and found the C Drive inside the Computer folder. He opened an Admin folder and clicked on a document titled 'Catalog'.

The file opened to reveal a huge table of numbers with notations next to each. The bottom left corner of the document listed Page 1, Sec 1, 1/38. Only 38 pages. Great.

"Try doing a 'Find' search for 'aquakinesis'."

"There's nothing," said Ilya as the document reported zero results.

"Try aquakinetic instead. It might have to be an exact match." I watched as Ilya did the search and the computer jumped to page 37 and highlighted the word in one of the cells. The passage read:

Twelfth iteration of stabilization formula for patient J, self-induced aquakinetic. Solution of serum and carrier 1:10. Formula viable. Dosage 0.5ml weekly.

I wrote the serial number next to the note. 205207x. I started reading vials. Row after row passed with no match. They were not in numerical order, so I had to go vial by vial. 303375b, 11128g, 008739a, and so on. Determination pushed me through the maddening tedium.

"I'm going to copy network files to this thumb drive. As soon as I finish, you better be ready to go," said Ilya.

I reached a row of pearlescent blue vials and I saw it.

205207x. There were half a dozen vials with the same number.

"It's here! I found it!"

<h1 style="text-align:center">Chapter 28</h1>

I searched the cupboards and found an empty plastic tray designed to hold a dozen vials. I packed the half dozen vials of 205207x and then I stopped to think. I rummaged through the drawers until I found a box of syringes.

"Okay, two things," I said.

"What now?" Ilya asked.

"They left so many formulas. Don't you think we should take a few extras? It could be a bargaining chip down the road." Dizziness clouded my head but my inner voice told me to pause, think for a moment, and be smart.

I remembered the chills on my spine when I saw Tatiana talking about her turn for something. Instinct told me she had concocted a serum for herself. She was an expert in manipulating variant abilities. She wouldn't just sit on the sidelines if variants took over the planet. And she could succeed where Jonah failed in engineering a stable mutation. If she could do it to herself, maybe she would do it to others, a valuable asset in a world no longer habitable for people without variations. The chances of returning to this lab were near zero, so the opportunity was now or never.

"Which ones do you want? It'll take hours to read this file and figure out what's what." Ilya leaned into the monitor, peering at a text-heavy document.

"We can be strategic and fast. Search for terms like 'adaptation' and 'transformation' or anything like that. I think Tatiana might have experimented on herself."

"If they've got a formula to convert Aunt Tat into a variant, it wouldn't have been left behind here," Ilya said confidently.

"Try anyway." The walls around us groaned with a CREEEEEAHH. "I'll print the document. The transfer I started is almost done. Grab a handful of vials and let's get the hell out of here." Ilya pulled his thumb drive out of the tower. "I guess that'll have to be good enough."

A printer whirred to life on the side table between Ilya and the partition next to him. I plucked another half-dozen vials from the fridge and set them into the plastic tray. I removed a cooler from the bottom level of the fridge and opened it. I gently lowered the tray of vials into the empty cooler. I found an ice pack in a freezer compartment and tucked it under the vial tray. I put the box of syringes on top and closed the lid.

When the print job finished Ilya scooped up the pages and we jogged down the hall. The walls creaked behind us until a CRACK-SNAP sounded overhead. We ran to the entrance. As we burst out into the bright light of the parking lot, we turned around to see what remained of the building fold in on itself in a cloud of dust.

"Irina!" Jonah ran to me and sized me up. Satisfied I was unharmed, he grabbed me and hugged me hard.

"We found it! I don't know if it's a cure or a treatment, but there were notes about an aquakinetic, patient J. It has to be you," I said emphatically.

"Assholes," muttered Jonah.

"Buddy, we went to some trouble to get this," said Ilya.

"I meant Ivan and Tatiana. For holding out on me." Jonah's eyes were full of anger.

"Forget about them," I said. "Does anyone know how to give an injection?"

"I'll do it myself," said Jonah.

I handed him the cooler and he opened the top. He took the cooler and sat down on the curb. The dust from the collapsed building continued settling behind him. Faith, Cole, Bruno, and Nellie all got out of the cars to see the action.

"The blue vials are for you. You're supposed to get half a milliliter a week," I said.

Jonah assembled a syringe and removed a blue vial. I sat next to him and watched as he drew a full milliliter of blue liquid through the needle.

"I'm going to get a head start," said Jonah.

"Don't you think you should ration it until we can find out what's in there?" I said. We had barely enough information to point to this being designed for Jonah. The question of whether it was a cure or simply a maintenance treatment was eating at my brain.

"There's no point in reproducing the stuff if it doesn't work. A small dose will take days to have an effect. Trust me. This isn't such a huge risk," said Jonah.

He stood up and unbuttoned his pants, folding one side of his jeans down past his waist to expose his hip. Everyone watched as Jonah twisted slightly and squeezed his hip flesh with his left hand, the needle poised and ready in his right hand. I flinched as he stabbed himself firmly.

"That should make a difference before sundown." Jonah winced and sat back down to recover.

"So where to now?" said Nellie.

"We should stop for the night before we head into the desert. We don't know where exactly they are," I said.

"The Mojave is huge. We need something more to go on," said Cole.

"Thorn was supposed to be in Bakersfield tonight. I didn't hear who he was supposed to meet, but I'd bet Ivan and Tatiana would be waiting for him there," said Ilya.

"That's good enough for me," said Cole.

"Bakersfield it is then," I said.

Faith traded me spots so I could stay with Jonah in the back of Cole's car. We sped back the way we'd come off Bay Farm Island and back to the interstate. Traffic coming out of the city slowed us down, but we kept moving.

I held Jonah's hand as he sweated and moaned. Working or not, the serum affected him. We could only hope for the best.

The dusty countryside unraveled in front of us as we drove south. Worry crept up my sides. The farther inland we went, the more dangerous it would be for Jonah if this treatment had adverse effects.

I looked over at Jonah and saw him asleep. The sheen of sweat cleared and he looked healthy, peaceful even. Was his complexion misleading? Would there be a horrible outcome on the other side of this dream?

I stared back out the window at the dry yellow grasses and sage bushes punctuated by the occasional country home on the hillside.

Bakersfield appeared uneventfully on the horizon, rising

above the bleak landscape with a fringe of concrete and glass. Palm trees and a few other pieces of greenery popped up as we neared the city limits. I took heart. With irrigation infrastructure came water for Jonah.

"Does anyone care where we stay?" said Cole as we passed a large salmon-stucco Super 8 Motel.

"Somewhere without a lot of tourists," said Ilya.

"How about this one," said Cole, gesturing at a brown strip motel titled Desert Breeze.

"That'll do," said Ilya.

Cole promptly turned in and parked.

"Jonah's still asleep. Let's leave him for a while. He needs the rest," I said.

"We need to dig through the folders on this thumb drive anyway," said Ilya.

"Give it to Faith and let her pick through it," said Cole.

"Will do. And I'll check us in," said Ilya.

My brother popped his head into Josh's Jeep to give the drive to Faith and headed for the motel office. Jonah slept soundly, leaving Cole and me alone in his car.

"So I guess you'll be back together with Jonah now," said Cole, staring at me in the rearview mirror.

"He's not out of the woods yet. We haven't exactly discussed what's going to happen," I said.

"I want you to know there's no hard feelings. Not on my part anyway," said Cole.

My stomach twisted. The state of Cole's heart mattered to me. I cared as much about him as I did my brother. I stared at the back of Cole's headrest, pleading silently for him not to hate me, or Jonah. The life we were living wasn't conducive to Cole meeting someone himself, but I wanted that for him all the same.

"I do care about you. You're as important to me as my brother. Faith too. You're all like family now," I felt a lump in my throat at the word 'family' and I had to stop talking.

I wanted to reach out and hug Cole. Ilya came back and put us out of our misery.

"Four rooms for one night and we're three hundred and sixty-eight dollars poorer," said Ilya.

"For this dump?" I said.

Cole yanked his keys out of the ignition and exited the car. "Who cares? We've still got lots of cash."

"Not at this rate," I muttered under my breath.

"He's more hurt than angry, you know," said Ilya.

"I know." I gently eased Jonah's head off my lap. He snoozed soundly, so we left him in the car and cracked a window.

"How long before Faith knows if we've got more info about Jonah's serum?" I said.

"I'm not sure. We might know before he wakes up," said Ilya.

"I can't stand not knowing if this is a cure or just a treatment. Because if it's the latter, and we can't make more …" I pushed my hands into my hair. I pulled out my ponytail and retied it.

I followed my brother through the door to his and Faith's room. She sat on the far bed, typing furiously on her laptop.

"Anything so far?" I said.

"Can't talk. Writing script," said Faith.

"We should leave her to it," said Ilya.

I followed him back out the door and into the next room where Bruno, Nellie, Josh, and Cole were watching television. Each couple had a room, leaving bachelors Josh and Cole to bunk together. Distance from the pairs around him was bound to improve Cole's mood.

I looked around Nellie and Bruno's room. The motel's dingy flower bedspreads and cheap wood-panel walls were a sharp contrast to the brand-new flat-panel television on the dresser facing both beds. Cole sat at the room's small table. Nellie and Bruno lounged on one queen bed while Josh had the other.

I didn't recognize the movie they were watching. It looked like a B-grade sci-fi. Under other circumstances, I'd make some popcorn and lose myself in it. After the last few months, no movie would be able to distract me properly as long as I lived. Josh left to get burgers and fries for everyone while the show droned.

When Josh came back the sky had darkened and our room was dim. Nellie flicked on the lamp on the nightstand between the queen beds.

I looked out the window with a view of the motel's florescent-lit courtyard. A flash caught my eye. I got up and ran to the window and scanned the courtyard. It happened again. A column of water surged up into the air from the center of the pool.

At the top of the column, water gathered until nearly the entire pool's contents hung in the air. I watched, full of panic that a civilian might see this display, as the water reversed direction and retreated down into the pool.

The pool's water started to settle and a figure swam up to the edge of the tile and crawled out. Naked except for his boxer briefs, Jonah stood tall and shook his black hair. I could see his bright aqua eyes from across the courtyard.

"I think we got him the right serum," Faith said behind me.

I whirled around to find everyone staring at me. I looked at Jonah and back at my friends. I ran out the front door and around the building past the motel's office looking for a break in the exterior to access the courtyard.

I reached the gap and Jonah was already there. I looked into his glowing eyes. He rushed forward and pulled me into his arms. I ran my hands up into his wet hair and he pinned me against the wall, kissing me with a fierce craving.

His arms were strong around me. I felt warmth radiating from his chest up through his tongue. I pulled back to take a breath.

"Everyone's waiting to see if you're alright," I said.

"I'm alright," said Jonah breathlessly.

"We've got our own room," I said and smiled.

"Good." He smiled back at me and kissed me again.

Chapter 29

I pulled my key card from my back pocket and led Jonah by the hand to our door. My stomach twisted into a knot of nerves as we walked. I had worked so hard to stop thinking about him. I'd blocked my desire to touch his tall lean body and toned arms.

Our moment had finally come and as I slid my card into the slot on our motel door, all I could think of was that we had no idea how much longer the world around us would be normal and safe.

No sooner than I opened the door and stepped inside, Jonah turned me around and kissed me. I backed up as he pushed forward. Our mouths connected and our arms wrapped around each other.

"Slow down," I said, stepping back.

"I don't want to slow down," he said, tracing my jawbone with his pointer finger. He took a plastic and foil packet out of his pocket.

"This is so new. You've had one dose," I said cautiously.

I gently took the condom from his hand and put it on the nightstand.

"It was a double dose, remember." Jonah leaned in to kiss me but moved to my neck. He dragged his lip across my skin and I shivered.

"You were so sick though," I said shakily as I fought to concentrate. "Seriously, we don't have to rush this," I said.

"I want you now, but only if you're ready. Please don't hold back because you think I'm still sick. I know my body." Jonah gently pulled my ponytail out and ran his hands through my hair.

I touched him back, running my hand across his chest and around his waist. He grunted and kissed me, leaning into me as he held the small of my back.

I pulled away again and sat on the edge of the bed. I sighed and smiled through my frustration.

"Have I ever told you that I love the way you smile? Your pink lips twist like you know something I don't." Jonah looked at me intently, cradling my jaw in his large hand. He touched my bottom lip with his thumb. I looked up at him, doubting his eyesight and perception. He tilted his head and a lock of his wet hair fell forward.

"I love how you look at me like I have something you need." He sat down next to me. "I love that your cheeks glow when you're embarrassed." He touched either side of my face.

"I hate being embarrassed," I said, turning away and palming my face.

"You're strong too. You've lost so much, but you keep going. You know right from wrong in every bone of your body. You're more powerful than you think. And no one can tell you what to do." Jonah ran his hand along my shoulder blade, tracing the outline of my bra through my shirt. He came to the scar his hand left months before. "I will never, ever, forgive myself for hurting you that day. I lost control and I moved too fast."

"You're doing the same thing right now. But it won't work. You're trying to sell me; you don't need to. I know you love me. And I love you, but this is too soon. You need time to get well." I kissed Jonah on the cheek. I paused to take in his scent, expecting pool water or sweat. "You smell different now. Like the first day of spring. Chlorophyll and flower buds."

"I feel different," said Jonah. He kissed my mouth, softly this time and I let him. I'd wanted him to get better for months. And now he seemed healed, but I didn't trust it.

On cue, my brain delivered a flash of Jonah and me, walking on a tropical beach that looked South Asian. He wore a linen shirt. I had shorter hair. It could only be the future. Which meant he really would live. I drew my mind's eye back into the motel room.

I pulled Jonah over me as I lay back on the quilt. I welcomed the weight of his long chest and strong hips as he kissed me deeply. I saw flashes of Jonah's past as our bodies moved together.

He played volleyball on a beach, still pale, but grinning in the sun. He wore a tuxedo at a graduation. He walked along the Inner Harbour in Victoria as the wind played with the loose curls of his hair. Surges of adrenaline coursed through me as I flashed back and forth between Jonah's past and his present, with me.

The warmth of his breath was charged with electricity, healthy and greedy. He rolled me over on top of him and gripped my backside firmly.

As Jonah pulled my pelvis against him, I leaned down and kissed his neck, nudging my way up to his earlobe. He lost patience and lunged for my mouth. He reached down to my waist and unbuttoned my jeans. I sat up and peeled off my pants, sitting on top of him in my T-shirt and panties. I looked down at his face in the dark. I wanted to savor the night. I flicked the lamp switch on the nightstand next to us.

His smooth pale skin glowed warmly in the yellow light. He smiled and ran his fingertips slowly from my neck to my hip. My skin tingled at his touch, sending delightful prickles down both arms. He gripped my thighs with both hands and kissed me again with intensity. I kissed him back with abandon, wrapping my legs around his waist. I gave in and let heat overtake us both.

Dawn light poured in through the gap in the heavy canvas curtains of our motel room. My naked body curled snugly up against Jonah's back. I moved my hand up along his bare thigh under the sheets.

"I could get used to waking up like this, next to you every morning," said Jonah as he rolled over.

"Do you ever think about what we'll do after all this is over? I mean, will we go home to Victoria and look for jobs again? Or start somewhere new?" I propped myself up with an elbow and pulled the sheet up to my chest.

"I don't care where we land, now that you're finally picturing a future with me," said Jonah.

"You make it sound like I put up a fight. But I did see a snapshot of our future," I smiled. This time I did know something he didn't.

"Really? What did you see?" He sat up, giving me his full

attention.

"Just us walking on a beach, somewhere I've never been. And we looked different." I felt uneasy about trusting the image in my mind.

"I can handle a walk on the beach. Taking you on a tropical vacation will make whatever we have to get through all worth it." He smiled and kissed me, artfully sliding over top of me.

"Shouldn't we make an appearance, you know, for breakfast?" I pulled back from him.

"After all the waiting *we* did, they can sit there for another ten minutes," said Jonah.

"Ten minutes?" I said, overly incredulous. "Is that all?"

"Okay, an hour." He kissed my neck and I gave in to the rush of heat.

Josh had made another fast food run by the time Jonah and I knocked on Nellie and Bruno's door. Our friends looked at us with mixed expressions of knowing guile and awkward approval. Everyone except Cole. His stone-cold face deterred me from making eye contact with him. A pang of guilt passed through me. I wondered what my poor brother heard from our minds.

"I got you each a bacon and egg bun. Should be cold by now though," said Josh through an irrepressible grin.

"Okay, back to reality," said Faith.

"Good idea. We need a plan of attack before we head into the desert," said Ilya.

"What exactly do we have to go on?" said Nellie.

"I know Ivan and Tatiana were on their way to the Mojave Desert and they took my sister with them. I don't think she's in danger, but I don't know if they want her because she's a variant or if it's to use her against me."

Bruno gave me a long, steady look. "Are you sure it was the Mojave? If we head into that desert and get stuck ... I don't want to think about it."

"I saw them pass a sign for the 'Mojave Desert Joshua Tree Road Scenic Backway' which is pretty specific," I said confidently.

"We'll head down that road and see where it takes us," said Ilya.

Nellie picked up her tablet, swiping and tapping away.

"I'll still need a decent supply of water, but that's mostly for offensive purposes now," said Jonah.

"I'm glad we're all match-fit, but we shouldn't let our guard down. Adelaide and Ralph may be actively helping the enemy now," said Bruno.

"I found the Backway. We need to cross over into southern Utah via Nevada, but it's not too far," said Nellie.

"Everybody pack up. We leave in twenty," said Josh loudly enough for the whole room.

"Works for me. I've seen as much of Bakersfield as I ever wanted to see." Cole marched out of the room. I grabbed Josh's arm.

"Would you mind taking me and Jonah in your Jeep?" I said sheepishly.

"I don't think Cole's going to let a little drama ruin the bigger picture," said Josh.

"Humor me. Faith, Nellie, Bruno can go with Cole and we'll take Ilya," I said as firmly as I dared.

"Fine. Out front as soon as you're packed," said Josh.

We stuffed our bags quickly, checked out, and pulled away from the Desert Breeze motel, headed east. Jonah and I sat in the back of Josh's Jeep. I put my head on Jonah's shoulder and held his hand as though the battle lay straight ahead. But only a dusty desert stretched around us as far as the eye could see. I pleaded to the universe with every fiber of my being that we had enough serum to keep Jonah well, if not cure him outright.

"He's fine. Stop worrying already. He HATES it when you worry about him," Ilya called out from the front seat. Josh stared at the road ahead.

"Did I ever tell you that *I* hate it when you invade my head uninvited?" I said. My cheeks betrayed me, filling with heat, and I wondered if Jonah could tell.

"Let's worry about the day ahead. We'll need more food. There's no better place to hit a buffet than Las Vegas. We'll stop for lunch and be in southern Utah before dinner," said Josh.

"Try to get some sleep, sis. Dream about the enemy, if you can manage it," said Ilya.

"Thanks," I said sarcastically.

"It's not a bad idea. We need all the information we can get right now," said Jonah.

"Okay, but no chatter until I fall asleep," I said.

I fished my tarot cards out of my backpack and shuffled them. I ran my fingers over the cards. When I was satisfied, I curled up with my head down in Jonah's lap and let the vibration of the road lull me to sleep.

Inside the same trailer where I'd seen Ivan and Tatiana, Rose and Gemma sat at the tiny dining table. Rose was on the far edge, her wings angled into the cramped kitchen. Sage stood steps away tending a boiling pot on the stove.

"We had another healer in Victoria. She knew your sister too," said Rose.

"Do you think you can bring your sister around to work with us?" said Sage to Gemma.

"I don't see why she isn't on your side already. Ivan is her father. And he got justice for my parents. That's enough for me. Once Irina finds out what *really* happened to Mom and Dad, she'll get on board fast enough," said Gemma.

"We're lucky to have you here, not just because you're Irina's sister. If anything happens to us – or your sister – you can help us recover if a couple of hotheads shoot first and ask questions later," said Rose.

"I'm happy to help. I don't know what happened to Irina to make her run away, but she'll listen to me," said Gemma enthusiastically.

The trailer door opened and Tatiana stepped off the metal stairs with an air of contempt. She wore her crisp camping khakis with a lavender collared shirt. She looked fresh from the fields of a country club.

"Gemma, it's time for my first trial injection. I need you ready, should something go wrong," Tatiana snapped at my sister.

"Do you know what the serum is going to do to you? Healing is still new to me. I don't want to screw it up and let you down, so the more I know about what's happening inside your body, the better," said Gemma.

"It's hard to say what the reaction will be, but I'm expecting a plant-based ability of some sort." Tatiana rolled up her sleeve.

Rose, Sage, and Gemma watched closely as Tatiana removed a glass vial of green liquid from the trailer's small fridge. She opened a drawer, pulled out a plastic package, and unwrapped a syringe. She turned the vial upside down and pierced the top with her needle, drawing green liquid into the syringe.

"I may lose consciousness. That's fine. Let me rest and monitor me. Make sure my heart keeps beating and my lungs keep breathing." Tatiana set the needle down on the counter and prodded the inside of her left elbow with her right hand.

Satisfied, she picked up the needle and slowly, carefully, pierced a vein in her forearm. She pushed the back of the syringe until the green liquid disappeared. She stood confidently for a moment and then faltered. She gripped the kitchen counter and steadied herself against the cupboard opposite her.

Gemma wiggled out from between the trailer's bench seat and dining table. She put her hand on top of Tatiana's. They both closed their eyes for a moment. Tatiana suddenly opened her eyes filled with opaque emerald green. Her skin flushed a pale leafy hue.

In the daylight, Las Vegas looked anticlimactic. I had always wanted to visit the city and I knew it was best seen at night. We'd agreed to visit the Strip, so Josh turned off the highway and into the heart of Vegas. I looked out my window, craning my neck up to a row of giant palm trees dividing the road. I touched the glass and felt the warmth of the summer sun. Josh's air conditioner ran full blast and it wasn't enough to fully counter the mid-day heat.

I thought we would walk through an air-conditioned casino to find a grimy all-you-can-eat buffet. Instead, Josh pulled into the parking lot of a Denny's. Cole turned in behind us. The retro-style diner was simple enough, an angular red roof and flat stone siding. Behind the restaurant, a long rectangular building striped with dark windows stretched into a giant spire. Jonah and I followed Ilya and Josh inside to an empty corner booth.

"What can I get for you, gentleman? And lady, sorry," said a gum-chewing red-headed woman who looked to be about the age my mother was.

"Do you serve breakfast all day here?" said Josh.

"And all night too," said the waitress.

"Let's do Grand Slams for everyone. Eight total. We've got four more friends coming," said Josh.

"We had breakfast this morning," I said.

"Grand Slams are simple. And you can never have too much breakfast," said Josh.

"We need to make it a quick stop," said Jonah.

"Y'all want the same thing then? Eggs? Toast? Bacon or sausage?" said the waitress.

"Over-easy, wheat bread, and bacon for everyone," said Josh.

The rest of our group arrived at our booth and slid into the seats. Bruno and Cole nodded at the waitress signaling their approval of Josh's order. The waitress scratched her notepad and left.

"Anyone interested in Tatiana's latest achievement?" I said to the table.

"Are you sure you're pronouncing 'abomination' correctly?" said Faith.

"Okay, her latest abomination. Does it count if she does it to herself?" I said rhetorically.

"Yes," said Cole flatly.

"She's started dosing herself to cultivate a variation. The metamorphosis may already be complete," I said.

"Aunt Tat, what have you done now," said Ilya shaking his head.

"She's become something plant-oriented," I said as quietly as I could and still be heard.

"Will she be dangerous?" asked Nellie.

"I'm sure if she can manage it, yes," said Cole.

"Few creatures in the plant kingdom are actively dangerous," said Jonah.

"How about passively poisonous?" said Cole.

"Let's assume she's dangerous, poison or otherwise. Are she and Ivan still in the desert? What'll we do when we catch them? And what do we do if we miss them, again," said Bruno.

"Ideally, fight, incapacitate, and obtain a copy of *The Compendium* so incidents like the Sutro Baths don't ever happen again," I said.

"If we miss them in the Mojave, we'll keep chasing them," said Ilya.

"All doom and gloom aside, it's too bad we can't stay in Vegas longer. Not because of the gambling though," said Faith.

"I'll bite. Why is that?" I said.

"This is the perfect city for variants!" Faith exclaimed excitedly.

"I think you're overestimating people's tolerance for weird things," said Jonah, evaluating a tent card advertising pie and ice cream.

"She may have a point. Ralph moved in public on a limited basis as long as he was in an urban area and added elements of the ridiculous to make his lizard self look like a costume. The tactic worked in regular cities," said Nellie.

"Some variations look like magic tricks. And this is the city of magic," said Bruno.

"It's the city of horseshit," said Cole.

"I'm willing to bet that if one or even all of us displayed our abilities, any onlookers would clap thinking it's street magic," said Faith confidently.

"I'll take that bet," said Jonah.

"If I win and the people stay chill, you will personally locate and bring me a pint of genuine cotton candy ice cream," said Faith.

"Shouldn't be too hard in Vegas. And if I win? What'll you bring me?" said Jonah.

"What do you want?" said Faith. Jonah paused to think.

"Ten liters of distilled water. Not filtered water, not spring water. Distilled," said Jonah.

"Where do I find distilled water?" Faith frowned. "Never-mind. It doesn't matter 'cause I'm not going to lose."

"This has *got* to be a bad idea," I said to Jonah. "You've only just bounced back. Now that you're at your fighting weight, you're ready to take on the world?"

"Yep." He smiled, then reached around my waist and squeezed my body into his. It felt good to let him in so close.

"This should be interesting," said Josh.

"Aren't we supposed to be on a timeline here?" I said.

"There's time for *this*." Faith cuddled up close to Ilya, mirroring me and Jonah. I felt another pang of guilt as I caught Cole's face in my peripheral vision.

"Let's hit the Mirage. Faith, you could use the volcano and the flame throwers, and Jonah, you could use the water feature beneath them both," said Ilya.

"Been to Vegas often?" I asked my brother with a tone of surprise.

"I'm a mind-reader. What can I say? Poker comes naturally to me," said Ilya. He arched his eyebrows and grinned mischievously.

"That's not poker, it's cheating," said Jonah.

"It was practice. And a study in human nature. We passed both those casinos on the way here, so it's not like I've got a Vegas map tattooed on my eyelids," said Ilya.

Our waitress reappeared with our breakfasts-for-lunch on a giant folding tray. She set it down and served us while Ilya and Jonah glared at each other.

We ate quickly, headed back out to The Strip, and backtracked until we came to the front of the Mirage casino and hotel. As we pulled inside The Mirage's parking garage, I realized why so little outdoor parking existed in Las Vegas. This was going to be an intensely hot experiment.

"Are you sure you're okay to be out in such intense sun like this?" I said quietly to Jonah.

"Stop worrying! This won't take long anyway," he replied and squeezed my hand with his.

Ilya led us to a shady patch under a cluster of palm trees in the Mirage's front yard.

"Okay, it's your show, Faith, so fire first. After you're both done, if it's not obvious who won, the group will put it to a vote," Ilya said to Faith.

We stood shielding our eyes as Faith stretched out her arms and concentrated. Only Bruno seemed to share my level of apprehension.

Faith closed her eyes. She rolled her head around, stretching her neck as she did so. She opened her eyes and squinted, narrowing her eyelids, focusing intently on the fake rock volcano ahead. The volcano roared to life belching a handful of fire plumes into the sky. A cluster of tourists at a covered bar whipped their heads at us.

"Hey Madge, check it out," a bald man called to his wife. "They're doing a surprise early show!"

"What? Who wants to see a fire show in the middle of the day?" she called back.

Faith sized up the bar patrons to make sure they were

watching. She gestured with her arms coaxing flames out of the tubes mounted in the pond around the volcano. Streams of fire shot out in a ring around the volcano, climbing taller and taller. The streams of fire moved around each other in pairs, like corkscrew-shaped dance partners. The crowd at the bar ooooohed and ahhhhhhed.

"Look at that! This is not the normal show!" said the bald husband.

"It's that girl there!" said the wife.

"She's an illusionist," said another man in the growing crowd at the bar.

Faith detached four streams of fire and linked them into interlocking hoops, like a short chain of fiery rings. After more ooooohing and ahhing, Faith erased the rings remotely and the fire disappeared. The crowd clapped.

"They won't be so accepting of this." Jonah stepped forward and stretched his arms out to the water. He gestured upwards, as Faith had done, coaxing streams of water up in front of the flame throwers.

Unlike the flames, the columns of water couldn't be accounted for by jets or fountain parts. The rippling surface of the water spat four streams up into the sky. Mimicking Faith's display, Jonah created four corkscrews spiraling upward. He then moved the streams into four interlocking rings of water.

"How are they *doing* that?" squealed the wife still watching from the bar. I turned my attention to the spectators. The group at the bar had doubled.

Jonah moved the rings into one long plume of water and looped it around to one ring, spinning faster and higher, faster and higher. He brought one of his arms down and the spinning ring of water spun into a funnel, connecting back to the pond.

"Does the hotel allow this?" said the husband.

"Hey, you there!" called a man addressing Jonah personally. "You're screwing around with private property. This isn't funny!"

"Sir, excuse me, Sir!" said a man in a navy blue uniform. His arm had a patch with SECURITY written in bright yellow.

"Guys, I think it's time to go," I said nervously.

Jonah dropped the water and we all stood, still as statues, as another two security guards ran to us.

"You think you're funny? You're about to get a rude wake-up call, kid!" yelled the man who'd shouted at Jonah. "We don't let vandals run around free in this country!"

"Screw this," said Cole. He uprooted the palm tree beside him and dropped it between us and the security guards. Screams erupted from the bar.

"They're not vandals. They're terrorists!" screamed the wife.

Nellie ran to the edge of the lawn and hopped the fence. She grabbed the pole of a streetlight with both hands and grimaced. Sparks exploded CRACKLE-ZAP-POP from inside the glass sending shattered light cover raining down around her. The lights of the Mirage's billboard went dark, followed by the signage on the building. Neon lights, signs, and traffic lights went dark like a ripple flowing along the strip in both directions.

"Time to go!" shouted Ilya. We turned and ran together back into the covered parking where Nellie had run to meet us.

"No ice cream for you," said Jonah as we reached Josh's Jeep and Cole's car.

"You're both idiots," said Cole as he slid behind the wheel of his car. He shut the door and started his car as Josh did the same in his Jeep. Doors slammed in succession and we peeled out of the covered parking in time to watch a fire engine and two cop cars roll past us to the Mirage entrance.

"That was a stupid idea!" I shouted over the passing sirens.

"No point in yelling about it now." Josh swerved through traffic and stopped in the confusion. "What's the best way out of Vegas?" Josh handed his phone to Ilya.

More flashing blue and red lights raced towards us along the strip. Ilya fired off directions and Josh lurched into traffic when the police lights passed.

We zipped away and kept speeding out into the desert, leaving the dusty dark lights of Vegas behind us.

I fumed at Jonah and my brother as we drove. Playing with the elements was too risky. Why hadn't I been able to talk them out of it?

"Josh is right, there's no point in staying mad all day," Ilya said to me.

Stay the fuck out of my head! I yelled internally. Ilya laughed at me.

I clenched and released my fists, berating myself anyway. I had to get better at managing people if I wanted our group to listen when I had the next vision and the next.

Our best-case scenario included somehow unraveling the complicated puzzle that was *The Compendium*. Our worst case would be that Ivan stopped us and ruined the world as we knew it, possibly killing some of my friends, and definitely killing most of humanity. If eight people couldn't take potential catastrophic change seriously, the rest of the world stood little chance.

We kept driving northwest and Josh cycled through radio

stations while the rest of us stayed silent, rattled and relieved. We crossed the state line into Arizona and dusty, flat beige earth stretched ahead of us. We crossed another line into Utah. Having started our day in California, our trip had included four states in one day. It was probably a record for all of us.

I nodded off briefly and snapped my head back up in time to see a road sign announcing an exit for the Mojave Desert Joshua Tree Road Scenic Backway.

Chapter 31

Mountains fringed the horizon ahead, slate gray under a clear blue sky. Josh's Jeep rumbled along the graded gravel road. The only vehicle in either direction was Cole's car behind us.

We passed the brown wood sign I'd seen in my vision and a bird of prey cried overhead. The sound of chainsaws erupted in the distance, shrouded in a dust cloud. Figures on bikes trailed out of the dust and formed a line zipping perpendicular across our route and my brother shouted at Josh to stop.

"Hold it here," said Ilya, as though listening to the air around us. The BRAAA, braaa, of the dirt bikes faded in the distance.

"What?" said Jonah.

"Shhhhh," said Ilya, irritated.

Gravel crunched behind us as Cole's car caught up and stopped.

"They work at a research farm. They're heading there now. I'm pretty sure they're variants," said Ilya.

"Good enough for me." Josh turned ninety degrees to the

right and followed the bikers into the bumpy brush of the rough landscape. "We're not trailing them over the open plain. We'd be sitting ducks."

"Are you sure anyone is watching?" said Jonah.

"Can Cole follow us?" I peered out the back window. He followed, but slowly.

"Text Faith so they know where we're going and why," said Ilya.

I frowned and picked up my phone to tap out the message.

Josh kept his eye on the sky for puffs of dust. Ilya listened to the bikers' thoughts. Our route wove through the sage and then curved around a bank of eroded sandstone. The dust cleared and we saw row upon row of tarp-covered plants and a large translucent plastic greenhouse butted up against the rock wall behind it. Unfortunately, the trailer from my vision was nowhere in sight. We were in a natural cul-de-sac, closed in by small steep hills made of layered red, brown, and tan clay deposits.

Josh drove up alongside the rows of tarps and I could see they were more like mesh screens, not solid black as they'd seemed from far away. The screens were propped up by countless poles roughly ten feet up off the ground. I recognized the plants growing in the shade.

Seedling versions of the evergreens with venus-fly-trap-style mouths ran in two columns back to the greenhouse. The rest of the plants were the teal ferns I'd seen in BC, with pearl flowers, in various stages of growth from tiny sprouts to large bushy shrubs.

"This is what they were growing in Vancouver and the valley where we found Kingston," I said to Jonah.

I got out of the Jeep and walked under the mesh screen

closest to me. A fly trap snapped closed around a tiny purple butterfly. A sucking sound followed and the mouth opened, releasing a cloud of white powder that lingered around the plant. I took a step back.

Buzzing from within the ferns drew my attention. Movement flickered around the taller plants where the pearl flowers were in bloom. As I drew closer to the ferns, I saw one of the large iridescent oil-slick bees land on a flower and feed.

"Guys!" I called out, not taking my eyes off the bee.

Jonah and Ilya came to my side.

"These are the bees Innoviro developed, the bees Kingston thought were so important," I said in a hushed tone.

"Are they dangerous?" said Jonah.

"They're probably not harmless. Look at them! Have you ever seen bees with metallic coloring?" said Ilya.

"We should catch one and save it for testing," said Jonah as Josh joined us.

"What kind of lab do we expect to work in?" said Josh.

"If we can't get a hold of *The Compendium* documents, we'll have no way of knowing what Ivan's going to do. The only alternative is to piece it together ourselves," said Jonah.

"That could take years. We don't have time," said Ilya.

Cole, Faith, Bruno, and Nellie inspected the plants as well. Ilya stepped away from us looking thoughtfully at the greenhouses and up to the sky.

"Did you see anything about what these bees are used for?" said Jonah.

"These plants reek of decay," said Bruno as he peered at the evergreen seedlings.

"Where did those bikers disappear to?" said Faith.

"They drove to that greenhouse on the far edge of the

property, but then they disappeared. It was weird. It's not like something violent happened to them. More like someone switched off a light. Their minds were there and then popped out of existence," said Ilya.

"They must have gone over the hill. Look, you can still see the dust cloud," said Jonah.

"Why is there no security here? Shouldn't this place be guarded? How are we able to walk right up so easily?" said Cole.

"I'm sure Ivan's got eyes on this place. We may have company soon," said Josh.

"When Irina and I found the Innoviro farm outside Hope, there was no security there either," said Ilya.

"Maybe these things protect themselves," said Nellie, eyeing up a bee as it flew past her.

"Careful, an animal is coming," said Ilya. No sooner had the words left his lips, than a flash of fur caught my attention through the plants.

"It's only a coyote," said Bruno, sniffing the air as he stepped forward. Jonah put his arm out to stop Bruno.

The coyote yelped and broke into a run, swerving through the ferns. It yelped again and broke free of the plants. Two oil-slick bees clung to its side. The coyote snapped helplessly at the bees, flailing around as it tried to bite them. It fell to the ground convulsing and whimpering.

Blood sprayed from the animal's mouth as he flung his head back and forth. The coyote stopped moving and emptied its bowels.

"Jesus," said Josh.

"I think it's dead," said Bruno.

"You think?" said Cole.

"Someone should examine it," said Nellie.

"You examine it!" Tears filling her eyes, Faith retreated from the dead animal while I watched the bees shimmer and quiver.

"Guys, shut up! Look at the bees." As the words left my lips, the quivering accelerated until the bees melted into a liquid and slid off the coyote's fur. The liquid dropped into the dust on the ground and dried up.

"They change. They're like the beetles. Oh my god, the beetles! A mechanism of change. That's what they were cultivating!" I shouted, to myself more than anyone else.

"What's music got to do with bees?" said Bruno.

"Not the band, the insect. I saw chameleon beetles in Victoria. I saw them in San Francisco too. These beetles didn't merely blend, they disappeared into the surface they imitated. I have no idea how it works, but those bees look like liquid because they turn into liquid!" I said, still shouting.

"To what end?" said Nellie, confused.

"To deliver whatever contagion killed that coyote into an urban area without being detected. Not until it's too late. I wonder how they make the first transformation, from liquid to insect. Timed exposure to air? A radio signal?" Jonah's calm surprised me.

"It doesn't matter how they do it! We need to get the fuck away from these things if we don't want the goddamn plague ourselves!" Faith backed away from the ferns. Nellie, Bruno, and Josh followed suit, backing out of the covered plant rows.

"I'm pretty sure we can relax. Everything Ivan and his partners are working on is engineered to remove humans and anything else they perceive as unwanted from the Earth. But they made a point of leaving variants alive when they killed humans in San Francisco. I don't think *The Compendium* attacks are meant for us. They're meant for them." Cole gestured behind himself, back towards civilization.

"How the hell are we supposed to stop something like this? We couldn't even stop them from starting an earthquake–with one big clunky machine!" Fear crept slowly up my sides as I visualized places where a rainbow-colored oily sheen would go unnoticed. Almost any urban area.

I pictured what our lives would become with endless empty cities. No power. No internet. No restaurants. No malls. No music. We wouldn't even have pets if the coyote on the ground in front of me was any indication. Fear evolved to panic. My lungs tightened and my heart raced faster and faster. *This is happening.*

"We're still going to fight him, them, whoever," said Ilya as he put his arm around my shoulder.

The sound of the mesh fabric screen flapping overhead seemed to be concealing a faint crackling somewhere far away. I remembered the people on dirt bikes and I wondered if they were coming back. I stepped out from underneath the screens, away from the flapping and bee-buzzing.

A chorus of snarling growls sounded on the hillside. I whipped around and saw a group of Innoviro's horrible hybrids, copies of the creature they'd used for security in the Victoria lab. In the full light of day, these abominations were more than disgusting, they were terrifying.

Black and dark brown fur and the face of a Rottweiler composed the creatures' front halves. Their back ends were the shiny black exoskeleton and tail of a scorpion. They were much bigger than the large dog breed they were based on. Each animal approximated the size of a small cow. I counted five of them.

"Cole! Josh!" I shouted. They were already next to me.

"I think we could use a little electricity here," Jonah said to Nellie. "I'll tap the irrigation line and soak them, then you add power." Nellie nodded, not taking her eyes off the dogs up on the hill.

"Or we could kill them with fire," said Faith. She unleashed two thick powerful streams of fire in the general direction of the dogs. They scattered instantly bolting in different directions before the fire hit the ground. The sagebrush and dry grass where they'd been standing went up like paper. The snapping and popping of burning brush accompanied the whoosh of fire as it spread across the hill.

Cole picked up one of the mesh screen support poles and threw it at a dog as it charged us. The pole speared the dog through the side and pinned it to the ground where it continued to claw the dirt and fight for freedom.

Josh charged another dog whose tail flung and stabbed at his back. CLING! CLANG-CLING! Josh's skin deflected each blow as he struggled to wrench life out of the creature.

Faith took on another animal with a fresh fire stream. The dog yelped in pain and fell to the ground, curling into a charred heap.

The apparition of a bear charged another dog. I knew the bear wasn't real when it flickered briefly and I saw the look of concentration on Ilya's frightened face. The dog stood its ground and my brother had no choice but to continue intimidating and stalling with his bear. Faith rounded on Ilya's dog and quickly created another blackened lump.

I caught sight of a large jagged piece of bedrock. I concentrated on levitating it over to where Cole circled a thrashing dog speared to the ground. I dropped the stone next to Cole who promptly snatched it up and crushed the dog's head with the pointed end. He stepped over to Josh's dog and finished it with the same devastating blow.

Out of the corner of my eye, I saw Nellie shoot an electric current into the dog charging her. The dog kept coming despite the charge. Bruno roared, bearing fangs I never knew he had. Thick black claws curled out of Bruno's fingertips as he leapt onto the dog before it could reach Nellie. A giant black scorpion tail rose above Bruno's back and pierced him squarely in his spine. Bruno roared again and fell to the ground, limp and lifeless.

"NOOOOO!" cried Nellie as she jumped onto the dog's back, instantly electrifying the creature with every ounce of her life force. The dog's tail lunged and missed, lunged and missed as it convulsed with the intense current passing through its body. The tail lunged again and struck Nellie's side. The electricity stopped. Nellie and the dog creature dropped into the dirt and lay motionless.

Chapter 32

Ilya and I saw Nellie and Bruno fall. Everyone else was still distracted. Faith had turned her fire on the mutated ferns and evergreen seedlings under the mesh tarps beside us. A ravenous blaze devoured the entire crop in moments. Jonah doused the brush fire ignited by Faith's clumsy first attack on the dogs. He turned his attention to the burning crops and extinguished them as well.

Cole made the rounds to each dog, crushing heads and tails with the giant piece of bedrock I'd given him until they were all definitely dead.

I ran to Bruno and felt his wrist, and then his neck. Both spots had a weak pulse. He wasn't gone, but without Camille or Gemma to heal him, there was nothing I could do. I turned to Nellie. I felt her wrist. Nothing. I felt her neck. No pulse at all.

"Bruno, can you talk? Can you move?" I said.

"Nellie. Save Nellie." Bruno gasped for air.

"Don't worry about Nellie. We'll take care of her. Rest. Be

still." I held his hand.

Whether he felt comforted or not, I couldn't say, but Bruno relaxed his grip. I brushed the hair off his forehead. Bruno took one more rattling gasp and went completely still. I felt his neck to find his pulse gone.

I looked up and everyone gaped at me. Ilya took a step towards me with his arm reaching out for comfort. Josh and Jonah hung their heads.

"I thought he didn't want to kill variants!" Faith shouted at Cole. She looked fierce in charred clothes with charcoal smeared across her face. She shoved her brother, who allowed the blow to move him.

"I'm sure he's willing to kill us if we get too close or destroy too much. *The Compendium* must mean more to him than our lives," said Cole. Dejected, he looked at Nellie and Bruno.

Faith let out a howl of rage and reignited the blackened crops behind her.

"Calm down! That's not helping anyone," said Ilya.

Jonah doused the fire again.

"We need to think fast," said Josh. "We've probably attracted some attention. If these crops and whatever facility is nearby have more security than five variant dogs, we need to get moving. Now!"

I looked at Nellie and Bruno's bodies. I looked at each of the crushed dog carcasses. I couldn't be sure we'd survive another attack, especially not if it came soon.

"Can you create an illusion to hide us?" I said to Ilya.

"It might not fool anything that can smell us," he replied, glancing at a dead dog.

"We need to get out of here and come back with a plan," said Jonah.

"Let's fall back to the main road and look for a spot to hide and camp." Josh stepped forward and picked up Bruno's body. He nodded at Cole and down at Nellie.

"We'll put them in the back of my Jeep. They deserve better than to stay with this garbage," said Josh.

I risked one last glance around the landscape before I got back into Josh's Jeep. The charcoal-blackened field was as unrecognizable as the bloody lumps that used to be variant dogs. How could we possibly sneak up on this place again?

The return journey to the Backway went quickly. We knew where we were going and fear spurred our drivers.

Back on the main road, such as it was, we continued northward rather than backtracking south. Josh felt we should look for somewhere secluded to dig in for the night. We had passed nothing on the way up the Backway which fit the description.

The sun crept down to the mountains as we drove, igniting the rocky landscape with hot orange, vibrant pink, and radiant yellow hues, complimenting the natural reds and browns in the earth. The plateau and the mountains on the horizon looked like they were sketched in chalk. If we weren't on the run, I would have wanted to stop and stare at the world around us until the light left entirely.

As soon as we rounded a corner and found a cove in the rock to satisfy Josh's military mind as a defensible spot, we pulled over and Ilya went to work on replicating the sandstone and clay rock wall in the air around our campsite.

The rest of us set up our tents inside Ilya's barrier. From inside the site, we looked out as though there was no barrier. I watched Ilya visually scan the rock wall behind me and Josh evaluated his progress.

When the tents were ready, we joined Josh on the outside of Ilya's illusion to admire his handiwork. His camouflage worked masterfully. Once we had crossed out of the campsite and looked back to where we knew the tents were standing, a wall of rock defied us with texture and color capable of fooling any onlooker. A gentle slope connected the wall to the hillside behind, perfectly enclosing our camp. Exactly like Sombrio Beach, passing through the illusion felt like a thick, cold fog.

"How much scrutiny can this withstand?" said Jonah.

"As long as nothing comes sniffing around this exact spot during the night, we'll be safe until sunrise," said Ilya.

"What about our heat signatures? Ivan may have acquired a drone or two since I worked for him," said Josh.

"I don't know if a drone can see through one of my illusions. I ran from the lab before they could test me with all that tech," said Ilya.

"Do you have to stay awake all night?" asked Cole.

"Not awake, I just have to stay here. And alive. If something snuffs me out during the night, you'll lose the wall," said Ilya.

"If something gets at you here in our campsite, your wall is going to be the least of our problems," said Cole.

"I hate to be the one to bring this up, but we should bury Nellie and Bruno. I'm sure this isn't where they wanted to be laid to rest, but we can't carry them with us when we go back," said Jonah.

"I'll do it," I said. Faith and Cole looked at me with furrowed brows. I tapped my temple and they understood.

I took a deep breath and approached the wall at the back of our campsite. I visualized giant hands scooping into the earth, effortlessly lifting huge handfuls of dirt up into the air. And it happened. A long SCRUUUSSHH preceded a mound of dirt dislodging from the ground and floating up. I concentrated harder, willing the floating earth off to the side of the hole. I repeated the process with another hole and dirt pile, a mirror of the first so Nellie and Bruno would be next to each other at rest. I took a step backward.

Guilt surged in my belly. I had once believed in heaven and life after death, but that time was in the clearly defined black-and-white years of my childhood. Even if I had not spent the last year confronted by a world of underground fringe science, my beliefs had already been muddled by the exponential growth of human knowledge. How could I continue to 'believe' while humanity probed out into a universe no longer compatible with traditional spirituality? But I *wanted* to believe. I wanted to believe in *something* with a need that grew exponentially with every loss.

Where were Nellie and Bruno now? Where were my mother and Darryl? Would I ever have contact with them again in any form? Once I died too, would I or could I care? Why had I seen my mother in my 'happy place', whatever that place was, along with Gemma, who still lived? It had to be more than my imagination or my visions wouldn't be true and I would be sitting in a locked room staring out at a treed yard through barred windows.

I looked up and my eyes focused on the stars popping out and twinkling on an expanse of flat black. I felt small. And feeling small felt right. I would have to make peace with knowing nothing about the fate of my friends and family who had died. I turned to see that Josh and Cole had retrieved Bruno and Nellie respectively from the Jeep's storage. I stepped aside.

"We should say a few words before we cover them. And

mark their graves. It seems like the right thing to do," I said.

"It's only the right thing because everyone else does it." Cole gently placed Nellie in a grave and retreated. Josh did the same with Bruno's body.

"You don't think they deserve a remembrance of some sort?" said Jonah.

"Of course they do. It doesn't make it better though," said Cole.

"Avenging them is all we can offer," said Josh.

"When we started this journey, I wanted to put Ivan out of business. Now, I'm going to burn him until he's a pile of ash," said Faith darkly.

"You knew Nellie best," I said to Faith. "Let's start there."

Faith looked around at each of us, at a loss for words. She looked down at Nellie's face.

"I knew Nellie because we were both hackers. She came from a bad scene. When she was a kid, her mom worked three jobs and her dad wasn't in the picture. I don't know if there were other variants in her family. Maybe Nellie didn't know either. She was quiet and kept her variation a secret until Rubin found her. I mostly knew her online. I only ever met her in person once when she came to Victoria. A couple of years ago, Ivan had a meet-and-greet type social for all the research and office variants to meet all his contractors and freelancers. Nellie wasn't good with people. I was still new to Innoviro, but I talked to her and tried to make her feel like she belonged. We emailed back and forth when she returned to Portland, but I thought I'd never see her again. It wasn't until we hit the road leaving Vancouver for San Francisco that I remembered her. She was smart and she cared about making the world a better place," said Faith.

We all stood silently, listening for more.

"I wish I could say something about Bruno. Nellie mentioned him, but we never met until a couple of weeks ago," said Faith.

"I'll speak for Bruno," said Josh. "He was a brave man. You get to know a person when you fight alongside them. He had a strength of character that I admire. He took a mortal wound for the woman he loved. Dying for love is a good death, of all the things I've seen in my life," said Josh.

We stood in silence under the weight of Josh's words.

"Cover them up," said Faith.

I wiped the tear streaks from my cheeks and concentrated on telekinetically nudging the dirt quickly back over my friends' bodies. Cole and Josh patted down each of the mounds to make them neater and more secure. Cole ripped a slab of rock from the bedrock in the wall and slammed it into the ground at the head of Nellie's grave. He did the same for Bruno. After she consulted her phone, Faith followed behind with a molten fingertip inscribing their full names and dates.

"We should get some sleep," said Jonah.

"When do you want to go back to the farm?" I asked Josh.

"We'll take tomorrow to rest and plan. Then we'll go back after dark," he answered.

"If we beat Ivan and derail everything he's doing, no one will ever know," said Cole. "We'll have done all of *this* for all of *them*," he pointed at the graves and made a sweeping gesture at the distant hills. "You're right; nobody will say as much as 'thank you' to any of us. Are you looking for recognition?"

"That's not what I meant. It's going to be weird, falling in with civilians when we're done," said Cole.

"If we get the chance to go back to 'normal' lives, that's the best outcome," said Ilya.

"Don't we all have people in our lives who aren't variants? At least the memory of those people," I said. "They all deserve a chance. Everyone does."

"We know that. It's hard to stay focused when you lose good men," said Josh.

"And women," said Faith.

Josh nodded.

Jonah drew moisture from the air and doused our campfire. We retired to our tents and I fell asleep to the sound of wind in the desert.

Chapter 33

Seedlings in various stages stretched away from me inside the translucent plastic greenhouse at Innoviro's Mojave research farm. The two species looked like a purple cactus and palm tree hybrid. The smaller cacti were mere spiked balls. The larger ones were bristly cylinders that glittered with a powdery coating. I suppressed the strong urge to touch the spindles. I didn't trust being safe from Innoviro even in my dreams.

I turned away from the spiky plants to face a rock wall with a flat glass panel of sand mounted beside me. I faced a cross-section of an insect colony. Albino ants streamed through the sand. A long yellow tendril shot through the sand picking up ants with its sticky surface before it retracted out of sight.

Beside the colony was a steel door with no handle. A woman dressed like a dirt biker walked past me and swept a card through a reader beside the door. The door slid sideways into the wall, and the woman walked forward. My gaze followed behind her as she descended into a fluorescent-lit corridor.

We went down and down until we hit level ground. Stairs quickly reappeared, and we went up and up and up until we reached another closed door. The biker slid her card through another reader, and the door opened into a desert plateau, bright under the Mojave sun. We faced a mobile home alongside Ivan and Tatiana's fifth-wheel trailer. A giant carnivorous evergreen loomed over the yard. The biker crossed through the shadow of the tree and entered the mobile home.

As the biker shut the home's front door behind her, the trailer's door opened. Tatiana, Ivan, and Gemma stepped out. Tatiana approached the evergreen. Oil-slick bees hovered around the open flytrap mouths. They seemed to know not to land inside the glistening deadly pods.

Ivan and Gemma stopped to watch from a distance. Tatiana passed the evergreen, looking at a seedling about ten feet away. I resisted the urge to zoom in on my sister. I concentrated on seeing Tatiana's face. My disembodied self rushed ahead and whirled around to face my aunt. Her skin's green tint startled me, more vibrant than at first. Her eyes had normalized but she now had vivid emerald irises instead of her once dark brown hue. Streaks of chlorophyll had stained her hair from root to tip around her face.

Tatiana knelt on the ground, reached forward, and rammed her fingertips into the earth around the seedling. She wiggled her hands and the seedling grew. Green flushed across her face. She looked as though she would throw up any moment, but she kept burrowing her hands into the dirt and the evergreen grew taller until Tatiana had to stand up and back away. She rubbed her temples with dirty hands and knelt back down in front of her young tree. She gripped the evergreen's trunk and opened her mouth. Pale green fluid shot out of Tatiana from the back of her throat and the evergreen's bark absorbed it, growing again, becoming as large as the tree next to it. Tatiana let go of the tree trunk and collapsed on the ground.

"Tatiana!" shouted Gemma as she ran to my aunt's aid. Golden light flowed out of Gemma's hands into Tatiana's chest. Gemma continued massaging my aunt's collarbones while Ivan watched calmly. Tatiana sat up with a gasp, weak, but restored.

"You're not stable," Ivan said to Tatiana.

"I will be. Given time and resources, I'll stabilize this variation as well," said Tatiana.

"Ilya and Irina will be coming back," said Ivan flatly.

"They're *your* children. The decision is yours," said Tatiana.

"She doesn't know she's on the wrong side! You need to give her a chance. She's my sister! Your daughter!" said Gemma.

"We gave her a chance in Victoria," said Tatiana coolly.

"She will be safe unless she threatens our lives. *The Compendium Transmuto* is the future, the life, of every variant in the world," said Ivan.

"If Irina has her way, variants will continue to live in hiding, pretending their gifts don't exist. She thinks our guardian bees are weapons. She thinks our research is intended to harm the very people we are fighting to protect," said Tatiana.

"Your sister's secondary ability has been activated. With telekinesis and remote viewing, Irina will be our biggest threat if she refuses to align herself with our work," said Ivan.

"Combined with the boy's mind reading and illusory abilities, there will be no level of security that can keep them out. She could be watching us now for all we know," said Tatiana.

My aunt stood and turned to face me where my disembodied

gaze originated. As she looked me in the eye, I felt her anger. Tatiana's mouth curved into a subtle smile.

I awoke surrounded by a dome of navy blue nylon. Jonah slept soundly next to me. I grabbed his shoulder and shook him gently.

"Jonah. Jonah, I know how to get to the other side of the Innoviro farm," I said.

"Huh. What?" he said sleepily. He yawned.

"We have to wake everyone up," I said.

"Be my guest." He rolled back on his side.

I shoved my arms into my hoodie and zipped it up before I exited the tent. I went tent to tent shaking them by the frames.

"This better be good," Faith said angrily from inside her and Ilya's tent.

"I know how to get to Ivan and Tatiana's trailer! We can catch them now," I said.

I still had no idea how we would stop them from unleashing their disease and their variant animals and plants on the world. The more I saw, the more I became certain I had only seen the tip of the Innoviro iceberg.

"Ilya, you have to get us into the greenhouses with some kind of cover. Can you make us look like something else? Can you make it so they don't see us?" I said to my brother as he exited his tent.

"I can't make us invisible if that's what you mean," said Ilya.

"Do we want to come face to face with them? What will that accomplish? I think we've established there's no talking them out of Innoviro's secret work," said Faith.

"We don't know the plan, in its entirety. We still need to get a hold of *The Compendium* document, folder, or whatever it is, so we know what we're up against. Otherwise, we're groping in the dark until the next catastrophic natural disaster or disease puts another dent in the planet. I'm sure they've got it stored electronically, just not on a network or anything you can hack," I said.

"So why do we need to get into the greenhouses?" said Cole.

"There's an underground corridor connecting one of the greenhouses to a plateau on the other side of the hill. That's where they've parked their trailer. I saw one of the dirt bikers there too," I said.

"You're hoping to steal something like a laptop or a netbook and then level the place?" said Josh.

"I'd like to find anything truly useful, but either way, I think we should leave nothing behind," I said.

"Are we prepared to kill to get *The Compendium*? Are we willing to keep killing to shut down Innoviro projects? We know the Krylovs are willing to take lives to bring their vision to life," said Jonah.

"We've come this far without saying it out loud, but I think it's time. This mission will likely require deadly force," said Josh.

"I always hoped my father would come to his senses once his projects were shut down," said Ilya.

"There is still that possibility, however remote," said Jonah.

"If this is bigger than our own lives, it's bigger than theirs too," said Cole.

We sat in silence for a moment. All loss of life around us so far had been in the heat of the moment. We had never entered a situation planning to end lives, or willing to sacrifice them. The image of Nellie and Bruno lying beside smashed variant dogs, surrounded by a charred landscape stayed fresh in my mind. One field of carnage already haunted me. Ivan wanted to remake the entire world. What would that atrocity look like afterward?

"I'll conceal us as coyotes. It's an animal they'll expect to see around here," said Ilya.

"Hopefully by the time we're inside the underground passage, we'll be past the worst of their security," said Josh.

"I'll listen for those variant scorpion dogs as well. I'm sure I won't confuse those primal brains for anything else around here," said Ilya.

"What if they have something worse on the other side of the hill?" said Faith.

"Let's hope they don't," said Josh.

Faith and Ilya made a breakfast of baked beans and toast while Jonah and I disassembled the tents. Cole repacked his car and Josh repacked his Jeep. My stomach turned over as I watched Josh rearrange the tarp inside his Jeep's trunk. He had flipped it over to put the bloody side down, so as not to stain our tent bags and backpacks. About an hour later we were parking at the edge of the ruined farm field.

"We'll need to walk in," said Josh.

"I suggest we talk as little as possible until we're inside the greenhouse. Sound is harder to convert than images," said Ilya. Nobody argued.

The autumn smell of burnt leaves blew off the ground. My heart had no room for nostalgia. The adrenaline of fear rushed through me tingling in my limbs like circulation returning.

We marched with determination, following Josh's motions and signs. He used two fingers, pointing to his eyes and then a sweeping all-clear gesture.

The greenhouse had only a simple screen door to enclose the entrance and it was only latched, not locked. The hair stood on the back of my neck, but I kept silent, as per my brother's instructions.

The glittering purple plants I had seen in my mind were exactly as I'd pictured them in all stages of growth. And at the far end of the structure where it jutted up against the hillside were the insect colony and the smooth steel door.

"Okay, what now? Rip the door off?" said Cole.

"Refresh our memories as to exactly what's waiting on the other side," Josh said to me.

"Behind that door is a stairwell leading under the hill and back up to a plateau on the other side. There's a mobile home. I have no idea what's inside the home. And Ivan's fifth-wheel trailer with all his gear and specimens is parked alongside. There's an exceptionally large one of the carnivorous evergreens next to the trailer. Tatiana grew it with her variation, but she weakens herself every time she uses her ability. She's unstable, like Jonah was. Gemma has been healing her, but she needs more gene therapy," I said.

"In terms of threats, did you see any animals or weapons?" said Faith.

"No, but I mostly saw Tatiana growing her trees. I'm not sure why I saw it, but I don't think she's a physical threat right now. Ivan appears to be in perfect health. I'm sure Gemma healed his arm and any other lingering injuries, including his outrageously strong telekinesis. He's got my sister fooled, without a doubt."

"Are we ready then?" said Jonah.

"Ready as we'll ever be," said Cole.

We crossed the greenhouse to the steel door, which Cole stopped to evaluate. It had gone unspoken that he would be the one to rip it open. Suddenly, the steel door slid open, unbidden, and an enormous mass of muscle filled the frame. In one fluid motion, the huge man flipped open his second set of arms and grabbed Cole and Josh by the collars, tossing them to the far end of the greenhouse.

The four-armed man turned around and I came face to face with Casey, the bouncer from The Looking Glass and what felt like another lifetime back in Victoria.

Chapter 34

Casey picked up Faith by a handful of her purple dreadlocks and flung her through the plastic wall behind me. From overhead a WHUUUPUNKSHHH announced the arrival of Rose and Sage. They burst through the plastic sheeting and wood rafters of the roof, swooping down in a shower of debris. One of Rose's wings crashed into the ant farm spilling sand and large white ants everywhere. The winged sisters grabbed Jonah and Ilya from behind and heaved, leaping up into the sky with a captive each.

Casey and I were left face to face and I froze. I cringed, waiting for a blow, but he stood there. He glared at me, speechless. Had he been instructed to spare me? I noticed a familiar talisman. He wore a rune necklace, exactly like the one I had been given when I lived at my Innoviro apartment.

"Where's my sister?" I blurted at him.

"She's with your father, where you should be. He'd forgive you, even now, if you pledge to join us. Your brother too. This doesn't have to be a fight," said Casey.

Cole and Josh picked themselves up and ran back to me.

"I'll never understand why Ivan thinks wiping out most of humanity is justifiable. He may have brainwashed enough variants to help him, but he'll never count me among them," I said.

Casey opened his mouth as a rush of fire consumed the nearest wall of the greenhouse. The acrid smoke from melting plastic bellowed around us like a thick fog. I ran out of the greenhouse to where Faith, Jonah, and Ilya stood catching their breath. Cole and Josh detoured around the fire and burst out of the building.

Rose and Sage swooped into the fire and carried Casey out and over the hill back to where I expected to find a mobile home and Ivan's trailer.

"That's right, run back to your boss!" yelled Faith as the trio disappeared over the hilltop.

Jonah diverted irrigation water again, dousing the greenhouse completely.

"Well, they botched their ambush," said Cole.

"Not necessarily," said Josh.

"How do you figure? We've still got access to the tunnel connecting to their compound," said Ilya.

"There could be something waiting for us in the tunnel," said Jonah.

"I can't hear anything. If another one of those scorpion dogs was in there, I'd hear its primal brain," said Ilya.

"I'll test it." Cole walked through the still-smoking remains of the greenhouse, back to the steel door into the hillside. He ripped it off like an old paper poster and stepped through the doorway.

Cole took two steps into the tunnel and fell to his knees.

He retched violently and the contents of his stomach spilled out onto the ground. He clutched his stomach with one arm, pulling himself along the floor with the other until he crawled back out through the doorway.

"Anyone else wanna to try?" said Faith.

"This is probably going to suck." Josh crossed the charred structure and helped Cole to his feet. Josh braced himself for a moment and then stepped into the stairwell.

"It's not too –," Josh's words were cut by the sound of vomit lurching out of his mouth.

"Can you get out?" Jonah stepped forward as if to help and I grabbed his arm. We watched as Josh too crawled back out of the tunnel.

"What the hell was the point of attacking us if they've got some kind of hex on their tunnel?" said Faith.

"My father used to refer to 'curses' as security measures. I never took him seriously," said Ilya.

"I'm sure it's not some form of witchcraft. I worked security for Innoviro and I never heard of anything like that," said Josh.

"Ivan hid something from everyone. But I know what this is. I mean, I know how to stop it," I said.

I ran back to Josh's Jeep leaving everyone scratching their heads. I rummaged in my backpack until I found the copper and glass rune necklace I had to wear when I lived in Victoria. I put it on and marched back to the greenhouse.

"Don't you remember having to wear these at my building in Victoria?" I said to Jonah.

"What is that?" said Cole.

"Irina lived in an old walk-up in Esquimalt. We were supposed to wear these in the building. I figured they used it as a form of identification. I didn't think it mattered," said

Jonah.

"But you wore it anyway," I said to Jonah. To everyone else, I continued my explanation.

"When Rubin moved me in there, he told me to wear it at all times. He didn't say what would happen if I took it off and I didn't ask. I figured I'd learn more in time, but that time never came," I said.

"How does it work?" said Josh.

"I have no idea," I said.

"Are you willing to risk your breakfast to find out?" said Faith.

"It's not like I've never barfed before," I said. Now Jonah grabbed my arm. "I'm right about this, I know it." He let go and I walked to the doorway.

I took a moment to size up the bare earth in front of the stone steps. The space ahead seemed empty, harmless. Cool air floated out. I looked to my right where Cole and Josh – the two strongest men I'd ever known – were sitting up against the rock wall, recovering their composure.

I closed my fist around the small copper oval on my chest and I stepped into the tunnel. Nothing happened. I took another step and another until I had descended several steps. I turned and ran back to the greenhouse.

"I can go!" I said excitedly.

"What about the rest of us?" said Josh.

"There's no way you're going alone," said Jonah.

"We can't use the tunnel, but we might be able to cross over the hill," said Cole.

"That'll take all day to go up and over on foot. We should take the Jeep and the car," said Faith.

"We've already lost whatever element of surprise we had

going for us," said Josh. He threw up his hands and walked back to his Jeep. We followed quickly.

"Shit!" yelled Josh. We caught up and I saw why he was upset.

Both the back tires on the Jeep and the car were flat. We weren't going anywhere on wheels.

"Those fuckers!" yelled Cole.

"The attack was a diversion so they could take out our cars?" said Jonah, perplexed.

"I don't get it either," said Ilya.

"They could be buying time. If Ivan's working on something he doesn't want to walk away from, but he doesn't want company, he might be stalling," said Josh.

"They are willing to kill. Casey was still trying to sell us on joining their 'team' back in the greenhouse, but I saw Tatiana and Ivan talking with Gemma. They're flat-out ready to murder us before sacrificing *The Compendium*. There's no question about it now," I said.

"If we go over that hillside and find critical research and specimens worth destroying, we will be risking our lives to do it," said Jonah.

"I'm still in," said Faith.

"Me too. I still feel responsible for my father," said Ilya.

"This isn't our first trip into the lion's den. We're all in it until the end," said Cole.

Josh nodded. "Everybody grab a bag. Take only what you need for the day. Whatever happens on the other side of this hill, we won't be going any farther anytime soon."

"What happens if we all get sick? I mean everyone but Irina. That 'curse' thingy might extend up into the hill," said Faith.

"If I have to go alone, I'll pretend I'm joining their side.

It's the only chip I've got to play. Ivan might not know I've inherited his telekinesis, so I could have a surprise to spring if needed," I said.

"You haven't learned to use or control your telekinesis very well yet," said Jonah.

"It's still better than sending her in armed with visions," said Cole.

At the word 'armed', I felt numbness in my chest. I had never considered myself armed with anything. But Cole was right, an offensive ability, even a clumsy one, made a better weapon in a fight than mental images.

We walked away from our vehicles with a sense of foreboding. Nobody spoke. As we trekked up the hillside, I looked for loose rocks and practiced remotely throwing them at tree trunks we passed. Under other circumstances, I would have been amused. I would have looked for smiles on my friends' faces. Today, it was all I could do to keep my breakfast in my stomach, even with my protective rune pendant.

Dry grass and dusty clay earth with a sparse growth of little round cacti, sagebrush, and small pine trees covered the hillside. No clear trail presented itself. Several times, someone cried 'ouch' and had to dislodge a small prickly ball from a pant leg.

We crested the hillside and looked down into the second half of Innoviro's Mojave research farm. The mobile home, fifth wheel trailer, and two freshly grown carnivorous spruce were exactly where I'd seen them. Josh knelt on the ground where we still had the cover of a few pines. We all copied him.

"Ilya, can you give us a read on how many people are down there?" whispered Josh.

Ilya frowned, concentrating. He looked back and forth

between the mobile and the fifth wheel.

"What is it?" I whispered.

"Seven people. My father, Aunt Tat, four girls and I think Casey," he whispered.

"Where are they?" said Cole.

"In the mobile – wait, no. What the?" said Ilya.

"What's happening?" hissed Jonah.

"My father is gone. No, Aunt Tat too. Now the girls. There's only … There's no one left!" said Ilya at regular volume.

"They're underground again?" said Josh.

"No, they disappeared out of existence. Their minds, just, blip, gone!" said Ilya, bewildered.

"Could it be some kind of panic room?" said Faith.

"I don't think so. I've never been locked out like this except for a variant like Rubin. Even then, he couldn't shut me down like this or put up a wall around so many people. They're … gone," he said confidently.

"We might as well investigate," I said.

Josh put his finger to his lips and gestured for us to follow him. We all trusted his military expertise more than ever. Every crunch made by one of our missteps sent a dagger of fear through my heart, but we kept walking. I reminded myself over and over that Ilya was probably right. They had escaped somehow.

"Wait," said Ilya as we arrived down on the plateau. "I can hear someone. It's one of the girls. She popped out of thin air! She seems familiar but I can't place her."

We all stopped short. Ilya took another couple of steps as though listening and suddenly vomited all over himself. Faith ran to pull him back and the sickness hit her too. I ran out in front of both of them and concentrated with all my heart on lifting them up and back to the hillside.

Faith and Ilya both rose a few inches off the ground and floated a few feet until I accidentally dropped them. They were still recovering, but the sickness had lost its grip.

"Don't come any closer, anyone," I said.

"The girl is in the mobile home. Hurry! While she's still there," said Ilya, wiping his face in disgust.

I ran to the front door of the mobile home. I hesitated for a moment before I opened the door.

The building was an office and storage space with several cubicles nearest me. A wall of cabinets stretched along one side of the mobile and a row of walk-in freezers hummed along the other. Rows and rows of canisters sat in quiet stasis.

I forced myself to continue inside, remembering that I was supposed to be looking for a live person before trying to make sense of files or specimens. And then a rustle of paper inside one of the cubicles sent a shock of panic through me.

Chapter 35

A flash of a brown-haired bun caught my attention at one of the cubicles. The girl stepped out from behind the divider. Melissa had come a long way from her days as a preppy downtown receptionist. She wore a white thermal shirt, still dressed in the stiff vinyl dirt bike pants I had seen in my mind. A stone pendant hung from a leather cord around her neck.

"You bitch!" I snapped at her. Melissa whirled around with a shocked expression. Her features relaxed as she evaluated me.

"Nice to see you too, Irina. Don't you want to know why I'm here?" she said.

"I should have known you were still with him. Fine, talk," I said.

"I'm not with him anymore. Not now. That's why I'm back in this godforsaken desert," said Melissa.

"And what made you change your mind at this point?" I said.

"I overheard Ivan and Tatiana talking about releasing a virus," said Melissa.

"You didn't know that's what those variant bees are for?" I said.

"No, I didn't. I knew they were working on some kind of variant colony. I could get on board with that. But once I saw what their virus will do to anything not a variant, I came back," said Melissa.

"Came back … from where?" I said slowly. "More to the point, where is everyone else who works at this farm? Where are Rose, Sage, and Casey? And my sister!"

"London," said Melissa flatly.

"England?" I said.

"Of course, England. You think I'd send them to Ontario?" said Melissa.

"Send them? You've lost me again," I said.

Melissa looked me squarely in the eye and turned to face the wall beside her. She traced the outline of an oval about three feet wide and seven feet high. The air shimmered with liquid silver following the outline made by her finger. When she closed the loop a rippling metallic window hung in the air.

"It's a portal. Not to where I left them in London, that's too dangerous. If you step through here, you'll be back in our old office in Victoria. If the landlord hasn't leased the space, it should still be empty," said Melissa.

My jaw dropped. My eyes widened. Of all the variations I'd seen, this one took the trophy for most bizarre. How had I never seen this before? Why hadn't anybody told me that Melissa could do this?

"Do the others know?" I said.

"Jonah, Cole, and Faith – *your* buddies? No, they don't. Ivan asked me to keep it confidential and I did. I did whatever Ivan asked me to do, without question."

"So if I walk through this … thing, I'll end up back in Victoria?" I said.

"Test it. You'll be in Ivan's office. More or less," she said, not as confidently as I would have liked.

I went closer to the portal and touched the surface. It felt like liquid on my palm, but when I pulled my hand away, the skin was perfectly dry. I ventured a larger test, pressing my hand into the liquid, and pushing my arm through to my elbow. I couldn't see where my arm went, but I felt dry air on the other side.

I took a deep breath and pinched my nose as though I'd be plunging underwater. I glanced at Melissa. She rolled her eyes. I turned to the liquid portal, closed my eyes, and plunged in until my head submerged.

I opened my eyes and I was in Ivan's abandoned office, precisely as we'd seen it last. I felt a push from behind and I stumbled the rest of the way through the portal. Melissa followed behind me.

"And here we are. Innoviro Industries, Ivan's office specifically," said Melissa.

"Did we travel through time?" I said uncertainly.

"Of course not," said Melissa.

"No, of course not. Silly me," I said sarcastically.

"So now you understand me. I already know everything about you, including your newly developed telekinesis. Now you need to decide if you want my help. Do you still want *The Compendium Transmuto?*"

"What!? You've got it?"

"I will have it. Once I complete the file transfer from the Mojave network to the hundred-twenty-eight gig netbook I left in the mobile," said Melissa.

"What is *The Compendium?*" I said.

"As I said, I thought it was a plan for a variant colony. But based on the virus test I just witnessed, it has to be a planet-wide takeover. Ivan has counterparts at two other variant research firms, Evonatura in Europe and Jinhua in China. They're rich and powerful variants who want dedicated space," said Melissa. She rubbed her face. "I just hadn't realized how greedy their reach had become. They want all of Earth."

"And you've made a snap decision to jump ship?" I said.

"All along, talks were about a colony for now, and then sowing seeds, reaping changes on a generational level. Humans are doing no less. But if they're starting a war, humanity won't recognize it for what it is. They don't stand a chance. I could see letting humans do it to themselves, but I can't be a part of a planetary extinction," said Melissa.

Car engines and the sound of a saxophone busker drifted up from the street. We were definitely in Victoria.

"We need to get back to the Mojave," I said.

Melissa and I whipped our heads around at the sound of a door opening down the hall.

"The property manager!" whispered Melissa.

"Open another portal!" I hissed back.

Melissa created another shimmering oval and we hopped through it.

We were back in the Mojave, only this time we were outside the trailer with my friends looking on from the edge of the property.

"Irina!" called out Jonah.

"Who is that?" yelled Faith.

"It's me! Melissa," she shouted back.

"Is there anything worth salvaging in the trailer? After we download *The Compendium*, of course. Should we bother picking through the specimens and files?" I asked Melissa.

"In terms of files, everything is covered by *The Compendium*. But specimens are another story. Your crew showing up here rushed his transfer to London. Ivan left material behind that I know he still wants. He took my loyalty for granted, assuming I'd bring him back after seeing the horrific plague he's ready to turn loose. Without me, he can't return quickly, but there is enough work in progress here that he'll come back at some point."

"Then we're better off to wipe it all out, even the species or projects we think are benign. You finish the download. I'll see what I can do about the fifth wheel."

Chapter 36

Melissa turned on her heel and marched into the mobile. I ventured a quick peek inside Ivan's fifth wheel. The foul odor of decay hung in the air. I flicked the light switch next to the door. Nothing happened. I heard a scratching sound from inside a cage at the far end of the trailer. A shrill SQUAAAAK pierced the air. It sounded like a cry of pain. I backed out of the trailer and closed the door.

The solution was for Faith to burn the trailer to the ground. But she couldn't get near it without being stricken by that mystery curse. An idea struck me. I needed to challenge my telekinetic skills, to push the boundary of what I could do with my mind, before my next encounter with my so-called father.

An idea struck me. I moved to the front of the trailer and the exposed hitch. I pulled on it. Of course, nothing happened.

"Irina, what are you doing?" called Jonah from the edge of the site.

"Moving a trailer!" I called back to him.

I let go of the hitch and tried to pull the vehicle forward with my mind. More nothing happened. I pulled with all my focus, walking backward, visualizing the trailer wheels rolling. *You are not using muscles to lift this thing. A rock, a person, a trailer; it's all in your mind.*

I felt the weight of the thing resisting, trying to remain stationary despite my draw. Against everything I knew of physics, the wheels rolled forward, picking up speed as I did. I reached the edge of the property where my friends waited.

"Faith …" I stopped to catch my breath. "Burn it to the ground. Turn it to ash."

Faith smiled. "No problem!"

She leveled her arms at the trailer and from her upright palms, two thick hot streams of intense fire blasted the siding. The blaze consumed the fifth wheel quickly. The windows shattered and curtains on fire flared out in front of us. Another cry of SQUEEEE sounded briefly, silenced by the WHOOOOSH of flames racing upward. Tinkling and crackling continued as the trailer's exterior blackened. Moments later, the roof fell in and a fresh plume of smoke billowed above.

"I think you got it," said Ilya as he placed his hand on Faith's shoulder.

Melissa ran to us with a netbook under her arm.

"We should burn the mobile too. If you want to be sure." Melissa walked over to Faith and placed her necklace around Faith's neck.

"Why didn't I think of that?" I said with my hand on my face.

"You needed practice anyway." Jonah burst an irrigation

pipe several yards away and funneled the water onto the crispy husk of the one-time trailer.

Faith ran to the mobile and kicked in the door. Without so much as a glance around, she unleashed an inferno on the interior. She backed out and went to work on the exterior.

I removed my rune necklace and placed it around Jonah's neck so he could follow behind and douse her flames as he now automatically did. Every time I watched them work together, I knew I would always be reminded of their romantic connection, however far behind them it might be. As they burned and doused, we waited.

"So what's the story with the portal thing?" said Josh. He looked intently at Melissa.

"I can open a connection between two known locations. It's not time travel. It's just bending space," she said.

"Just bending space!" said Cole.

"It's the coolest thing I've seen in a long time. And we're in the business of seeing seriously weird shit!" said Ilya.

"More importantly, why are you with us now? Weren't you working for Ivan literally moments ago?" Josh eyed her with palpable distrust.

"You all used to work for Innoviro!" Melissa accusingly stared around at all of us. "I supported a variant colony; it made sense to me. Now that I know about the pathogen those bees carry – he calls it *Terra Nova* - I'm done!"

Jonah and Faith rejoined us and I was relieved to see a healthful glow on my boyfriend's face. Finally, after so much worrying and caution, he'd become stronger than ever.

"So where to now?" said Jonah.

"London," I said.

"What if she's leading us into a trap?" said Josh, to me,

ignoring Melissa. The latter crossed her arms angrily.

"I believe her," I said.

"Ilya, listen to her. Dig as deep as you can," said Cole.

"If you don't trust me, then screw off and let *The Compendium* roll ahead," said Melissa.

"What's a little hand-holding among friends? I can hear you whether you let me in or not, but it's easier this way," said Ilya.

He reached out to Melissa, looking at her with a playful grin. My brother was hard to resist when he felt like charming someone. Melissa relaxed, rolled her eyes, and offered her hand to Ilya. He closed his eyes and held her hand with a thoughtful expression. I wondered how Faith's temper fared.

"It's okay. She's telling the truth," said Ilya after a long moment. "My father tested his bee serum on a stray dog right in front of her. He scared the hell out of her. She really didn't know. And now she's livid. He underestimated his hold on her."

All of us looked from Ilya's concerned face to Melissa, still uncharacteristically casual in her dirt bike gear.

"Can we get on with it now?" Melissa demanded impatiently.

"Where, exactly, in London are we going," said Josh.

"I sent everyone, including Gemma, to an alley outside Piccadilly Circus. It's a nice secluded spot that's within walking distance to Evonatura's London office," said Melissa.

"So we follow them to Evonatura and throw down?" said Cole.

"No, we'll hide in Soho. That's where Evonatura's office is, but Ivan hates the neighborhood. It's too 'weird' for him. He won't be there any longer than he needs to be. We'll case the office and come up with a plan before we make a move," said

Melissa.

"Is there any chance that Ivan could accelerate some of the more catastrophic elements of *The Compendium* if we spook him? Is he ready to release this *Terra Nova* virus to the public?" said Cole.

"I think that's exactly what he'll do. And I think he's in a position to do it now. I'm sorry. I didn't know how far this had gotten. I'm kicking myself now and I will be for years to come," said Melissa.

"You're doing the right thing now. That's what counts," said Jonah.

"Do you need to go back to your cars? Are you all ready to go now?" said Melissa.

I looked around at my friends' faces. I saw apprehension mixed with uncertainty.

"We've got everything we need to be in a city. The stuff we left in the Jeep and Cole's car is camping gear," said Josh.

"I'm game," said Faith.

"Me too." Ilya grabbed Faith's hand.

"Yeah, sure, why not," said Cole.

"Fire up your portal," I said to Melissa.

She swooped her arm through the air, up, down, and around re-creating the liquid silver oval. Smiling, she stepped through her portal.

The rest of us stood gawking at each other for a moment. Melissa's hand reappeared, floating mid-air through the portal, beckoning us to come.

I took her hand and let her pull me through. I emerged next to a greasy dumpster in an alley reeking of rotting meat and diesel. Traffic sounds replaced the white noise of desert winds.

I looked to my left and saw a brick wall. To my right, a party was going on. Pedestrians cleared and I saw a slim man dressed in a black speedo and a black policeman's hat, dancing to club music in a shop window. Another man stepped into view in the window, dressed in a giant white feather boa, silver glitter makeup, and bright white short shorts. They danced together grinding groins and hips.

"Welcome to SOHO," said Melissa.

"I can see why this is the perfect place to hide from Ivan and Tatiana," I said.

"You'd better hope we can stay hidden, especially if he finds out the Mohave facility was destroyed. Now that I've betrayed him, he'll be as dangerous as a coiled cobra if we meet him," said Melissa. "Or should I say, when we meet him."

I reached my arm back through the portal, as Melissa had done, and beckoned to friends I couldn't see. I felt someone take my hand and I knew the wildest leg of our now international quest was about to start. We had a lot left to do, but somehow I felt fresh hope that we could defeat Ivan.

About the Author

Christine Hart is a metalsmith and mother who writes speculative fiction. Her backlist includes The Electric Girl (MG) and The Variant Conspiracy (NA) trilogy. Her debut Watching July (YA) won a gold medal from the Moonbeam Children's Book Awards.

She holds a BA in English and Professional Writing, as well as current membership with the Federation of BC Writers. When not writing, she creates wearable art from raw stones, vintage glass, and unique gems. She shares her eclectic home with her husband and two children.

Also by Christine Hart

Terra Nova (The Variant Conspiracy)
The end of humanity and an unrecognizable future Earth are days away. After their first glimpse of the Terra Nova virus, Irina and her friends know that Ivan's scheme is almost complete.

After surviving a catastrophic earthquake and destroying a secret viral testing facility, Irina's crew has traveled by a variant portal to London. On the other side of the world, they know stopping the Terra Nova virus is only the beginning.

In Irina's Cards (The Variant Conspiracy)
Irina leaves small-town life behind after a strange deck of tarot cards propels her into a supernatural mystery and a world of fringe genetic science.

Working for Innoviro Industries, she falls in love while uncovering the dangerous nature of the company's business. Meeting other 'variants' brings Irina closer and closer to a frightening plot that could threaten all life on Earth.

The Electric Girl (Middle Grade Novel)
Polly is trying to forget that her mom has cancer. Until a freak electrical storm and a unicorn arrive. Sy'kai wakes on an orchard floor. She doesn't know where -or what she is.

Polly and her friends find Sy'kai and two questions hang over their heads. Can an alien deliver a miracle for a human mother? Can a group of teens defeat an interdimensional demon?

Her Experience Connection (Short Story)
Anna is a stay-at-home mother, nearing her fortieth birthday. She is considering a transition either back into the workforce, or on to a slower phase of motherhood.

Until she is offered a third option. Another restless mother recruits her into a world of virtual escapes and customized fantasies.

Has she discovered an exciting new lifestyle? Or will she fall head-first into a bottomless digital hole?

A Charmed Woman (Short Story)

Barb is a weary divorcée running a thriving vintage boutique on Vancouver Island. She uses her work to help her heal while she rebuilds her life.

Until a friend of her son comes to visit with an unbelievable story and a strange gift for her to pass along.

Can Barb take the opportunity to reconnect with her reclusive son? Or has his retreat into the wilderness reached a point of no return?

The Crystal Miners (Short Story)

Paige and Randy are on their second round of pandemic-era vacationing. The first time, they toured filming locations around BC's Lower Mainland.

Now that they can travel within the entire province, they're touring weird properties for sale. They started with a former rural school and then moved on to a northern lake island.

Their last stop is an abandoned mining community. Paige is apprehensive. Are they in for one more eccentric outing … or something truly bizarre?

Stalked (Sidestreets Novel)

It's the summer before her final year of high school, and Amy and her best friend Elise are stoked about their summer job. Two months, no parents, a dreamy twenty-something boss, and a remote Vancouver Island resort. It sounds like the perfect opportunity for shy, artistic Amy to reinvent herself. But when her dream boss turns creepy, Amy has to decide how far she's willing to go to get the recommendations she needs for her future.

Best Laid Plans (Sidestreets Novel)

Robyn's family has always struggled to make enough money to survive. When Robyn's grandmother leaves them an apple orchard in British Columbia, Robyn thinks things will be different, but Robyn's father still can't pay the bills. He asks Robyn for her own hard-earned money and encourages her to drop out of school to work in the orchard. Robyn desperately wants to go to university, but to make a better life for herself, she'll have to leave her family behind.

Watching July (Young Adult Novel)
16-year-old July has been through hell. Her mom was killed in a hit-and-run. Her other mom packed up and moved them to the middle of nowhere. And then July meets the boy down the road.

Surprised to find herself falling in love and making friends at school, she starts to see the possibility of building a new life. But when it is revealed that her mom's death was not what it seemed, July finds herself in a world of danger.